I0618788

Love Across the Pond

By

Amy Corwin

Copyright

Synopsis

Which will they choose; love or money?

Edward Archer walks into the den of lioness Charity Stonewright when he is sent to South Carolina to resolve a property dispute for his cousin, the Duchess of Peckham. Astute and devoted to the law, Edward isn't prepared for dealing with Charity, a strong-willed woman determined to uncover a secret hidden in her family's Charleston mansion. The lost Stonewright fortune lies hidden somewhere within the walls of the sprawling mansion. Finding it would end the grinding poverty she's endured, but she needs time to find it.

Drawn to the attractive woman, Edward is increasingly torn between duty and his growing love for her. But even when he allows her to stay, she stubbornly maintains her distrust of him and keeps her secrets to herself.

The mysteries of the mansion soon threaten to tear Edward and Charity apart before they can learn to listen to their hearts and find the love waiting for them.

Chapter One

November 25, 1822, London

Edward Archer watched as Miss Denholm drew off her green gloves, glanced at him, and calmly stated, "It is not a matter of love, of course. Never has been. Nonsense to base a marriage on such whims, as I'm sure you agree."

He gave an ambivalent grunt. Marriage might very well do without love, but one at least needed respect and some sort of affection.

"I am convinced we shall rub along tolerably well together," she said, smiling in satisfaction as her gaze roved around the elegant furnishings of the large, bright Ivory Drawing Room. Her glance dwelled for several seconds on the gilded moldings and high, coffered ceiling, with its exquisite painting of dawn breaking over Olympus, before coming to rest on Edward's face with proprietary pleasure. "What say you, Mr. Archer? You are not getting any younger, you know, and neither am I. Shall we consider the matter settled?" Her smile widened. "I am not without resources of my own, you understand. I shall bring you a generous settlement—very generous. And I have no objections to your interest in the law. You may even have a legal practice, if that is your desire." She snorted with laughter and shook her head, dislodging several bright red curls. "Frankly, I am convinced you will see that it is not necessary after we are wed, of course, but every gentleman must have his trivial pursuits."

"How very kind of you. Very rational. I'm sure most gentlemen would be pleased to hear such a sensible proposal. But alas, I must say no," Edward replied dryly. When she opened her mouth to speak, he held up a hand. "I assure you, I have given the notion all the consideration it deserves."

She laughed heartily and shook her head, her brash, red curls bouncing over her wide shoulders. "It is the lady's role to be coy, Mr. Archer. We both know the arrangement would be a good match for both of us." She slapped her gloves against her left palm. "My father is waiting to hear from you. I would prefer to get the wedding over with as soon as possible."

"I have no doubt of that," Edward said.

"Mid-December would suit me. Think on it." Miss Denholm had a peculiar inability to hear anything that she didn't want to hear. "I will return tomorrow, never fear."

"I have no fears on that score," he murmured, smiling gently.

She gave him a bland look and nodded, snapping her gloves against her palm again. She also seemed incapable of understanding the concept of accepting defeat, graciously or otherwise, and he wondered if stronger measures were required.

If he hadn't been hampered by the fact that she was his sister's friend, he would have made it completely clear to her in a way even she could understand that he would not be forced into a marriage he didn't want.

"If you will excuse me, I have an appointment," he said at last, gesturing toward the door.

"Of course." She drew on her gloves. "Tomorrow, then."

He sighed. "Tomorrow."

He waited until Latimore escorted her to the door before he donned his hat and gloves and strolled outside, examining the hurrying pedestrians. No sign of Miss Denholm's tall figure. For once, the excuse of an appointment was not a social expedient designed to end an interminable visit. He'd received a request from his cousin, the Duchess of Peckham, to call on her today, though he couldn't imagine why.

First Miss Denholm and now the Duchess of Peckham—both strong-willed, red-haired women. It was growing difficult not to associate that particular hair color with an annoying slide of his normally good luck into bad.

After fifteen minutes of brisk walking, he came to a halt in front of the vast, columned façade of Her Grace's London home. He studied the imposing frontage. A dark cloud floated overhead, casting shadows over the gray panes of the windows and sinking the dark green door into gloom.

He straightened and climbed the four stairs to the stoop, entering the cold shadows. No matter the cost, one didn't ignore a duchess, particularly if that duchess were also a cousin.

With a sigh, Edward knocked on the wide door and was soon ushered into the huge, crimson and gold sitting room on the first floor.

Her Grace was seated near the bow window, with a view of the busy street below. She was dividing her attention between eying the passersby and a magazine she held in her lap.

Bright sunshine gleamed off the red-gold curls clustered against the duchess's long neck, and stray beams sparkled over the gilded moldings. The brilliant light enhanced the Egyptian-inspired designs, including sphinxes, jackal-headed men, and urns, painted on the walls and high-domed ceiling, reminiscent of Adam's Etruscan Dressing Room that Edward had seen at Osterley Park. While impressive, it was a bit too ornate for his taste.

Various ancient vases and Egyptian statuettes in onyx, gold, lapis, and clay were distributed around the room, echoing the wall decorations. They stood on various small marble and gold-trimmed pedestals and delicate tables, vying for attention with the crystal vases of hot-house flowers that perfumed the air.

No visitor could mistake the interest the duchess had in Egyptian art and history.

"Mr. Archer, Your Grace," the butler intoned before closing the doors behind Edward.

"Your Grace." Edward bowed deeply.

Her blue eyes—remarkably similar in color to the small lapis scarab on the table at her elbow—flashed, and a small frown pinched her brow as she glanced at him. "Come in—and stop that title nonsense. I have no patience for it." When he moved closer, she looked up at him and grimaced. "Pray, don't hover over me. It would be best if you would take a seat." Her sharp gaze drifted to the door. She let out a long-suffering sigh. "I suppose you would like some tea?" She sounded as if she considered such a desire to be quite incomprehensible.

Then she sneezed and sneezed again. Her color faded, and she pressed her fingers over her mouth, staring at the floor with an intensity that warned him that something wasn't quite right. She swallowed several times and grew even paler.

After a swift glance around the room, he picked up one of the vases of flowers from a nearby table, ruthlessly dumped out the contents, and pushed the vase into her hands.

While she was violently ill, he yanked the bell pull and moved to the door. When the butler arrived, Edward shrugged out of his coat, handed it to the butler and gave him a series of terse orders.

"May I remove this?" he asked gently when he returned to the duchess, who was leaning back in her chair with her eyes closed, the vase clasped loosely in her hands.

She nodded, and he took the vase away, placing it on a table near the door.

"I took the liberty of ordering some mint tea," he said when he joined her again.

The duchess grimaced before she delicately touched her handkerchief to the corners of her damp eyes and her forehead. "I should apologize." Her mouth twisted again.

He held up his hand to stop her. "There is no need. Sir Bernard spilled his snuff over my sleeve, I should have removed my coat before entering." He smiled. "That filthy rose-scented mixture of his is enough to make anyone ill."

She returned his smile, although her lips wavered.

"Does His Grace know?" he asked at last when she remained silent, swallowing repeatedly.

"Yes." Her eyes flashed with a touch of malice when she looked at him. "And there is no need for you to concern yourself over my brief weakness. His Grace's pleasure at the prospect of another child is enough to make anyone quite ill, I assure you."

Edward chuckled. The duchess was famous for remarking that she considered even the drabbest moth to be more interesting, vastly more intelligent, and far more presentable than most children. But her words were as false as the fashionably hard exterior she cultivated. She was far more devoted and loving to her first child than she pretended, and her second would no doubt be just as cherished. No amount of badinage could hide the fact that she was a doting mother.

"Sit, please." She waved Edward to the chair across from her as the butler entered, followed by a maid carrying a large silver tray.

The aroma of mint wafted into the air, and he glanced at the duchess again.

The scent didn't appear to affect her. Her color was slowly returning, and she appeared to have regained her composure.

"Thank you, Your Grace." He bowed again before sitting on the edge of an elegant gold brocade chair facing her.

After busying herself with the tea, she poured the pale green liquid into one of the china cups and handed it to him before preparing her own. She gazed at him over the rim as she took a cautious sip. "I am told you have studied law. Is this true?"

"Yes. I have read a bit," he answered cautiously. The duke had an experienced man of business already and had no need of Edward's limited expertise. He could only hope that the duchess hadn't gotten into some sort of legal scrape that she wished to keep secret from her husband.

Getting embroiled in such matters and withholding information from the duke would not be a wise course of action.

As if divining his thoughts, the duchess smiled, her blue eyes gleaming. "Afraid I will involve you in something untoward?" She waved one hand negligently while her other balanced the cup of tea in mid-air. "His Grace is perfectly happy to deal with any small transgressions of mine—if any should occur."

Somehow, he thought she was a little optimistic about His Grace's pleasure concerning whatever it was that she'd done. But apparently, she wasn't going to burden him with awkward confidences.

"Then you don't require advice?" he asked.

"Not I," she confirmed. "However, I—that is—*we* do have a slight problem, which both the duke and I feel sure you are well-suited to resolve." She rested one hand on her belly briefly. "I would have gone, myself, but it is awkward at the moment."

"Then I will do my best," he murmured when she eyed him, obviously expecting some kind of a reply.

She grinned. "I have no doubt of that. We would like you to go to Charleston—in South Carolina—the United States of America, you know, to represent our interests."

The light dawned. The duchess was having difficulties with her inheritance in that distant colony. He'd heard that her previous guardians had mismanaged the estate, and it could not be an easy task to straighten matters out when an entire ocean separated one from the property or properties in question.

"I apologize, but I have not read law for the colonies—that is—the United States of America. I am not a barrister, nor am I in a position to represent you in a court of law, should the need arise. Perhaps the duke's man of business can recommend someone—"

"No." She raised a hand to cut him off and sniffed with exasperation. "It is not a matter for the courts, either those in England or in South Carolina. At least, not yet. There is a dispute over some property I own in Charleston—specifically a house."

"I understand, however—"

6

"Our ownership of the house is contested," she continued speaking relentlessly, her gaze fixed on him. "Some strange person claims that not only was the property never part of the Haywood estate, but that it was illegally sold by one of my guardians—before my marriage to His Grace—and that the purchaser has no right to the house." She sighed, and her blue gaze released him as she shook her head. "At a minimum, I believe we may need to refund the purchaser's money—that is not difficult." Once again, her eyes glowed with a wicked light as she studied him. "I am sure my previous guardian will be more than happy to return the money paid to him for the wretched house. But beyond that, we must determine who is the true owner. I wish to know if it is my home—my childhood home—or not. I believe that it is. If so, the person infesting the place must be removed. She has no right to be there."

"Very well, Your Grace," he said, considering matters. "However, as I perhaps mentioned, I am not versed in the property laws of South Carolina—"

"As a member of the family, I'm persuaded you will pursue this matter much more diligently and honestly than any stranger in another country. Even if that stranger were well-versed in the law. Perhaps *particularly* if that person were well-versed. I have no desire to be cheated again." The duchess's smile grew positively evil. "Both the duke and I have given this matter a great deal of consideration. We believe this is the best course of action."

Her request might seem simple to her, but it presented myriad difficulties for him. While he could act as her agent, he was not an expert. "As I mentioned, I have no knowledge of the local property laws."

"When you return to Archer House, you will find several books concerning the subject of property law and inheritance delivered to you. They will give you something to read on board the ship. We have booked you a first class cabin on the *Hercules*, which leaves Liverpool on the eighth of December. That allows you two weeks to make preparations and arrive in Liverpool. Ample time, I should

7

say." One of her red-gold brows rose, daring him to object. "Two weeks is also long enough to allow you to obtain a special license, if you wish to marry before you depart. Lady Olivia gave me to understand there might be something in the way of an understanding between you and a friend of hers—a Miss Denholm, I believe." Her head tilted to one side as she studied him. "A long sea journey to South Carolina could be very romantic as a honeymoon."

If she were looking for an effective way to prod him into accepting her request, she couldn't have picked a better stick than the persistent Miss Denholm.

Two weeks. Despite his exasperation, he was intrigued by the problem Her Grace had thrown at his head, and two weeks was more than sufficient time to pack and travel to Liverpool.

"Have we an agreement, Cousin Edward?" the duchess asked.

"Yes," he replied. "I shall do my best to represent your interests."

"Excellent!" She smiled sunnily. "You and Lady Hildegard must be in Liverpool by no later than the seventh of December to depart on the *Hercules*."

"Lady Hildegard?" He studied her. Surely, she was simply making a deplorable jest. She had long been known to cherish a taste for such things.

She laughed so hard she had to grab for her magazine again to keep it from sliding off her blue silk dress to the floor. "Oh, did I forget to mention? Lady Hildegard expressed a desire to see the city of my childhood, and I could not say no. She is so very excited about the prospect. And your brother, Lord Wraysbury, approved, as well. So the matter is quite settled. It will be very educational for her, and we can put off her curtsy to Society until her return."

Apparently, his entire family had been involved in this decision, except him. He eyed her, considering the disadvantages of making an enemy of the duchess.

The duchess grinned at him and placed her cup on the table next to her, knocking against the blue scarab. The lapis bug wobbled on the edge for a breathless second before an errant draft knocked it over.

Edward caught it before it hit the floor and placed it on the table, next to the cup.

There was little point in arguing. With a grunt, he nodded. "Very well. Have you any documents relating to the property in question?"

"Several pounds of the stuff," the duchess answered gaily. "I have sent it along with the books. Do you have any other questions?"

"Should I?" he asked dryly.

"Not if you wish to leave without any further surprises." Her voice shook with laughter.

"Then I believe I have none," he replied.

"Excellent decision." The duchess stood, forcing Edward to stand as well. "Now if you will excuse me, I have another crate from Cairo I wish to unpack." She cast him a questioning glance. "Unless you would like to assist me? Are you interested in Egyptian art?"

"No, Your Grace, and I'm afraid I must leave you to enjoy your treasure in peace." He bowed and backed to the door.

"If you need anything, be sure to let me know," she called to him.

"I'm sure you have already thought of everything, Your Grace," he replied wryly. Then he paused at the doorway. "Did I understand correctly that there is someone living in the house?"

"Yes." Her eyes darkened and her mouth turned down. Pale of cheek, she sat down again and swallowed. The expression that had crossed her face briefly could have been either sadness or worry, and when she spoke, her voice was low and troubled. "Mr. Tarte's most recent letter indicated that a member of the previous owner's family—Stonewright is their name—has taken up residence on the assumption that the family still owns the house. It is sad—

unfortunate." She looked at him and frowned as her hands restlessly rubbed the upholstered arms of her chair. "It is awkward—I have no wish to leave anyone destitute, and I have no idea how many may be living there. Perhaps it is merely a widow and her children—I really don't know." She gazed at him, her eyes searching his face. "You must promise me that you will see them settled in another apartment, if at all possible. I know what it is to be homeless—I will not have that happen to an entire family, or a widow and her children. Or anyone, for that matter."

Her request might have struck another man as unusual, but knowing the duchess's difficult upbringing and her constant moves from one guardian to the next, concern over another woman's possible homelessness was understandable.

A twinge of unease settled in his chest. "I give you my word, Your Grace. I will do my best to ensure all parties are treated fairly." His lips twisted in a wry smile. "I don't fancy myself as a cruel evictor of women and children."

"Thank you." She smiled, relief bringing her natural radiance back to her cheeks. Her vivid coloring glowed in the sunlight streaming in through the window. "I've always liked you—I knew we'd made the correct choice. Have a good journey, Cousin Edward, and good day."

A good journey? With Hildegard doing her best to inconvenience him, a trunk full of law books to study, and a strange woman to relocate? Her Grace was either being far too optimistic, or suffered from a gross misunderstanding of the situation.

Unlike her, he had no delusions. Traveling to the colonies and trying to determine the legal status of a house purportedly owned—or once owned—by the duchess was going to be an exercise in tedium and frustration, even if his younger sister decided to behave rationally for once in her short life.

And the lady currently occupying the house would no doubt do her best to prevent him from ascertaining the truth if she thought it might be to her benefit to obscure it.

On the whole, he suspected the experience would be rather like sticking one's hand into a bag of scorpions; not immediately fatal, but certainly a bit uncomfortable.

Chapter Two

January 20, 1823, Charleston, South Carolina

Charity Stonewright pointed her pistol halfway between the lawyer, Mr. Tarte, and the front door. "I am sorry you felt the need to visit Oldwood—"

"Uh-um." Mr. Tarte cleared his throat and frowned, cutting her off. "Haywood Mansion, if you please," he said in a fussy, precise voice. Although his small, close-set brown eyes remained fixed on the weapon in her hand, his pinched mouth and cold, firm expression told her that he was determined to do his duty, no matter the consequences.

Or maybe he was aware that the pistol wasn't loaded. The thought made her return his frown with an icy vengeance.

The lawyer shifted his feet uneasily although he didn't quite retreat.

"Oldwood," she repeated.

"I will not argue the matter, Miss Stonewright." He eyed her. "Will you *please* give me that weapon?" He held out his hand. "We do not want another accident, do we? Poor Officer Carmichael—"

"I never hit him—that shot never even came close to hitting him," she said, interrupting him. Her gaze strayed momentarily to the hole the bullet had left in the white column to the right and slightly above Mr. Tarte's shoulder.

That wild shot was precisely why her pistol was currently *not* loaded. She had no intention of accidentally murdering anyone, even if she were seriously tempted.

"Which, young lady, is why you are not currently under arrest, though I must say you should be grateful to Officer Carmichael for not pressing charges. Women are ill-equipped to handle firearms, and if I may say so, Miss Stonewright, you should not consider yourself an exception to that rule." Mr. Tarte shook his head.

Charity widened her eyes in a thoroughly insincere expression of amazement. "Is that a rule? Truly? I had not heard that. Clearly, my knowledge of the rules of etiquette is incomplete."

Mr. Tarte flushed and stared fixedly at the edge of the door with such an accusing, sour expression that she glanced at his small feet in expectation of a sharp kick at the offending piece of wood. Instead, he took a deep breath and transferred his gaze to her face. "This property does not belong to you or your family, and you must vacate the premises immediately." He shifted the leather case he held in his hand, holding it against his stomach as he opened it and fished around inside. Paper rustled, and he mumbled under his breath before he pulled out a much-folded letter. A portion of a broken red wax seal clung to the top edge. He placed the case between his feet and held up the paper with a flourish. "The Duchess of Peckham, the former Miss Charlotte Haywood, has written to our firm. She is sending a representative to verify the title and ownership of this property. The sale to our previous client by one of her guardians has come under question and, in fact, has been rescinded by agreement between the concerned parties. The matter must be resolved."

Charity clamped her mouth shut and worked very hard to keep from waving her pistol impatiently. "Then the duchess will discover that this property never was hers to sell. It is mine. It belongs to my family, and as I inherited all properties and goods possessed by my father upon his death a year ago last September, I am therefore the rightful owner." *There.* If Mr. Tarte wanted to converse in the stuffiest, most legal-sounding terms imaginable, she was more than pleased to oblige him.

"The Haywood family—"

"No," she interrupted him. "While they *claimed* my grandfather sold Oldwood to Mr. Haywood, no one has ever shown me a legal document signed by my grandfather, authorizing such a sale. And my father never said a word about such a sale." She smiled triumphantly at him, hiding a ripple of doubt.

If they still owned the mansion, why had they lived in near poverty in Philadelphia? They could either have sold it to obtain the money, or returned to Charleston, as she had done, to live. The fact that they hadn't, and that her father never even mentioned returning home to Charleston, left her with the niggling worry that Mr. Tarte might be correct.

A ripple of emotion raced over Mr. Tarte's face, revealing that even he had his concerns over the title. She suspected it was the sole reason why, despite numerous attempts, no one had actually forced her to vacate the premises. Charity felt a quick flush of victory before the lawyer's mouth tightened again.

"While the original document, or documents, may have been misplaced, I assure you, the property was sold and is part of the original Haywood estate." He cleared his throat and straightened, and although it may have just been the shifting late afternoon light, his little eyes seemed to glow for a second with sympathy. "That is precisely why the duchess is sending a representative to study the matter." He coughed into one hand. "Although I could have taken care of this question for her, as I indicated in my reply."

"I'm sure you could have," Charity said, amused by his reaction to the implications and his subsequent affront to his dignity and competence. "And I'm sure you will therefore agree that until the matter is resolved, there is no need for me to leave."

Even if she wanted to go, she had insufficient funds to find a new home. It was Oldwood or nothing.

"You are trespassing," the lawyer stated. The firmness of his voice indicated he felt that statement concluded their discussion to his satisfaction.

She fluttered her eyelashes at him. "One could say *you* are the one currently trespassing," she said in a sweet voice. She raised the barrel of her pistol an inch, just to catch his attention.

"Miss Stonewright, *please,* try to be reasonable. You cannot be here when the duchess's representative arrives."

"I don't see why not."

He picked up his case and frowned at her. "I cannot allow you to remain."

"You cannot stop me from doing so." She lowered her weapon and reached out to touch his arm briefly. "I'm sorry, Mr. Tarte. I know this places you in a difficult position, but I have difficulties, as well. I'm sure I can find the truth of the matter, given enough time. And whoever the duchess sends can't really blame you for my presence. I'd be more than happy to explain to him that you've made every effort possible to oust me from Oldwood."

"I am sure that will impress him," Mr. Tarte replied in such a dry voice that Charity couldn't suppress a small laugh.

"The duchess won't fire you—I'm sure she still has faith in you."

He shook his head, clearly disagreeing. The woebegone expression that flashed over his face almost made her want to assure him she'd leave—almost, but not quite. She couldn't forget that she had nowhere else to go. Poverty forced her to remain where she was. As a result, she felt her own woebegone expression settle over her features.

"Please reconsider, Miss Stonewright. That is all I ask." Mr. Tarte turned and descended the few steps leading to the sidewalk. His narrow shoulders were bowed as if he carried an unbearable burden instead of a small leather case containing a few papers.

She watched until he disappeared around the corner before she shut and locked the front door. Maybe they would leave her alone for a few days so she could continue her search. There had to be something hidden in the house that would prove she was indeed the owner as she claimed. Her father would have said something if the property had been sold, wouldn't he? Certainly, there would have been more money after such a sale.

A sudden hot surge of tears burned her eyes. She wiped them away with the heel of her hand and sniffed until she could breathe again. He'd been dead over a year—why did this crushing grief hit her now, making her want to crumble onto the floor and wail? She was so alone and so tired, trying to manage on her own. She just wanted to feel her father's arms around her for a few minutes and hear his laughing voice telling her not to be such a silly mouse, shivering in the corner with fear.

The problem was, no matter how confident she sounded to others like Mr. Tarte, she actually did feel like a little mouse, all alone, trapped in a corner with a cat sitting a whisker's breadth away.

An English cat, coming all the way from London.

Chapter Three

January 25, 1823, Charleston

Edward and his sister finally arrived at the disputed property in Charleston, South Carolina, on a rainy evening, a little after nine. Although there was a streetlamp on the corner of the block, the misty rain obscured the light, and all Edward could see was a dark, hulking building, partially hidden behind trees and overgrown shrubbery.

Drenching swaths of rain and black shadows concealed the mansion's architectural details, but Edward got a distinct impression of overwhelming decrepitude. The faint glow of candlelight shone in two of the windows, one on the first floor and one he'd noticed toward the rear of the building as they'd come around the block.

"I thought we would never arrive," Hildegard said in a tired voice. "I certainly hope the cook has something better than biscuits and cheese. I shall consider myself fortunate if I never have to eat another such meal again." She stumbled on the uneven walkway as they made their way carefully to the front stoop.

"I'm sure they will have something suitable, Lady Hildegard." Edward held out a hand to help his sister climb the shallow front steps.

White columns on either side of them gleamed dully in the fitful light cast by the streetlamp. Hildegard leaned tiredly against one of them, her gaze fixed upon him.

Hildegard snorted. "*Lady* Hildegard—who are you trying to impress? I only see two of us here, and no one in this country uses titles."

"I fear I am unable to escape from the persistent delusion that using your honorary title of *lady* will one day encourage you to act like one." Edward's mouth twisted into a lopsided grin.

"That certainly is a lamentable delusion." She laughed. "Resign yourself to disappointment, dear brother, and think, instead, about how to convince the cook of this wretched place that we require a decent meal. And beds that are not so damp they are actually sprouting mushrooms," she said, reminding him that she'd actually found a tiny fungus growing quite happily in a dark corner of her bunk on the clipper that took them from New York to Charleston. That particular leg of their journey left them all feeling bruised, cold, and slightly mildewed.

He chuckled. "*Touché.*"

But they both knew that a journey overland would have been longer and much worse. They had arrived in New York at the height of what appeared to be a very unpleasant winter. Local reports indicated that the Hudson River had frozen in December, and although the weather had moderated somewhat in January, Edward had no desire to be mired in snow and muck on their slow way to South Carolina. So he'd chosen the quicker route by sea, assured Hildegard that they would see a bit more of the country after the spring thaw, and ignored her subsequent complaints about their tiny quarters and the wretched food.

A series of loud sniffles caught Edward's attention. The increasingly morose silence of both Hildegard's personal maid, Louisa Nettle, and his own valet, Brian Atwood, spoke volumes about their opinion on travel in general and sailing in particular. They stood dejectedly behind Edward and Hildegard, sneezing and dripping on the walkway.

"You were a beast not to change rooms with me," Hildegard said.

"But I had a trunk full of valuable books. The damp would have ruined them. What else could I do?" he asked, struggling not to laugh as he stepped closer to the front door.

"You could have changed rooms with me—that's what you could have done," she repeated with exasperation.

"Just be thankful our quarters on the *Hercules* were relatively comfortable."

"And *relatively* first class. I had no idea they would be so cramped and mean."

"They were perfectly comfortable."

"Only if you'd never slept in an actual bed before. With decent pillows."

After a final exasperated glance at his young sister that she undoubtedly couldn't see because of the darkness of the stoop, he raised his walking stick and rapped sharply on the door.

They waited. His sharp ears caught no indication of any footsteps within. He walked back several yards and glanced up at the window on the first floor. The dim candlelight still glowed faintly through the rain-smeared glass panes. Cold droplets spattered his cheeks and dripped down his neck as he studied the mansion.

Sighing, he returned to the door and beat a louder tattoo with the gold knob of his stick.

"There are servants, are there not?" Hildegard asked, peering up at Edward and tilting her head in an effort to see his face. "There was a light, was there not?"

"Yes. There is still a light." He glanced over his shoulder at their two servants, shivering in the mist, and at the street beyond. There were a few passersby, but they were hunched beneath the heavy folds of coats and shawls, scurrying past to their destinations. None of them seemed interested in the four people standing forlornly in front of the Haywood Mansion.

He gripped the doorknob and rattled it, but the door was securely locked.

Using his cane, he knocked again, listening as the loud noise echoed and finally faded in the depths of the house. It sounded empty, completely deserted. While finding the house empty did mean he wouldn't have to evict anyone, it did mean that he'd have to find the lawyer, Mr. Tarte, in order to obtain the key and enter.

With a sigh, he half-turned. A flicker of yellow light caught his attention. The wide fanlight above the door glowed with the faint, wavering illumination of a candle.

After a minute, the doorknob rattled as someone struggled to unfasten the heavy lock.

The door creaked open a few inches, spilling light through the gap.

"Finally! Where have you been?" a woman's breathless voice asked.

She peered around the edge of the door, holding a candle above her head. The golden gleam of red hair curled over the woman's pale face. Below the tangle of hair, eyes blinked, lost in shadowed hollows beneath her arching brows. A sprinkling of freckles leapt over the bridge of her straight nose and high cheekbones.

"We would like to speak with Mr. Stonewright," Edward said, hoping his cousin was incorrect when she said the woman lived here alone. "If he is available."

"Mr. Stonewright? My—" She broke off before asking sharply, "Who are you?" Then, as if she suffered sudden doubts about the wisdom of opening the door to strangers, she started to slam it shut.

He shoved his booted foot into the gap and thrust the door open, forcing her to retreat into the dim hallway.

Clearly nervous, she glanced around the near-empty hallway, her mouth set in a grim line.

Edward held up his hands, although the cane gripped in his right hand marred his attempt to appear harmless. "I am Edward Archer." He reached through the door and dragged Hildegard over the threshold. "This is my sister, Lady Hildegard Archer. I believe we are expected. Is there a Mr. Stonewright? Is he available?"

"Archer? I don't know anyone named Archer," the woman said, gliding back another yard, her feet invisible under the long hem of her pale gray gown. Her gaze flicked to the candle in her hand, as if she contemplated blowing it out and escaping in the resulting darkness.

"No, but I am sure if you speak to your master, he will recognize our names. Or your mistress," he amended. "We sent him notice of our pending arrival weeks ago."

"Master?" A harsh laugh broke from her mouth. "He—he is not here." She lifted her round chin, daring him to argue otherwise.

Switching the cane to his left hand, he held up his right in a gesture of surrender. "Please—we mean you no harm. We simply wish to speak with Mr. or Mrs. Stonewright. He is expecting us. We are cousins to the Duchess of Peckham—"

"We don't know any duchesses," she threw back, her chin set at a stubborn angle.

He studied her. Her straight back and air of defiance suggested she was not a servant. "You—and your husband? Father?—may have known her as Miss Charlotte Haywood."

"I didn't know her at all, and I would appreciate it if you would leave immediately. This is my house—you have no business here."

"Mr. Stonewright—"

"I own this property, and I am the head of this household. If you wish to speak to someone, then you must make do with me."

Behind him came the soggy squelching of their servants' footsteps as Atwood and Nettle sought the relative dryness of the stoop. Another volley of damp sneezes echoed through the door. Nettle blew her nose noisily and heaved a heavy sigh.

Mr. Stonewright or no Mr. Stonewright, they were not going back out into the foul weather to look for an inn if Edward had anything to say about it.

"As we informed Mr. or Mrs. Stonewright, the ownership of this property has yet to be determined," Edward replied calmly.

The red-haired woman leaned forward, body rigid with tension as she held the candle out slightly above shoulder-level. "It *has* been determined—it is mine."

"Then we will certainly be able to verify that," he replied. "May I ask when Mr. Stonewright will be available, and whom I am addressing?"

"No." The woman tilted her head to one side and eyed him with her lips compressed into a thin line.

"Oh, please, must we argue *now*?" Hildegard asked, interrupting and stepping forward with her hands holding the edges of her wet shawl tightly at the base of her neck. The feathers of her bonnet sagged down to her chin and contributed a steady, soaking drip of icy droplets onto her rain-darkened shawl and pelisse. "We are awfully tired, and it is raining, and we are simply *miserable*."

The woman's mouth twisted to one side with quickly suppressed amusement. "I'm sorry—"

"Don't say no," Hildegard pleaded as more water dripped slowly from the hem of her dress onto the wide oak floorboards. The pool spread around her until it merged with the puddle that had formed around Edward's boots. She shifted her feet, and her short walking boots squelched damply. "*Please.* I'm sorry we haven't been properly introduced, but truly I am Lady Hildegard Archer, and as he said, this is my brother, Mr. Edward Archer." She sketched a curtsy, staring hopefully at the red-haired woman.

"Miss Charity Stonewright," the woman said with a sharp nod. "I *am* sorry—"

"Please, don't make us leave, Miss Stonewright," Hildegard interrupted her. "I'm positively *famished*. And it is raining." Her voice quavered with misery. "And *cold*. I didn't think it would get this cold here."

Nettle crowded in after Hildegard, holding a drenched handkerchief to her red nose and sniffling as a third puddle formed around her worn, black boots.

The poor light from the candle and the shadowed hollows under her golden brows made it impossible to determine the color of Miss Stonewright's wide-set eyes, but Edward got the impression they were blue when she blinked and took a step back.

She studied each of them in turn. Despite her rigid, unwelcoming attitude, her high cheekbones and softly rounded chin gave her a very young, very appealing appearance. Dimples lurked in her plump cheeks, and she looked like the kind of woman made for laughter and warm kisses.

Her gaze rested on Edward for a long time before she flicked a quick look at the door behind them.

Indecision curved her mouth downward. She chewed on her lower lip for a moment before she said, "There may be some cheese."

A soft moan broke from Hildegard, and she glanced over her shoulder at Edward.

It was all he could do not to chuckle at the look of absolute revulsion wrinkling his sister's brow and puckering her mouth at the mention of cheese.

"Very good," Edward said, motioning to Atwood to enter and shut the door. "We are much obliged to you. If you show us to the kitchen, we can find something, I am sure, while we wait to speak to your father. Or brother." Surely, she didn't live here alone.

"My father is deceased," she flung at him. A flush crept over her cheeks, and she dropped her gaze to the combining and spreading puddles darkening the floor. She clearly regretted her impulsive admission.

Interesting. If it was not her father she'd expected to find at the door, then who was it? A brother?

He frowned. Was she bold enough to live here alone, then? Defenseless? No wonder she was nervous about allowing strangers to enter the house. The thought made him uncomfortable.

Perhaps they should have found rooms at an inn rather than arriving here so abruptly. But they'd all been tired from traveling, and he'd been impatient to take the measure of those who had reportedly taken up residence illegally in the Haywood Mansion.

Now, he had discovered that the family he expected was actually *Miss* Stonewright, presenting even more difficulties than he'd anticipated. He didn't relish the role of the wicked lawyer, forcing a destitute woman out of her only home and into the storm-ravaged street.

23

Ignoring her inadvertent admission, Edward gestured to the servants standing behind him. "You must have received our letters. We sent several notices of our impending arrival. So perhaps you will allow Atwood to bring in our luggage." When Miss Stonewright's arched brows rose, he continued, saying, "We left a hired cart around the corner, near the rear of this house." He drew off his damp leather gloves. "I trust this will not inconvenience you unduly?"

"Not *unduly*," Miss Stonewright replied dryly. "I am not so cruel as to turn you out on a night like this, and I'm always pleased to have guests, even when they can only stay a single night."

He smiled wryly. "Don't despair, Miss Stonewright. I assure you we intend to grace you with our company for far longer than a single night."

Hildegard kicked him sharply on the ankle. Thankfully, his stout leather boots prevented her from accomplishing her apparent goal of breaking the bone, and she only left him with what felt like a deep bruise.

Another series of sneezes came from behind him. Nettle sniffed and let out a long, despairing sigh that seemed to imply that though they had found shelter, it was far too late to do anyone any good.

"How reassuring," Miss Stonewright said, stubbornly remaining where she was.

"The kitchen?" he reminded her, gesturing toward the dark hallway beyond her.

She flicked one last glance over his shoulder at the door before turning. "This way, then. Mr. Atwood can use the kitchen door to bring in your trunks, though it seems like a great deal of trouble to take for a single night."

"And the stables?" Edward asked, following her down a short passageway, through another door, and into another hallway.

"Behind the house. He should find them easily enough." She cast a quick look at him. "You brought your own horses with you?"

"No." He shook his head. "We hired them. However, they need to be fed and given shelter. The weather is somewhat unsettled."

"Unsettled?" Miss Stonewright laughed. "What a pleasant description for this absolutely wretched storm. It has been raining for the last three days, and the entire yard is flooded. If you wanted to claim someone's property, you should have selected an estate where you didn't run the risk of drowning in your own bed."

"I am surprised you stay, then," he replied, the soles of his boots scraping over the dusty wooden floor.

The shadows obscured most of the furnishings, but he had the impression that there were very few pieces of furniture, and the floors were not overly clean or shining with care. Like the outside, there was a desolate, abandoned air about the place, as if too few people lived here to fill the rooms with a sense of life or to maintain it properly.

"I *own* this place, decrepit though it may be," she threw at him in a harsh voice. She came to a halt in the middle of a large room and held the candle up again, though the feeble flame didn't do much to scare away the black shadows. "Here is the kitchen. While the larder is not precisely bare, it won't be what you are used to, I'm sure." She sounded pleased at the prospect of seeing them starve.

While Miss Stonewright used her candle to light two oil lamps, Hildegard walked over to the large wooden table in the center of the room. She pulled out one of the sturdy wooden chairs, and brushed her gloved hand over the seat. After yanking off her shawl, she draped the dripping garment over the back of another chair and rubbed her face tiredly before flopping down onto the chair.

Nettle picked up the shawl, shook it out, and then replaced it over the chair back, glancing around with a worry wrinkling her forehead.

Frowning with misery, Atwood made his way to the door at the rear of the room. He glanced outside and then threw a black look over his shoulder at Edward. With a grunt, he pulled up his collar and dashed out to attend to the horses and their baggage.

Edward strolled around the room and managed to find the pantry in the far corner. The contents weren't nearly as bad as he anticipated, and ignoring the large hoop of cheese, he collected a few items.

"Where is your cook?" Hildegard asked, looking optimistically at Miss Stonewright. "I hope it is not too much trouble to fix us a small meal. Anything would do, as long as it is hot."

He glanced at his sister sharply as he entered the pool of light around the table. Surely she realized that a woman who answered her own front door wasn't plagued with a houseful of servants. In fact, he had the strong suspicion that Miss Stonewright might be making do with one maid, if that, given the gritty state of the floors.

Before she could respond, Edward laid the items he'd found on the table. "We have eggs, the remnants of a ham, and a few other supplies. I am sure we can put together a tolerable meal without disturbing Miss Stonewright's servants, Lady Hildegard."

"What you so optimistically call *tolerable* is unlikely to meet even that lofty standard for the rest of us, I assure you," Hildegard said, staring with irritation at the food. Her fingers tapped the edge of the table.

"Then I recommend you keep any criticisms to yourself," Edward replied, checking the coals slumbering in the bowels of a huge stove and adding a few sticks of wood from a nearby basket. A large cast iron pan sat on top, still warm, and he found a crock of lard nearby.

A simple, hot meal would not be impossible.

"I didn't know you could cook," Hildegard said, getting up from her chair to peer over his shoulder.

"There are a great many things you don't know, Hildie." he replied absently.

"I didn't know you were even interested in cooking," she said, persistently seeking an explanation for his unexpected behavior as she poked at a nearby cast iron skillet.

"I don't like relying on the whims of others." He glanced at Miss Stonewright, who stood nearby, arms crossed, watching him with her brows raised.

Her lips were partially open in a look of faint surprise, but when she caught his gaze, she shut her mouth and frowned with irritation.

He nodded to her. "If you wish to return to your previous employment, we will be quite all right here for the time being."

She flushed and looked down at the floor. "I—"

"You were expecting someone? A guest perhaps?" He raised a brow as he scraped a dab of lard into the pan, carved off a few slices of ham, and added them. As the ham began to sizzle, he cracked eggs into the liquefied fat and sprinkled them with salt.

He hadn't forgotten her remark when she opened the front door, even if she hoped he had. A small smile flickered over his mouth.

She sputtered, flicking uncomfortable glances at Hildegard and then at him.

"There is no need for concern, Miss Stonewright," he added, flipping the ham and eggs over. "We will be well occupied here for at least an hour. We will not intrude unnecessarily into your affairs."

"You have already intruded," Miss Stonewright said, her voice vibrating with anger. "*Unnecessarily.*" She swallowed and took a deep breath. "And I am not expecting anyone."

Edward shrugged and sprinkled a dash of pepper over the eggs. "As you say. And I do apologize. It is not our intention to pry or cause you difficulties."

"Then you have failed miserably—because you have." There was no mistaking the bitterness in her reply. "And will doubtless cause even more before you leave."

"We will do our best to cause no harm," he answered quietly.

Miss Stonewright shook her head, her golden-red hair gleaming in the soft lamplight. She studied him, opened her mouth, and then shut it.

As Edward removed the pan from the fire, she glided out of the room, her soft slippers making no sounds, despite the faint gray film of dirt scattered over the floor.

"Well," Hildegard pulled her chair away from the table, its legs scraping the floor, and sat down with a huff. "What did you think of her?" She cocked her head to the side, like a robin eyeing a likely worm.

"I think she is a woman in a difficult position." He shrugged.

"You said we were to see *Mr.* Stonewright—do you think she was lying?"

"For what purpose?"

"To avoid the inevitable, of course." She glanced at the ceiling. "He might be upstairs, hiding." She straightened, grinning with excitement, and her voice growing rushed and breathless as she said, "She might be his mistress, killing him for his money, and now we have interrupted all her plans. Or he might be an invalid, lying upstairs on his deathbed, brought low by our terrible demands that they vacate their house—the only home they have ever known!"

"Control your imagination. If there was a Mr. Stonewright, she would have no reason to deny his existence." He sighed. "Again—why do so? For what purpose?"

Hildegard shrugged. "Because he is ill and doesn't want to talk to us, of course."

"That may well be, but I suspect Miss Stonewright was truthful—at least partially truthful—with us. I doubt there is a sickly father upstairs, languishing in bed while his daughter tries to bar strangers from their door."

"Or mistress."

He sighed. "I doubt she is anyone's mistress." Mistresses were generally more fashionably dressed, for one thing. However, he didn't want to encourage his sister's imagination, so he didn't mention that fact.

She huffed, clearly disappointed with his prosaic response. "Well, you never answered me—what did you think of *her?* Were you expecting to discover such a woman here?"

"No," Edward admitted.

"So?" Hildegard grinned. "I thought she was very pretty. What was your impression of her?"

He studied the door through which Miss Stonewright had disappeared. "I have not decided, yet."

"You never notice anyone. Well, I think she's decided about us—and her assessment is not very flattering. Or pleasant."

Edward chuckled as he placed plates of food in front of Hildegard and Nettle, before taking a seat at the head of the table. "No. Regrettably, we may be destined to prove her low opinion of us if Her Grace is correct about the ownership of this property."

Frowning, Hildegard stopped eating long enough to look at him and say, "Maybe Her Grace is wrong, then. I think it is wrong to evict Miss Stonewright just because of some old law no one cares about."

"Someone cares about it, or we wouldn't be here," he said gently before pushing his plate away.

Hildegard snorted. "You mean *you* care about it."

"I mean we all care about it because Her Grace cares about it, and we know nothing about Miss Stonewright."

"Except that she is very pretty."

"If you appreciate red hair. And a dusting of freckles." He held up a hand to prevent further argument. "I suggest we all suspend judgment—at least until morning." He grinned when his sister snorted inelegantly, and he gently bumped her stubborn chin with his fist. "Tomorrow we may find that Miss Stonewright is nothing more than a specter created by the moldy cheese and weevil-infested biscuits we had for breakfast this morning."

"How amusing." Hildegard rolled her eyes and stood, her chair scraping noisily along the same grooves she'd left previously on the floor. "But I wouldn't be surprised if

29

there were ghosts here, too. I have never seen a drearier house in my entire life. I'm beginning to think Her Grace is quite mad to want this property. I'd be more pleased to be rid of it than to discover it was mine."

"Oh, Lady Hildegard! Spirits?" Nettle exclaimed, pressing a hand to her pale lips. Her pink nose twitched, and her red-rimmed eyes watered before she sneezed into her wrinkled handkerchief. "Please, don't say such things!" She looked around the kitchen, her reddened gray eyes wide, clearly afraid she'd find a phantom peering at them from the pantry, or blood dripping down the walls. "This place is not haunted—please don't say that it is! I don't know that I could stay here if that's so."

Hildegard shrugged and picked up her still-damp shawl. "I think we will be fortunate if it is *only* haunted."

Nettle moaned before sneezing again into her handkerchief.

Chuckling, Edward pushed his sister toward the door and picked up a lamp, leaving Nettle peering nervously at the flickering shadows as she cleaned up their dishes as quickly as humanly possible.

Chapter Four

Where is he? Charity went to the wide window in the sitting room and stared out into the darkness. The storm was gaining strength. Rain sluiced down the panes of glass, obscuring her view of the street. Howling wind whipped through the oleander bushes surrounding the house, and their wiry branches scrabbled and slapped against the brick walls and windowsill, seeking a way to escape the icy fury of the gale.

She cocked her head, listening for the telltale drip of water as it worked ceaselessly to find another hole in the battered roof, and hoped her cousin was drenched to the bone and completely miserable. As usual, Kevin was somewhere else when she needed his assistance. He *knew* that the Archers were coming—she'd shown him the letters from Mr. Archer and their lawyer—and yet her cousin was nowhere to be found when they had arrived.

If he'd been there, she might not have been so foolish as to open the door and let them inside. Once again, she cocked her head to listen to the muted, distant sounds of voices and footsteps competing with the sound of rain pounding the house. Charleston was not always quiet, it was too busy with the port and all the bustling traffic one finds in a thriving city, but she was used to the rattle of wagons, the clatter of horses, and the occasional shout in the street and no longer really heard them.

However, the noises made by strangers creeping around her kitchen made her move with nervous jerks, too ill-at-ease to remain still.

She wasn't used to it. She didn't like the faint sounds created by other people wandering around Oldwood as if they owned it. Other people meant a myriad of problems she didn't wish to face. Demands. Questions. *Explanations.*

Not that she lacked determination and spirit—she was frequently accused of having far too much of both—but the complications presented by others simply made everything that much more difficult.

She turned away from the window and grimaced at the feel of grit under the thin soles of her shoes. Yet another reason to resent the sudden arrival of the Archers. She'd been preparing to sweep when they'd knocked, so they had no doubt noticed the dirt everywhere. Tomorrow was the day for a thorough cleaning, so of course, they saw everything at its worst.

If Mr. Archer had come alone, it wouldn't have mattered so much. Men rarely noticed anything, unless there were actual plants growing between the cracks in the floor. But women were another matter entirely. She frowned and wiped her hands down the sides of her worn skirt.

Women noticed everything. Every tiny detail, like the outdated, much-washed dress she wore.

Who brings their sister to an eviction? Why on *earth* would Mr. Archer do such a thing? What he had been thinking to drag his young sibling along on what would certainly be an unpleasant journey? Particularly if Charity had anything to say about it.

That thought brought a twisted smile to her lips.

Miss Archer was most assuredly to blame for a great deal, already. She was the reason the Archers were making themselves at home in her kitchen. If Miss Archer hadn't looked so pitiful and bedraggled, Charity would have shut the door cheerfully right in Mr. Archer's dripping face.

Now, she had the two of them sneaking around with their servants, making themselves at home. The real surprise was that Mr. Archer hadn't already thrown Charity out into the driving rain. But no doubt he wanted to be well-rested when he strolled down the stairs tomorrow morning and evicted her.

Or tried.

A series of authorities, including Officer Carmichael, Mr. Tarte, and a nervous constable she'd never seen before, had tried several times in December and January, but she was still here, and here she would stay. Sending an Englishman across the Atlantic to force her to leave wasn't going to be any more effective than Miss Charlotte Haywood's lawyer, Mr. Tarte, had been.

Another twinge of irritation made her smooth her hands over her hips. Apparently, Miss Haywood was now a duchess, which made it even more ridiculous for her to persist in her attempts to claim ownership of this dismal property. Didn't she have sufficient palaces and mansions in England? Why cling to this forlorn little house?

It wasn't Miss Haywood's and never had been hers. *Haywood Mansion, indeed.* The house was Oldwood and always would be. The duchess was just being difficult, and Charity had no intention of being cheated out of her only home. The crumbling mansion should never have been part of the estate the duchess had inherited.

A footstep sounded in the hall. Charity glanced at the doorway and frowned as the glow of a lamp grew brighter. Mr. Archer held one of the kitchen lamps up at shoulder height as he stepped into the front sitting room.

"I apologize for disturbing you, but we would like to retire for the night," he said. His soft tone suggested he regretted his intrusion, but Charity was not fooled by his apologetic air or square-chinned, handsome face. He was not there to make friends with her.

Quite the reverse, in fact.

"There is an inn less than a mile away," she suggested, facing him.

A half-smile tugged at his mouth. "Must we cover the same ground again?"

"Not at all," she replied blithely. "Just go to your left when you leave. The inn is in the opposite direction from the docks, so you will have the opportunity to travel over quite different ground on your way there." She crossed her arms at her waist and raised her brows.

"Your wit may be a trifle more amusing in the morning, but for now, we would appreciate being shown to our rooms." He studied her, his dark eyes glimmering with flashes of gold in the lamplight. "Or we can simply select bedrooms at random, if you prefer." A slight hardening in his voice warned her that she would be unwise to push him much further.

"No need." She sighed and took a step toward the door. "There are two bedrooms that you and your sister can use. They are clean, and there are fresh sheets on the beds."

He nodded and moved out of her way. "I appreciate your patience with us. I know this is a difficult situation."

"Not as difficult as it will be," she murmured as she passed him and walked into the hallway. She picked up the lamp she'd left by the door while she still cherished the futile hope that her cousin might finally decide to visit her, and she headed up the stairs.

Mr. Archer didn't respond to her comment, and as they climbed the staircase, she thought he hadn't heard. But when she glanced over her shoulder, a twisted smile curving his mouth indicated that he'd heard her very well and simply chose not to comment.

When they reached the gloomy landing, Mr. Archer held his lamp higher and glanced around before fastening his perceptive gaze on her. "If you will recall, we also have two servants with us. I don't wish to inconvenience your staff, but they will also need rooms."

"There are plenty of rooms on the fourth floor. They can select whichever ones they want." She shrugged and stared at the doors lining the hallway, wondering which rooms she should use.

While she wasn't overly concerned about the comfort of Mr. and Miss Archer, she didn't particularly want her cousin, Kevin Stonewright, to stroll into one of their bedchambers if he decided to visit her later tonight. Her mouth twitched, imagining Miss Archer, nightcap askew, screaming in surprise as she held the blankets to her chest if Kevin should happen to totter into her room, no doubt singing at the top of his lungs, clutching a bottle of rum in his fist.

If Kevin wandered into Mr. Archer's room, she wouldn't put it past him to shoot her cousin.

The thought sobered her.

"Fourth floor?" Mr. Archer appeared surprised, his black brows rising to the damp curls hanging over his forehead. "I realize you might not wish for us to remain, but I'd rather not have Nettle and Atwood camp on the roof."

She faced him.

"I was given to understand that the mansion was only three stories," he added.

She sighed impatiently, shaking her head. "What floor do you believe you are on now?"

"The first, of course." His response was just as curt as her reply.

"The second by my count. She pointed at the staircase. "You entered on the first floor."

"Very well." He gave one sharp nod before glancing at the series of doors lining the hallway.

She pointed to the left. "You may use the bedchamber there—the second door on your left." She turned to the right. "My room is on the right, further down the corridor. Your sister may use the room next to mine, which is the third door on the right. I trust the rooms will suit you."

"If they have beds which are not tossed up and down with each wave, I'm sure they will be more than adequate."

She had to laugh before she said, "Seasickness will not torment you here. I can at least assure you of that, although after the last storm, the roof leaks a little. But I don't think the water will reach you on this floor—it's mostly confined to the attic. Is there anything else you require?"

"No. We have disrupted your household sufficiently for one night." He smiled at her, and the expression transformed his coldly serious face into one so handsome and magnetic with charm that her breath caught in her throat.

She stared at him until she realized what she was doing. She dropped her gaze, forcing herself to breathe. What was the matter with her?

It was late, and she was tired. It was the only reasonable explanation for her unnerving reaction to his presence.

When she caught his glance, she flushed before the sounds of voices and footsteps distracted her. She looked at the closed door at the end of the dark corridor stretching out to her left.

"I should warn you," she said slowly. "Others who have stayed here have expressed ... concerns. About hearing things." The last thing she wanted was to admit that her cousin frequently showed up in the middle of the night, unannounced and generally unwanted. "There is no need for concern. Just lock your door if you are worried by noises."

"What kind of noises?" He glanced up and down the hall with apparent interest.

"Footsteps, voices, doors slamming...." She waved airily as if it were quite normal to hear such things in the middle of the night. "It is nothing. Truly. You know how it is with old houses. And the sea breeze, of course."

"Of course," he agreed with an unsettling twinkle in his eyes. "And you suggest I lock my door?"

"Yes. If you're nervous. Or scared." Her chin tilted up. "I wouldn't want you to shoot anyone by accident."

"Indeed. I don't anticipate being troubled by such noises." His lips twitched into a brief smile as his brown eyes roved over her face. He nodded. "But thank you for the warning." His teeth glimmered as he grinned, dimples creasing his cheeks. "And I promise not to shoot any visitors who don't deserve it."

Well, her cousin certainly deserved it tonight.

She turned and stepped toward the staircase, thinking about Kevin's more annoying habits, such as his failure to be there when she needed him to help her repel invaders to her domain.

Then she paused and turned back. "Oh, I wouldn't say the ghost—or whatever it is—doesn't deserve such a fate, but I'd appreciate it if you didn't introduce them to a fate even worse than death."

Mr. Archer chuckled. "You have my word, Miss Stonewright. I dislike interfering in family matters, deceased members or otherwise. So you may rest assured that if your, uh, spirits meet a worse fate, it will not be at my hands."

She smiled and shook her head before she descended the stairs. No matter how hard she tried, she couldn't help but feel the tug of Mr. Archer's charm, and she didn't like it. She had to get rid of him and his sister as soon as possible, and he was only making it harder.

Well, tomorrow he'd find out that she wasn't some soft, wilting flower on which he could tread. Or even a little mouse shivering in the corner.

He'd be gone before another nightfall if she had anything to say about it.

Chapter Five

A woman's sobs woke him. The sound was so soft that at first, Edward thought he'd dreamt the sound. He lay in bed, listening, as the wind whipped around the corner of the building and rattled his windows.

Another low moan echoed around him. He sat up. The sound came from nowhere and everywhere, like water seeping around and filling a cup dropped in a bucket of water.

Was this what Miss Stonewright warned me about? He eyed the door, sighed, and slipped his feet out from between the warm covers. The four-poster bed had been surprisingly comfortable and smelled faintly of lavender, even though the linen sheets were well-worn, and the coverlet was an indeterminate color that seemed mostly gray.

The heavy furniture was sparse but functional: just a large wardrobe, a small chest with three drawers, a chair, a nightstand, bed, and a washstand with white bowl, pitcher, and thin, white towel draped over the washstand's rod. Draperies kept out most of the drafts from the two windows, and on the whole, he was satisfied with his assigned room, even if Atwood had sniffed several times disparagingly as he unpacked Edward's trunk and put his clothing away.

The floor was cold under his feet and the old oak planks felt rough. An icy current of air cascaded over his toes and pooled around his ankles, making him shiver as another faint sigh made him stiffen.

Hildie...

A sense of urgency made him move more quickly. He found his slippers and robe, struggling into them as he listened to the creaking of the house. Was she frightened? What would she think if she awoke to such a low, breathy moan echoing through the halls? He could well imagine she'd be terrified. A small smile flickered over his lips as he took the candle from the nightstand next to his bed and carried it to the fireplace. He blew on one of the small embers smoldering in the ashes and lit the candle.

Hildie tried so hard to prove she was completely fearless, but he knew she had at least one weakness: a very sincere fear of phantoms. He couldn't let her wake up alone to such frightening noises in a strange place.

The sounds seemed to fade as he strode to the door, but he opened it anyway and stepped out into the hallway, his head cocked to one side. Another gusty sigh filled the hallway. The noise descended into an unintelligible tangle of whispers that reminded him of the complexity of sound one hears outside a tavern. No individual voices or understandable words could be heard—just a dull, low thrum of sounds.

A footstep scraped nearby. He turned sharply and studied the shifting darkness at the edge of the wavering circle of illumination from his candle. Nothing stirred behind him. Then he realized that the floors were made of wooden planks. The eerie footstep had the harsh quality of a leather sole slipping across stone.

A distant echo from a forgotten past. He pushed the thought away and listened.

Silence. Or mostly silence. The windows of his room rattled again under the assault of another gust of wind. A second later, a small eddy of cold air caressed his slippered feet. The old house groaned with a complex series of snaps and cracks as it settled a bit more around them.

He took another step, hesitating and holding his candle aloft. The golden light only reached a few yards down the hallway, and made a dark pit of the central staircase. He walked toward Hildie's room at the far end of the corridor. The creak of another door opening made him halt.

A golden glow spread out of the doorway of Miss Stonewright's room, and he heard the rasp of a soft footstep before she appeared. A long, white robe draped her slender figure, trailing over the floor behind her as she walked into the hallway, holding an old brass lamp out in front of her. She glided a few feet down the corridor toward Hildie's room before she jerked to a stop, noticing Edward for the first time.

"Who is there?" she called, lifting her lamp higher.

Apparently, it was only his candle she'd noticed.

"It is just me. Mr. Archer," Edward said as he moved closer. "Did you hear that noise, too?"

She studied him, her eyes sunken into dark pools and her skin pale. The sprinkling of freckles over the bridge of her nose stood out starkly in the wavering light, and her rigid posture reminded him strongly of Hildie when she was terrified and determined not to reveal it.

He lifted a reassuring hand before he dropped it to his side. She would no doubt take it very much amiss if he tried to embrace her here in the corridor while they were both clad in nothing but their nightclothes.

"Yes," she said before pressing her lips shut, perhaps regretting admitting even that much. She partially turned away.

"Is that noise what you were warning me about?"

She nodded, her mouth tightening even further.

He looked down the corridor toward his sister's room. The house was quiet now, and even the wind seemed to have died down. Perhaps Hildie had slept through the noises.

"I can check the house, if you wish," he offered, studying her lovely profile.

She flashed a glance at him and opened her lips before shutting them again. Her shoulders slumped with exhaustion. "I have searched. There is never anything to discover."

"The front door—"

"Is locked." She waved a hand at the shadowy staircase. "I made sure before I retired."

"Someone may have broken in." He stepped away. "I'll make sure the windows and doors are secured."

She sighed. "Very well. I'll accompany you." When he looked at her, she gave him a wan smile. "It is the least I can do."

They descended into the gloom of the ground floor in silence, and Edward strode to the front door. The lock was set, and he rattled it to make sure before moving to the right to check the windows.

"How often does this happen?" he asked, keeping his voice light.

As she trailed after him, he sensed that she was still disturbed by the way she kept looking over her shoulder and holding her lamp aloft. Her head tilted to the side as she periodically stopped to listen while they made their rounds to all the windows on the ground floor.

"Occasionally," she finally whispered.

"Perhaps it is only the wind."

"It comes on still, windless nights, as well." She halted to stare up the staircase at the darkness of the first floor. "It comes without warning—it just comes and then fades away—all without warning. At night." She turned to look at him, her eyes lost in black pools of shadow.

He touched her shoulder, surprised at how fragile her slender bones and muscles felt. "There are no spirits—"

"How do you know?" she flung at him. "You don't live here—you haven't heard it—night after night until it drives you nearly mad." Her voice rose before she snapped her mouth shut again and swallowed. Gripping the lamp, her hand clenched around it, causing the flame to flicker wildly until she stared at it, and by sheer force of will, steadied her arm. "You know nothing about this house."

"I know, Miss Stonewright, and I apologize. I didn't intend to dismiss your concerns so lightly. You are clearly exhausted—we all are." He smiled at her and gestured to the staircase. "We should retire. In the morning, perhaps you could show me the rest of the house. Perhaps there are structural issues that cause the strange noises."

"Don't you think I've looked?" Despite her quick retort, she lifted her gown enough to allow her to ascend the staircase.

"Of course. However, perhaps another look may reveal something. Don't give up hope of an ordinary explanation."

At the landing, he wavered, looking to the right. Should he check on Hildie, anyway? No noises came from her room, and she would undoubtedly be aggravated if he woke her up just to ask if she were all right. Traveling had been hard on both of them, and she no doubt was in a deep restorative sleep.

He smothered a yawn and glanced at the open door of his room.

"I have always expected there to be an explanation," Miss Stonewright said, pausing on her way to her room. "However, you have not lived here as long as I have. When you hear those pitiful cries night after night, we shall see if you remain sanguine about a reasonable cause. I bid you goodnight, Mr. Archer." A grim smile stretched her pale lips. "Sleep well."

"Good night, Miss Stonewright. Pleasant dreams." He waited until he heard her lock her door before he returned to his own bedchamber.

After a brief consideration, he turned the key to lock his door.

The gesture was probably useless, but it did make him sleep better when he finally climbed between the now-cold sheets.

Chapter Six

The sky was still dark when Charity got out of bed again, desperately wanting a few more hours of sleep. She winced as her bare feet touched the icy floor next to her bed.

Why, oh why, had she impulsively taken the small rag rug from its spot next to her bed and placed it next to Miss Archer's bed, instead?

With a sigh, she lit her lamp, poured cold water from the ewer into the bowl on her washstand, and hurriedly washed until her skin turned red. Her shivering increased to the point where she had to clench her jaw to keep her teeth from chattering. The only consolation to the icy bath was that her chemise, petticoat, corset and gown felt particularly soft and warm when she dressed.

Her gaze strayed to her bed one more time. Her body felt numb with exhaustion, and the rumpled sheets and warmth of the coverlet beckoned her to climb back under them and pull the covers over her head. The hollow in the center fit her so well and promised a soft comfort that made her ache. Her hand caressed the spot before she ruthlessly made the bed, yanking the sheet and covers into place and smoothing out the wrinkles.

Temptation neatly set aside, she drew the window's curtains apart and studied the black sky. A few late stars twinkled overhead, proving that last night's storm had finally moved out to sea. It was still too early for the sun to make an appearance, and there wasn't even a comforting streak of pale blue and rose as a cheerful harbinger of the new day. She sighed and rubbed her tired eyes.

Her body ached for rest, and her nerves tightened like an old, frayed rope creaking as it strained to hold a ship at dock.

Why of all nights had those sounds returned to haunt them? She'd had a blessed month of silence, of decent sleep, and if she'd been awakened, she'd expected it to be her cousin, not ... whatever it was. Her shoulders drooped, hating the thought that it might be starting again.

Those same noises had crept through the house before on soft little cat's paws, stalking her night after night in the darkness. The sounds had worked on her nerves until she couldn't bear the whispers any longer and had curled under her covers, shaking from the terrifying thought of staring into the blackness and seeing something standing there, near her bed, watching her.

Then a few weeks ago, just when she thought she would go mad, the moans and footsteps stopped. As her spirits had recovered, she'd laughed and convinced herself that she'd imagined everything.

Peace had reigned. Until now.

Once more it had started, interrupting her rest and grinding away her peace until she wanted to scream. She rubbed her forehead and stared into the darkness beyond her window.

Last week had been so lovely and quiet. No noises at night and no strangers in her house. Once again, she'd half-hoped that she had imagined the sounds, even if that meant she was no longer in her right mind. Her rational side had considered the matter closed with Mr. Archer's arrival. Surely, no ghost would dare to interrupt *his* sleep. He was the cousin to a duchess, after all. But Mr. Archer had heard the moans and footsteps, proving that they were real and that the ghost was as democratic as any decent American.

So Oldwood was indeed haunted, unless Mr. Archer could come up with a better explanation.

Her night terrors seemed to be well-founded, but that was a cold comfort at best, even if she were worried about such things, and she had long ago decided that her state of mind was the least important matter to be faced. There were far too many other things over which to fret, matters which kept her at Oldwood, despite what happened at night.

She slipped out into the hallway and paused to listen. The rest of the house was silent. As drafts whispered through the corridor, she could almost imagine that the rustling noise was Miss Archer and Mr. Archer snoring in their beds.

A grin replaced her tired frown as she descended the staircase and made her way to the kitchen. Mr. Archer's presence still seemed to haunt the large room, even though he was upstairs in his room. She leaned her hip against the wide maple table.

There had been a moment last night when she thought Mr. Archer was going to put his arm around her in comfort, and for one wistful second, she'd wished he had done so. She'd been alone so long, and on nights like last night, when the terrible crying began, she just wanted to hold someone's warm hand in her own. Her throat closed with the sudden ache of longing for her father, and her fingers rubbed the smooth surface of the table.

Then she straightened. Her gestures became sharp and jerky as she pushed away her sorrow and pulled down the canister of flour from one of the shelves lining the inner wall. A cloud of white flour rose into the air as she yanked open the lid and scooped out enough to make bread for the day.

The darkness of the predawn hours always brought despair twisting through her heart. And like every other day, she just had to keep on performing all the tasks, large and small, that comprised her narrow life at Oldwood. A sense of duty and responsibility for her family home kept her going.

In a few hours, when the warmth and rosy glow of the rising sun chased away the gloom, the sunny beams would fill her once more with courage, and her life wouldn't seem so circumscribed and poor. Fleeting moments of happiness would return like the Carolina Wren continually trying to nest in peculiar places around the mansion, and she'd be able to enjoy her freedom.

The rhythmic motions of kneading helped her black mood too, and her confidence slowly returned like the tide returning to shore. By the time she'd built up the fire in the stove and placed the loaves nearby to rise in the warmth, the first thread of rose-red was glowing through the high streaks of thin clouds. Her heart lifted at the sight, and she stood near one of the windows to watch the sky brighten. A nearby wren called, *rattle-pate, rattle-pate, rattle-pate*, making her smile until she turned back to the kitchen.

She'd have to get something for the travelers upstairs to eat other than the cheese and scraps of ham in the pantry.

With a sigh at the lightness of her purse, she collected a shawl, a basket, and slipped through the kitchen door to make a brief visit to the early market. She honestly didn't know how she was going to provide food for four more people, particularly after the Archers made a meal of the ham she'd hoped would last her several days.

Breakfast first, then worry about dinner later. The thought was not particularly comforting. Like the ant of Aesop's fable, she preferred to be prepared and not leave the future to the vagaries of chance. But in this case, it was the vagaries of her nearly-empty purse that ruled.

Only a few pennies remained when she returned to the kitchen and placed her basket of food in the pantry. After donning her apron, she punched down the rising dough, shaped the loaves, enjoying the scents of yeast and flour that filled the room. She covered the loaves for their second rise before looking around the kitchen to decide which task needed doing most urgently.

"Good morning, Miss Stonewright. You are up and about early," Mr. Archer said from the kitchen doorway.

Startled, Charity jerked around, her palm pressed against her pounding heart. "Mr. Archer—I did not hear you enter."

She studied his handsome face with its square jaw, and thick brown hair curling over his forehead and proud nose. He looked freshly shaven and well-rested, although he had the kind of beard that always left a darkish shadow over the skin of his lower face, giving him a rakish charm that made her pulse race.

No dark circles nestled under *his* brown eyes as testament to last night's terrors. Bitter resentment filled her, making her forehead tighten as she frowned and stared at the gritty floor.

"Are you baking?" He glanced around the kitchen with interest, his sharp gaze resting briefly on the towel-covered loaves.

"Yes." She wiped the dusting of flour off her hands onto her apron. "I assumed you and your sister would like something to eat before you left today."

His brows rose as a gleam of amusement lit his rich brown eyes. "I'm sure we would appreciate breakfast, even though I can assure you we have no intention of abandoning you so soon."

Her back straightened, and she gave him a stern look. "As I mentioned last night, you can't stay here. For one thing, it isn't proper."

"Oh, I think it is." He chuckled and strolled over to the table in the center of the kitchen. "With my sister's presence, as well as her maid, I believe you need not worry about any assaults on your virtue."

The kitchen suddenly seemed very small with his broad-shouldered presence in its center. Charity stepped back before deliberately walking over to the stove to check the fire. After pushing the coals around in the lower compartment, she placed the loaves of bread inside the oven, all the while aware of Mr. Archer's gaze on her back.

When she straightened, she turned to face him. "Your sister is too young—it is still inappropriate for you to be here."

He studied her for several seconds before he shrugged. "Perhaps you are right." He ran his fingertips over the top of the table next to him and staring thoughtfully, rubbed his thumb against his middle finger as if testing for dust. "I had intended to meet with our lawyer, Mr. Tarte, and hire a cook and at least two maids today. I will request him to find a suitable woman to act as chaperone, as well."

"Until you do, you must see that you will have to stay elsewhere," she said, her chin raised in triumph.

"Not at all." He smiled at her. "And I should imagine you're getting quite tired of repeating yourself on the matter, so I suggest we abandon the subject." His gaze drifted past her to the oven as he took a deep breath. "That bread does smell good—much better than anything I could have thrown together."

"Is that why you came downstairs so early? To bake some bread?" she asked in astonishment. Surely he couldn't have intended to do their baking?

He chuckled "Well, I had intended to try, though I feel fairly confident the results would have resembled ship's biscuits rather than actual bread."

"Mine may be no better. You must reserve judgment until it is out of the oven." Despite her best intentions, she couldn't help smiling back and warming to him.

He was so calm and confident, so ready to share a laugh, that it was difficult to remember that he was not there as her friend. He was the enemy, a man sent from England with the sole purpose of proving that Oldwood was not hers and evicting her from the premises. He might show her a pleasant face as he went about it, but there was a certain steel in the depths of his brown eyes that warned her he would be a bad enemy and an implacable force when it came to attaining his purpose.

She wiped her hands on her apron again, thinking about his stated intention to hire servants. Thwarting him would be dangerous, but servants were the last thing she needed or wanted. She'd managed to survive in this house for months without help, and servants would only interfere. She studied him uneasily.

Before he'd died, her father had made her promise to remain at Oldwood and then, as he lay dying, he'd finally revealed the reason it was so important: *gold*. The house had never been sold, despite vague rumors they'd heard about people living there. He'd clasped her hand in his cold, thin fingers and swore on his life that the house was hers, and there had to be proof of that if she could find it. But more than just the title to the house, there was a chest of gold hidden somewhere within its walls. A fortune that had been lost for years.

The Stonewright fortune. Just thinking about it made her heart beat faster.

The Stonewrights hadn't always been as poor as Charity was now, and most of them had been far less honest, as well. Many of her swashbuckling ancestors had been more than happy to leap aboard any Spanish galleon they happened to run across on the high seas and rescue a gold doubloon or two from the clutches of their sworn enemies. And despite their devil-may-care character, most of them were remarkably tight-fisted once they wrapped their fingers around a coin.

Or so her father had claimed.

The result was that the Stonewrights of yore had accumulated a fortune in gold, and it had supposedly remained hidden somewhere behind the modest walls of their mansion in Charleston. The secret to the location had been lost after the untimely death of the father of Charity's grandfather. Her grandfather had only been two years old at the time, and his father had never had the opportunity to reveal the hiding place of the treasure before he died. The secret was supposed to be handed down from father to son on the son's eighteenth birthday, but the chain had been broken and the family's prosperity had suffered a severe decline as a result.

Charity gazed at Mr. Archer with hard eyes. If he hired servants, they would undoubtedly snoop around the house. If they discovered either the proof that Charity owned the house, or worse, found the treasure, they would give it to Mr. Archer. Since he paid their wages, he, not Charity, would have their loyalty.

If Mr. Archer obtained the title before she did, he could easily burn it, destroying any chance Charity had of proving her ownership. If he located the treasure, he could claim it belonged to Miss Haywood—the duchess—and Charity would have nothing.

Even her home would be gone.

The more she thought about it, the more her mood shifted into black anger. Her hands gripped the edges of her apron. Suddenly, she disliked him—*Mr. Edward Archer*—sticking his proud nose into matters that had nothing to do with him.

How dare he presume to hire servants for her house? Who did he think he was that he could interfere with her life and her domestic affairs? He'd ruin everything she'd been working for, and she had no intention of breaking her promise to her father. She wouldn't let someone else take their house or find their fortune.

She would *not* let Mr. Archer win.

"I sent Atwood out to return the hired cart and obtain some supplies," Mr. Archer said, gesturing in the general direction of the pantry. "He has also been instructed to deliver a note to Mr. Tarte to arrange for him to come here first thing this morning. I hope you don't mind."

"Mind? Why should I mind you taking over management of my house, ordering things we don't need, and inviting guests we don't want?" She raised her brows mockingly.

A shadow of anger briefly hardened his eyes, and his mouth compressed for a moment. He glanced away from her and rested his gaze on the oven before his harsh expression smoothed into one of controlled blandness. "I apologize if I seemed highhanded to you," he said with a bow. "However, if you consider the matter, I believe you will agree that I have done nothing that did not need to be done. You are clearly exhausted trying to manage this establishment alone." He deliberately scraped the sole of his shoe over the grit on the floor, the noise reminding her that she hadn't swept the floor yet as she'd intended last night. "You need assistance. It does no one any good if this house falls into disrepair because you lack the resources to manage it properly."

Her chest tightened with hot fury, but when she opened her mouth to protest, he raised his hand, tilted his head slightly to the right, and smiled at her.

"Wouldn't you like to have one decent night's sleep and see dawn from your bedroom window instead of down here in the kitchen?" he asked. "Are you truly so foolish that you'd argue against making your own life more comfortable?"

A sigh escaped as her shoulders slumped. She was not *that* foolish. But she would have to be smarter. She resolved to find what she was searching for before he did and ensure no changes he made would affect her or her future.

She caught his gaze and shrugged. "No. I see that you are at least partially correct, though I would appreciate at least having the opportunity to add my suggestions to any purchases you make for my home. And if you are so desperate to identify matters with which you can interfere, you might consider repairing the roof. It was damaged in the last hurricane, and I have never had the funds to repair it." Hands on hips, she eyed him, hoping he might realize that there were more problems associated with the mansion than he had any desire to tackle.

To her dismay, he merely nodded thoughtfully. "Perhaps you should make a list of the items that require attention."

"And if you're going to hire servants, I should at least like the opportunity to interview them."

"Of course. I had hoped you would find the time to conduct the interviews yourself," he said with a disarming smile.

"Why?" She crossed her arms and stared at him. "Because you will be too busy attempting to prove Oldwood doesn't belong to me?"

His lopsided, self-deprecating grin made her feel like a perfect shrew. "I had thought that you might know what is required better than I. However, if you don't wish to be disturbed, my sister and I can perform the interviews."

After a second, her frown started to slip. "Must you be so nice?" she asked with a small laugh. "It is cruel, you know."

"Ah, well, how about this?" His brown eyes twinkled, although he maintained a bland expression. "The very next time we have a terrible storm, I shall throw you out into the rain and bar the doors against you. Would that suit you?"

She couldn't help laughing. His deep chuckles joined hers, and unable to resist, she reached out briefly to touch his wrist before wiping the tears from her cheeks.

When Mr. Archer sobered, his gaze searched her face. "I realize this is a difficult situation, and I am sorry for it." He glanced at the sunshine pouring through the window above the sink and for a second, a wistful look passed over his features. "I should have been placing dusty tomes of law books on the shelves in my law offices at this very moment." He pulled out a pocket watch and smiled. "It is after two in the afternoon in London."

"It is not too late to return." She almost winced when she heard her reply echo in her ears. How rude. And it really would be nice to have servants and a roof that didn't leak.

And company like Mr. Archer and his sister.

Because truth be told and much against her will, she liked the Archers.

Somehow, that admission made her situation seem that much worse, because at some point, no matter what he said now, he would undoubtedly be barring the door against her, rain or no rain.

Unless she could find proof that the Stonewrights owned Oldwood. Her hands clenched the edges of her apron, twisting it. She'd been searching for months already and hadn't found anything except a few mummified rats. Her grandfather must have searched, as well, before he left and died in Philadelphia. How could she find something he could not?

What if there was nothing to find?

What if there wasn't anything that could prove her ownership of the sprawling house?

What would she do then?

Several times, she'd almost given up hope of locating the mythical Stonewright fortune. Anything could have happened to it. Some previous ancestor might have spent the last gold doubloon on a jug of rum and good company for the night. Everything she'd hoped and dreamed of might simply be that: a childish dream.

What child didn't dream of finding a treasure?

And it wouldn't be the first time her father had promised her the moon, only to give her a pint of cream and an embarrassed smile, instead. He'd been kind but untrustworthy when he was alive, but she had hoped that for once...

If wishes were horses, beggars would ride.

But he'd promised her on his deathbed that he was telling her the truth this time, and she had believed him.

As she looked at Mr. Archer, she wondered if she were allowing herself to be taken in by *his* charm. Perhaps he was another ineffectual male like her father; full of promises that were ultimately empty.

Before she could decide, the sounds of rapid footsteps cut off Mr. Archer's reply.

Lady Hildegard walked into the kitchen looking much refreshed and sparkling with good humor. Her muslin dress, embroidered with delicate yellow flowers and green leaves, looked freshly ironed, and her pale brown hair was braided and twisted around her head to form a crown, while a few delicate strands floated around her heart-shaped face. She looked very young and carefree, with a wide smile on her pink lips and her gray eyes flicking around avidly to take in everything in the room.

And yet despite her youthful appearance and the custom to eliminate titles in the United States, Charity couldn't think of the young woman as anything but *Lady Hildegard*. The way she held her head, her straight shoulders, and her carriage granted her a regal quality that Charity couldn't ignore. Her hands smoothed the sides of her limp dress, her gaze fixed on Lady Hildegard's rosy face.

Just looking at her made Charity feel old and worn out, and she was glad she was wearing a heavy linen apron. The wrinkled folds covered the dingy gray of her dress, washed so many times that its color had vanished long ago.

"Good morning, Miss Stonewright," Lady Hildegard sang out.

"Good morning. Did you sleep well?" Charity asked.

"Oh, yes. My room was exceedingly comfortable and very quiet. I never heard a thing." A second later, Lady Hildegard straightened rigidly and her eyes widened briefly, her hand fluttering up to press against her lips.

"You didn't *hear* anything?" Mr. Archer asked, studying his sister.

Her hands dropped to grip the sides of her lovely dress, and she stared at the dusty floor. "No," she said in a rushed voice. "Of course not. My room was very quiet—that's all I meant. After London and our voyage—there is always so much noise in London and, of course, all that creaking on the ship. Last night was the first decent night's sleep I've had in quite a while. Because the room was so quiet. That is all I meant."

Charity didn't know Lady Hildegard very well, but even she was aware that the girl didn't seem to be telling them the exact truth.

Perhaps she'd heard the awful moaning and was afraid her brother would tease her for believing in ghosts if she admitted it. She obviously didn't realize that both Charity and Mr. Archer had heard the same horrible noises.

She was about to explain that she had heard the same sounds when Mr. Archer said in a dry voice, "So you heard those noises, too."

"Noises? What noises are you talking about?" Lady Hildegard faced her brother and raised one dark brow in perfect imitation of her brother's expression of disbelief.

Mr. Archer sighed and raised his hands in defeat.

Lady Hildegard smiled sweetly and sniffed. "Is that fresh bread? Edward, your talents never cease to amaze me. You must have risen in the middle of the night just to bake our morning bread."

"Miss Stonewright is the one who rose before dawn," he said in a dry voice. "So you must thank her for her talent and thoughtfulness."

Flushing, Charity flicked her hand in embarrassment. "I always get up early. It was nothing." She looked at the flour and the dirty bowl on the counter and frowned. "Perhaps you two would like to go to the dining room, or the sitting room. I have a great deal to do." She picked up a linen towel and opened the oven.

The loaves of bread were dark brown, on the verge of burning. Using the towel to protect her hands, she pulled them out and after a quick glance around, placed them on the kitchen table.

Lady Hildegard rushed forward to grab the flour-smeared bowl. "You must let me help you, and we shall have breakfast in no time."

Mr. Archer took the bowl from his sister and placed it in the sink. "Ring for Nettle. She can finish any tasks here and bring us our breakfast in the dining room."

A flash of anger lit Lady Hildegard's gray eyes, and she straightened abruptly, opening and shutting her mouth before she finally shrugged and said, "I am as capable as you are of performing at least a few small tasks. But if you want Nettle to attempt to make your morning coffee, then let it be on your head. I have *had* her coffee, you know." She gave him an ironic smile. "Right before I was, um," she glanced apologetically at Charity before she murmured, "*sick*. If you will recall."

"And I had a cup, as well, if *you* will recall. I was not ill, so I am perfectly willing to take a chance on her cooking."

Lady Hildegard moved closer to Charity and laced an arm through hers. "At least we will have Miss Stonewright's lovely, fresh bread."

"And eggs," Charity said as Lady Hildegard pulled her toward the door. "We have fresh eggs in the pantry, as well as butter and honey. There is also a jar of strawberry preserves I put up last summer." The last jar. She almost sighed at the memory. She'd managed to sell the one remaining painting of any value that June and feeling rich, had spent some on the luxury of five pounds of sugar.

For a few brief months, one shelf in her pantry had held an entire row of an array of preserves, glinting with bright colors of red, amber, and purple. She had put them up using the sugar and fruits she'd surreptitiously harvested in the wee hours of the morning from several locations around Charleston.

"A feast, indeed!" Lady Hildegard called over her shoulder with a smile. She patted Charity's hand as she dragged her along the corridor. "I'm so glad you're here, Miss Stonewright. Can you imagine how boring and *stuffy* it would have been if I were here alone with my brother? I thought I'd die of boredom while we were on the *Hercules*. An entire month! Can you imagine? Sailing for an entire, dreary month with my brother?"

A month alone with Mr. Archer, with nothing to do but watch the waves rush by and be waited on by the crew. It sounded very nice to Charity. She smiled mysteriously and kept her thoughts to herself.

Mr. Archer's valet, Atwood, brushed past them on his way to the kitchen. Before they reached the dining room, Mr. Archer caught up with them.

"I sent Atwood to find Nettle. Between the two of them, they ought to be able to manage breakfast," Mr. Archer said.

His sister snorted. "Well, I wouldn't make plans on going anywhere today, then, until you are sure you'll feel quite well later."

"You are entirely at liberty to remain here and nurse your sensitive digestion if you wish, but I have every intention of accomplishing a great deal today." He smiled at his sister. "Not the least of which is to do sufficient shopping to provide for an adequate dinner and find someone capable of cooking it."

"You're performing the shopping?" Lady Hildegard asked, coming to a halt just inside the door to the dining room.

Her brother pushed her further into the room so that he could enter. "Yes. I had thought that you and Miss Stonewright might wish to accompany me. However, if you would rather stay here, I will have to muddle through alone."

"Oh no, not at all!" Gray eyes brilliant with excitement, Lady Hildegard caught Charity's hand. "You will go with us, will you not? Oh, do say you will, Miss Stonewright!"

Charity glanced from Lady Hildegard to Mr. Archer, pulse racing and feeling simultaneously trapped and excited by the prospect. "Of course. I would be more than happy to join you." She caught Mr. Archer's impudent, amused gaze. "However, I thought you said you must meet with Mr. Tarte here. Today."

"I shall preempt him." Mr. Archer's grin widened. "He shall be our first stop. I hope you will introduce us to him, and then we can continue on to the market."

"Perhaps another time." She frowned at him, her chin jutting at a stubborn angle. The last thing she wanted to do was to introduce Mr. Archer to Mr. Tarte and have the two men begin the process of proving she didn't own this house. Why should she assist in her own eviction? "Your business—"

"A longer meeting can be arranged later. Simple introductions will be sufficient for now." He lifted his head and tilted it to listen. "Now, if I'm not mistaken, Nettle is hard upon our heels with a breakfast tray." He waved to the dining room table in the center of the room. "Shall we be seated?"

She hesitated, suddenly wanting to do something contrary just to show him that he couldn't count on her being so agreeable all the time. However, when she caught his glance and saw the warm understanding in his eyes, she nodded before she could think of a scathing but witty reply.

Renewed resentment flared as he took the chair at the head of the table, and waved Charity to the place at his right. Frowning, she took her seat, her stomach growled, and she felt the heat of a blush burn her cheeks. She stared down at the dusty surface of the table and prayed he hadn't heard anything.

Well, if nothing else, at least she would be well-fed when Mr. Archer barred the door against her on the next stormy night.

Chapter Seven

His sister only kept Edward waiting in the hall a few minutes before she showed up wearing her bonnet, a warm shawl, and her gloves. He glanced up at the second floor landing and listened for a moment, but he didn't see Miss Stonewright.

While they were alone, Edward turned to Hildie, who had taken a seat on a bench near the front door. "So, you didn't hear anything last night, Hildie?"

She looked up at him with eyes wide with innocence. "No. Wonderful, is it not? An old house like this? One would think one would hear all *kinds* of things." She shifted on the bench and adjusted her bonnet's ribbon before grimacing, untying it, and retying it. "I hadn't realized how noisy ships are, and after five weeks, it was a pleasure to have such complete quiet."

What *he* realized was that she wasn't telling him the truth. He straightened the lapels of his coat as he studied her. She couldn't have slept through the noises he and Miss Stonewright had heard, and his sister gave the distinct impression that she was holding something back.

But why? If she were truly frightened by the eerie sounds last night, why bother to hide it?

After a minute of silence, Edward said, "One wonders why you find it necessary to remark on *not* hearing anything, if you truly heard nothing."

Flushing, she fidgeted and then stood and walked impatiently to the door and back to the bench. "I told you, did I not?"

"If you slept so well, I don't quite see how you could know that there were no loud noises," he said, refusing to allow her to change the subject. "Hildie, I don't wish to argue. I'm concerned that you may have been frightened if you heard some unusual sounds. I am right down the hall from you. If you are ever nervous, all you need do is knock on my door. Or scream." He smiled reassuringly and shrugged. "I heard something last night, and I don't mind admitting it was disconcerting. So I promise I won't tease or embarrass you if you were disturbed."

She stared at him, her lower lip projecting before she pulled it between her teeth. She turned her gaze to the floor and shrugged. "Well, I slept right through whatever you heard. My room was very quiet." She tapped her foot. "There is no reason to continue questioning me about it."

"If you wish to go to an inn—"

"No!" she exclaimed before forcing a smile. She paced between the door and the bench again and then faced him. "No. I have no desire to leave. I don't know what you imagine you heard, but I'm quite comfortable here. I have no wish to move to a noisy inn with lumpy beds and execrable food." She tilted her head to one side and eyed him saucily. "Not that your cooking is that good, mind you."

"Next time we are in difficult straits, you can do the cooking, and we'll see who has cause to complain," he said dryly before lifting his head. The soft shuffle of a footstep sounded overhead.

"Complain, indeed." Hildie sniffed and waved a gloved hand dismissively.

The clatter of footsteps above their heads grew louder, warning that Miss Stonewright's arrival was imminent.

He studied his sister. "I only wanted to assure you that if you are ever frightened, I'm here. You're not alone, Hildie."

Her face softened, and a fleeting smile touched her mouth. "I know, Edward, and I'm not ungrateful. But perhaps you ought to consider that I'm well over eighteen and outgrew my childhood terrors many years ago. I'm rarely frightened anymore."

"Good." He nodded and turned to greet Miss Stonewright as she stepped off the last stair.

She nodded at Edward and Hildie. "I've been considering your requirement for additional staff—"

"*Any* staff." Hildie snorted and pressed one hand against her mouth to suppress a reprehensible fit of laughter. Her eyes danced with merriment.

"Hildie," Edward said warningly before he turned to Miss Stonewright. "You were saying?"

"There is a woman who might be persuaded to cook for us." Miss Stonewright eyed him shyly, her gaze fluttering between him and his sister. "She is very good."

He sensed a *however* hovering behind her lips, and he waited, his brows rising in inquiry. "Yes?"

"Yes?" she repeated his question, her voice hesitant. "Oh. She might not agree, but I'm sure she needs the employment."

"Very well." Edward nodded and opened the door for the two ladies.

When they turned onto the walkway running along the busy street, Miss Stonewright paused. "Perhaps it would be better if Miss Archer and I went to the market while you visited Mr. Tarte. His office is in the opposite direction." She turned and waved vaguely to the south.

He studied her face, but the suggestion seemed innocent enough.

"Oh yes, that sounds like an excellent notion." Hildie pulled her hand out of the crook of his arm and held out one hand, palm upward, clearly expecting him to give her his purse. "There is no need for you to accompany us. You know how bored you get shopping." She flicked a grin at Miss Stonewright. "You can trust us." She wriggled her fingers with impatience, reminding him of her empty palm. "We shall get everything we need."

"And then some, I suspect." His mouth twisted as he pulled out his wallet and poured a few coins into her hand.

When the clattering stream of money slowed, she shook her hand and frowned at him.

He glanced at Miss Stonewright, but she merely shrugged and gave him a faint smile.

"That is more than enough," he said at last, folding his wallet shut and slipping it back into the breast pocket of his jacket.

Hildie tilted her hand back and forth like a robin eyeing a likely bug and frowned at the small pile of coins in her hand. Finally, she dumped it into the embroidered reticule she had tied to her wrist. "We need a great deal," she complained, hefting the small bag. "If you are going to be so parsimonious, don't expect to sit down to a feast tonight."

"If you were as good at household management as you believe you are, I should expect a very fine meal, indeed," he replied.

"And you shall have it," Miss Stonewright said as she linked her arm through Hildie's. "That is sufficient for our purposes, Lady Hildegard. Your brother has been very generous."

"Only because his stomach is involved." Hildie gave him one last, disgusted look, sighed heavily, and turned on her heel to walk away, arm and arm with Miss Stonewright. Her straight back and the tilt of her bonnet hinted that her nose was in the air with the full expectation that he was watching them walk away.

He shook his head and chuckled to himself before he turned where he was to get his bearings. He'd studied a map the duchess had included in the bundle of papers she'd given to him, and recalling Mr. Tarte's address, he started out in the opposite direction from that taken by the ladies. His sense of direction was fairly good, and it helped that Charleston was bounded on one side by docks and water.

The lawyer's offices were easy enough to find. Within minutes of the clerk taking his card and disappearing through another door, he returned to usher Edward into the small, cluttered office.

Edward's first impression was of towering bookcases, cabinets, and piles of paper stacked on every horizontal surface. A hedge of paper ten inches high rimmed the lawyer's desk on three sides, leaving only the center free for a well-worn leather blotter, a pot of ink, a brass cup holding several quills, and whatever documents Mr. Tarte was currently reviewing.

As soon as Edward entered, Tarte collected the papers in front of him, tapped them on the desk to align their edges, and placed them gently on the top of the stack on his left. He hurriedly removed a pair of wire-rimmed spectacles and tucked them into his pocket with his left hand as he held out his right.

"Mr. Archer," he said, glancing at Edward, beyond his shoulder, and then back to Edward. "It is an honor to finally meet you. I trust your journey went well." He frowned at something behind Edward.

"Well enough," Edward said, stifling the urge to look over his shoulder to see what had captured the lawyer's attention.

Hinges squealed and Edward heard the soft snick of the door shutting.

Tarte waved at a large, padded leather chair arranged in front of the desk. "Please, Mr. Archer, take a seat. I had not expected to see you here so soon after your arrival. I was intending to come to Haywood Mansion later this morning." He scurried around his desk and gestured again at the chair, giving the impression of nervous energy barely controlled. He opened the door, peered out, and then shut it again before returning to his chair.

"So you did receive word of our arrival. I wasn't sure the note would be delivered." Edward sat.

The wall of paper blocked his view of the lawyer. He was about to stand to move it when Tarte reached across the desk and removed the stack directly in front of him. After a moment's consideration, he placed it on the floor against the wall behind him. He glanced at Edward through the opening, frowned, and removed two more stacks before he sat and leaned forward, his clasped hands resting on the blotter in front of him.

63

"Note?" His small, brown eyes blinked several times. "Oh, yes, the note. Yes. I received that from the first mate. Very prompt." He frowned and stared down at his blotter. "I hope you found everything satisfactory."

Edward smiled and leaned back, resting his left ankle on his right knee. "We found the property without any undue difficulties, though I was surprised to find the house lacking in servants."

Tarte flushed and ran a hand over his balding head. "Well, yes. I beg your pardon—it was supposed to be unoccupied—of course I had no knowledge of your schedule or when you would arrive, so I did not engage any."

"And there was Miss Stonewright," Edward murmured.

Eyes blinking even more rapidly, Tarte's hands fluttered over his desk before he felt his pockets, withdrew his glasses, and put them on with fumbling fingers. "Ah, yes. Of course, of course." He cleared his throat and frowned at the blotter. "I trust you were not incommoded by Miss Stonewright's presence. She has been ... intractable. And of course, I did not wish to evict her bodily until we were very sure she had no legal claim to the property. It is a difficult situation for both Miss Stonewright and the Duchess of Peckham." He stared at Edward accusingly, as if he blamed him for the awkwardness.

His sympathy for Miss Stonewright and her anomalous state regarding her claim to the estate was obvious, despite his frustration in handling the matter. Oddly enough, this made Edward like the dry little man for his concern. Miss Stonewright's position worried him, as well.

"She has been exceptionally helpful and is company for my sister until I can resolve these matters," Edward said, watching Tarte with amusement. "Although it presents certain difficulties that require your immediate assistance. We are in need of a lady of mature age to act as chaperone while I am living in the house."

"Your sister?" Tarte ignored the matter of the chaperone. His close-set eyes focused on Edward's face, giving the lawyer a cross-eyed look of dumbfounded surprise.

"Yes. Lady Hildegard. The duchess thought the journey would be educational," Edward replied dryly. "Now, about a chaperone?"

Tarte waved his hand. "That presents no difficulties. There are any number of refined, widowed ladies who would be satisfactory. I shall have my clerk send over those we feel most appropriate."

"Very well." Edward nodded.

"Now where were we?" The lawyer cleared his throat and fussily adjusted his glasses before clasping his hands together on top of his desk. When he glanced up, a serious expression had elongated his face and deepened the creases running from his nose to the corners of his thin mouth. "Ah, yes. The duchess." The lines around his mouth deepened. "I regret she felt the necessity to send you on such a long, disagreeable journey," he said in a stiff voice. "I have been researching the matter, of course."

"Of course," Edward murmured. "Have you resolved the question of title, then?"

Tarte frowned and straightened his stooped shoulders. "There is a great deal of research to be done. Some documents appeared to be, um, misplaced." His fingers made a nervous gesture at the remaining stacks lining the edges of his desk. "I attempted to assure the duchess that I was happy to take care of this matter for her." A flush rose up his wrinkled neck, bloomed over his jaw, and filled his cheeks with a crimson tide of frustration and wounded vanity.

Edward smiled reassuringly and made a negligent gesture. "I'm sure she retains the utmost confidence in you."

Tarte coughed noisily behind a fisted hand. Clearly, he suspected the duchess had lost confidence in him quite a while ago, and he was not altogether wrong.

While the lawyer was coughing, Edward said, "Now that I'm here, I trust we shall make progress more rapidly. The duke and duchess were not altogether pleased when they had to repay the purchaser of the property due to questions about whether they actually owned the property her guardian had attempted to sell prior to her marriage."

The flush returned with a vengeance to Tarte's gray cheeks. A drop of sweat dripped down the side of his face. He wiped it away hurriedly with a handkerchief. "I must point out that I was not involved in that sale. When I heard the details, I felt it was highly questionable. If I had been involved, I would have advised against it due to the lack of a clear title on the part of the Haywood family." He frowned accusingly at Edward as if lumping him in with those he held personally responsible for the title confusion. "I do not know what I can do at this juncture. As matters stand." He removed his glasses again, methodically folded the earpieces, and laid them in the exact center of his ink-stained leather blotter.

If Edward were to make any progress, he needed to soothe the lawyer's ruffled feathers. He really couldn't blame Mr. Tarte for feeling the duchess didn't trust him. Edward would have felt precisely the same way under the circumstances. But without Tarte's cooperation, chances of successfully concluding the matter on her behalf were slim. At a minimum, he needed Mr. Tarte to assist him in the tedious process of collecting the relevant papers for evaluation.

"It is regrettable no one asked or heeded your advice, then," Edward said.

"Well, it was seven years ago, and I did not own this practice at the time. I was merely a junior partner." Tarte's stiff shoulders relaxed a fraction.

"What was your assessment of the situation? How did ownership of the property become contested?"

Tarte's brown eyes twinkled with excitement as he picked up his glasses again and placed them on his nose. He peered over the top edges at Edward before twisting around. His chair squeaked as he moved it, and he cast a glance at the piles of paper he'd placed on the floor. He picked up one of the bundles of papers held together with a black ribbon and placed it on his desk.

After untying the sheaf, he flipped carefully through the top several pages before flashing another glance at Edward. A passionate love of research and history glowed in his eyes.

"The original grant of land was enacted by our first governor, William Sayle, a little after Charles Town moved from the Ashley River site to its current situation." He adjusted his glasses. "Let me see ... that would have been in 1682. Are you familiar with our history, Mr. Archer?"

"In general terms." In hopes of forestalling a complete history of the city, he said, "I was interested in more recent events, of course, relating to the loss—"

"Misplacement," Tarte corrected him, peering at him over the rim of his glasses again.

"*Misplacement* of the title transfer to the Haywood family."

"Mr. Marcus Haywood, to be precise. The father of the current Duchess of Peckham," Tarte clarified.

It was clearly going to be a long, *long* morning.

"How—"

"If you will allow me to continue, Mr. Archer?" Tarte's thin, gray brows rose in gentle enquiry.

Edward nodded. Amusement pulled his mouth awry.

Frowning in concentration, Tarte carefully flipped through several more documents. "Ah, yes. 1682. That would have been Mr. Albert Stonewright who was granted the property in question by our governor for services rendered." His frown deepened and he pursed his lips. "It does not state what services, of course."

"Of course," Edward murmured.

"The main portion of the house was built between 1682 and 1684, although I understand subsequent owners expanded it greatly, as Oldwood—as it was known then—was described in Mr. Albert Stonewright's will as a two-story brick mansion with outbuildings and accompanying grounds when it was inherited by his son, Mr. Anthony Stonewright in 1712. The property passed to his son, Mr. Frederick Stonewright, in 1752 and passed to Mr. Henry Stonewright—the current Miss Stonewright's grandfather—in 1785. Thus far, we have wills and the necessary documents to prove the unbroken chain of inheritance and ownership through 1785."

"Then it is the last thirty-eight years that are in question? Did Mr. Henry Stonewright have no sons to inherit?" That didn't seem correct, since Miss Stonewright carried the family name which implied a father who also carried the name.

"Yes and no." Tarte removed his glasses and began cleaning them with a large handkerchief. "Mr. Henry Stonewright had a son, Mr. Bartholomew Stonewright, who was Miss Stonewright's father."

"Then was his will missing? Or was there any indication that the mansion had been sold?" The matter seemed simple enough, given how much history Tarte knew as documented fact from the papers in front of him.

"Well, Mr. Henry Stonewright grew ill in the autumn of 1798 and his son, Mr. Bartholomew Stonewright, took his family and ailing father to Philadelphia. They'd hoped to seek a cure from a physician Mr. Bartholomew had befriended while attending the College of Philadelphia. Unfortunately, there was nothing they could do for old Mr. Henry, and he subsequently died in Philadelphia in 1799."

A cold feeling settled in the pit of Edward's stomach, and he released a long breath. The longer he listened to the lawyer, the more he questioned the Haywood ownership of the property. "When did the Haywoods acquire the property? The duchess lived there with her aunt from 1800 through 1808. Unless the Stonewrights sold it when they moved to Philadelphia, it does lend credence to Miss Stonewright's claim, does it not?"

"That is precisely why I have not been more insistent that Miss Stonewright vacate the premises." Tarte picked up another sheet of paper and turned it to allow Edward to see the thick black writing. "We do not have any documents relating to a sale from that period. Curiously, the property was not specifically mentioned as part of Mr. Marcus Haywood's estate, either. But Miss Elizabeth Haywood, the aunt of the duchess, claimed the property had been acquired around the time the Stonewrights went to Philadelphia, and she lived there with the child, Miss Charlotte Haywood, until her death in 1808 when Miss Charlotte was sent to live with relatives in England."

"What proof did this Elizabeth Haywood have that the property belonged to her family?"

Tarte cleared his throat and shifted uneasily in his chair. "Miss Elizabeth Haywood claimed one of my previous partners had the sale documents. This partner unfortunately passed away during this period. However, Miss Haywood had a number of influential friends and one of them, Mr. Charles Cooper—who is a distant relation of Mr. Anthony Ashley Cooper, one of the original Lords Proprietors to whom King Charles II granted the chartered Carolina territory in 1663—sent this to us." He lifted the topmost document again. "Mr. Charles Cooper wrote this letter on Miss Elizabeth Haywood's behalf, stating that to his knowledge, the Haywoods did indeed own the property previously known as Oldwood and now known as Haywood Mansion."

"And you have questioned Mr. Cooper about this knowledge?"

"That was not possible. He wrote this shortly before his death." Tarte tapped the letter with one finger. A faint smile on his face seemed to say he was pleased that this problem now rested in Edward's hands. "You see the difficulty."

There were far too many deaths during that period from Edward's perspective.

"I do, and these circumstances certainly leave us with a puzzle missing several key pieces." Edward leaned back, jiggling his left foot as it rested on his right knee. "It is a pity we cannot question Mr. Cooper. I am very curious about this supposed knowledge of his."

"It is perhaps not so surprising. Mr. Cooper knew both Mr. Marcus Haywood and Mr. Bartholomew Stonewright very well. Their friendship does seem to lend credence to this sale, and my partner," he adjusted his neckcloth, "ahem, well, he did have certain peculiarities." Tarte sighed. "This is not the first document we have, um, mislaid."

Hence Edward's presence in Charleston.

Edward glanced at the window behind Tarte's back. The winter sunshine promised a warm day, and the bright rays penetrating the gray glass sparkled with dust motes. His thoughts went to Miss Stonewright and his sister wandering through the market. He rubbed the back of his neck, crushing his sudden desire to return to the mansion to see how successful the two ladies had been in spending his money to refill the larder. His stomach rumbled.

"Are there any other friends of either family still alive?" Edward asked.

Tarte's forehead wrinkled, and he pushed his glasses more securely against the bridge of his nose. "Most of those who were alive at the time of the supposed transaction are no longer with us. I am not sure how helpful she would be as she was a friend of Mrs. Henry Stonewright, but there is a Mrs. Eggerton. She is quite elderly, now, of course. I doubt she would have been privy to a business arrangement such as the sale of the property in question."

An elderly lady. Even if she had been a friend of the family, chances were good that she would not have been present when—or if—Henry Stonewright signed the property's title over to Marcus Haywood. Disappointment undermined the brief flash of hope he'd nurtured that he might locate a witness to the original transaction.

"I don't believe we need to annoy Mrs. Eggerton just yet." He smiled as he stood. "Thank you. You have given me an excellent start, and I already have a great deal to consider."

Tarte got to his feet abruptly, pushing his chair back so quickly that it knocked one of the stacks of paper on the edge of his desk to the floor. "You will wish to study the files, I suppose." He glanced at Edward before stooping to collect the scattered documents. "Do you propose to take them with you?"

Walking through the streets with an armful of legal documents held all the appeal of a moldy, weevil-infested hunk of bread. "No. I would appreciate it if you could send them to the Haywood—Oldwood—Mansion." He smiled. "I don't want to get in your way by going through them here."

"You will have questions," Tarte objected, his hands full of papers as he straightened.

"No doubt," Edward replied in a dry voice. "Perhaps we can agree to meet in the morning twice a week: Tuesdays and Thursdays?"

"Of course." Tarte bowed, still clutching documents. "I am at your service."

They shook hands, but on his way through the door, Edward paused and turned partway back. "Upon reconsideration, may I borrow the most recent documents, including the letter from Mr. Cooper? You can send a messenger with the rest later this afternoon."

"Certainly." The lawyer sifted through the mass of paper he'd collected from the floor and drew out several. After a quick glance at Edward, Tarte pulled out a fresh sheet of brown paper, placed the documents on top of it, and folded the packet together before neatly tying a black ribbon around the small bundle. "I hope this is satisfactory," he said as he held it out to Edward.

Edward took it and slipped it into his pocket. "Thank you, Mr. Tarte. Between the two of us, I'm sure we can resolve this to everyone's satisfaction."

"Or at least to the satisfaction of the duchess," Tarte replied with the first evidence of a sense of humor he'd shown. His brown eyes twinkled behind his glasses.

"Yes." Edward laughed. "That would certainly be most desirable."

His neck itched again in warning. He ran a hand between his collar and skin, frowning with an uneasy thought.

When he was through, it was highly probably that no one would be completely satisfied, least of all the duchess.

Chapter Eight

"Mrs. Granger is an excellent cook," Charity repeated in exasperation, irritated that Lady Hildegard seemed disinclined to accept her judgment.

"But she is so *thin*! I've never seen a chef or a good cook who was thin," Lady Hildegard protested, shifting her overflowing shopping basket from one arm to the other.

"And you have a great deal of experience in the kitchen with chefs and cooks?" Charity asked. Her own basket felt like it was full of bricks instead of the vegetables and jars of honey it contained.

"We had a French chef at Archer House, and he was enormously fat, though not particularly jolly. In fact, he was quite ill-tempered." Lady Hildegard frowned and shifted her basket again to rub her left wrist. "I don't think Shakespeare really knew that many fat people, frankly, if he thought they were all so jolly. Although I agree with him about those who are excessively thin, and Mrs. Granger is *excessively* thin."

"Mrs. Granger is excessively thin because she lacks the resources to be plump, not because she cannot cook. The matter is settled."

Lady Hildegard sighed and smiled as they turned the corner and Oldwood rose into view. "Well, I suppose we can always ask Edward to prepare eggs and ham, if necessary."

Suppressing the urge to *accidentally* kick Lady Hildegard's trim little ankle, Charity forced a laugh.

She liked Lady Hildegard—most of the time—but the girl could be unbelievably obtuse over the most trivial matters. Charity ascribed it to her luxurious childhood. Lady Hildegard had not had the privilege of managing the thousands of small difficulties encountered in a more restricted life. In Charity's experience, common sense always won over desire. One did what one *had* to do, not what one *wanted* to do, with limited resources.

It was difficult not to feel bitter. Each time she'd had to sell something from Oldwood, she'd felt a twinge of guilt. What if her father had been wrong and the house, along with its contents, truly did belong to the Haywoods? Her actions could be considered theft, even if she was fairly sure the objects she sold had been in the house for several decades. She could only hope no inventory had been kept, or that whatever documents were finally discovered failed to specify the contents as part of the sale to the Haywood family.

The more she thought about it, the tighter the skin across her forehead stretched. Even though it was not hot, the sun beat down on her bonnet, and a trickle of sweat slid underneath the knot of her hair and down the back of her neck.

"We were fortunate, though, to meet those sisters— what were their names?" Lady Hildegard asked as they entered the cool shadows of the front hallway.

"Kitty and Janet," Charity answered. With a sigh of relief, she untied the ribbons of her hat with one hand and drew it off. She felt an immediate rush of refreshing air cascade through the damp curls that framed her face.

"They were so pretty—I wish my eyes were dark like theirs, they were as deep and luminous as a fawn's." She sighed, gazing into the distance. "Anyway, they seemed very eager to begin, and I must say that I am just as eager to have them do something about these terrible floors. When I arose this morning, walking to the washstand was precisely like walking along a sandy beach." Her hand flew to her mouth, and she looked at Charity in horror. "I am *so* sorry. I did not mean to complain—I'm sure you have done everything you could. You must think me perfectly horrid."

Charity's lips twisted. "Not perfectly."

"Just horrid." Lady Hildegard laughed. "I always say too much and don't stop to consider my words until afterwards. You must learn to ignore me the way Edward does. He never takes any notice of my remarks."

"I daresay he never takes notice of anyone's remarks," Charity commented, leading the way to the kitchen.

Lady Hildegard hurried to follow and touched Charity's shoulder. "Oh, you mustn't think he takes no heed of opinions not his own. He is very kind."

"For a lawyer," Charity murmured, not convinced.

"He is not precisely a lawyer. Not yet, in any event. Though he does have a high regard for the law." Her last remark was made in such an irritated tone that Charity wondered if Lady Hildegard didn't appreciate her older brother's love of legal matters.

If things didn't go as Charity hoped, she suspected she might eventually hold the same opinion as Lady Hildegard.

Then she remembered the sympathy in Mr. Archer's warm, brown eyes, and her breathing juddered in a warm flush of anticipation at seeing him again. She placed her basket on the kitchen table and took a deep, deliberate breath, irritated with herself.

Was she so silly as to believe he was as attracted to her as she was to him? That he wouldn't evict her?

Did she *want* to be kind to the man who would soon decide whether she could stay or go? Common sense reminded her of the obvious answer: *yes.* If she could change his mind with sweetness, she would have to try.

Unfortunately, no matter what she did, a bleak future of poverty faced her, one way or the other. She had no money to maintain the house for much longer, unless she found the Stonewright fortune. Which made the search even more urgent.

She mechanically emptied her basket on the kitchen table and put away its contents, along with the few items Lady Hildegard contributed to the pantry. The bulk of the supplies would arrive later that afternoon; the large bags of rice and other goods had been too heavy and bulky for the ladies to carry back.

It gave Charity an odd sensation to see the pantry shelves begin to fill again and to imagine the floors and furniture clean.

"There is someone at the door," Lady Hildegard announced, standing in front of the stove. She stared at the kitchen door with raised brows.

Charity stifled the sharp suggestion that Lady Hildegard open the door, strode over to it herself, and yanked it open.

"Mrs. Granger." She stepped aside to allow the older woman to enter.

"Good day, Miss Stonewright," Mrs. Granger said as she walked into the kitchen.

As she glanced around, her thin lips pressed together, thinning even further. A small bundle drooped from the crook of her left arm, and she dropped that onto the seat of one of the chairs. She looked at Lady Hildegard, nodded, and yanked off her shawl, draping that over the bundle.

"You'll want a cup of tea, I suppose," she said in her dry, creaking voice.

Lady Hildegard moved aside, her eyes sparkling. "Yes, Mrs. Granger. That would be lovely."

"Then get out of my kitchen." Mrs. Granger pulled a well-washed, grayish-white apron out of the bundle, tied it around her waist, and bent over the stove to check the fire. "I will bring the tea to the parlor when it is ready."

"Thank you, Mrs. Granger," Charity said demurely, catching Lady Hildegard's glance.

Lady Hildegard cast her gaze heavenward and pressed her fingers over her mouth to hide her smile, although her fingers couldn't hide the dimples at the corners of her lips or the merry crinkles around her eyes. She nodded to Charity and turned to the hallway with Charity following behind her.

They hadn't even reached the end of the hallway when a shriek reverberated through the narrow corridor. Charity stumbled and pressed a hand against the wall to catch herself. Lady Hildegard whirled around and reached out to grip Charity's arm. The two ladies exchanged shocked glances before Charity jerked her arm free and ran back to the kitchen.

Mrs. Granger was standing rigidly with her back to the stove, one hand clutching her long, wrinkled neck and the other pressed over her heart. "Who are you?" she asked in a trembling, high-pitched voice.

Looking around, Charity's gaze fell on a small man dressed in a plain black coat, fawn-colored waistcoat, and black trousers. His gray eyes stared back at her, and he raised a shaking hand to slick back his already slick, well-oiled, brown hair.

"Miss Stonewright," he said, his nervous gaze flicking between her and the cook, whose expression was growing increasingly hostile.

Mrs. Granger's eyes narrowed, and she frowned. "Who are you? What are you doing, sneaking around my kitchen?"

"Who are you?" he flung back, like he was tossing her the remains of a rotten fish.

"Who are you—what are you doing here?" Lady Hildegard asked, placing one hand on Charity's shoulder and peering over it.

"Identify yourself immediately, or I shall send for the constable!" Mrs. Granger ordered.

The man looked at the kitchen door and edged toward it.

"Officer Carmichael, what are you doing here?" Charity asked, finally recognizing him without his hat and uniform.

Surely Mr. Archer hadn't already determined that the Stonewrights no longer owned Oldwood? Had he sent the officer to evict her?

Officer Carmichael smoothed his oily hair over the crown of his egg-shaped head again, and he used the sleeve of his jacket to wipe the sheen of sweat off his brow. His gaze dropped to her right hand.

Apparently, he had vivid memories of her inadvertent firing of her pistol.

"Well, ah..." He slid closer to the door.

Charity studied him before her gaze slipped past him to a narrow door in the far corner of the kitchen. A dark gap showed that the door stood partially open. "How long have you been here? What were you doing?"

He took two more steps toward the outer door, straightened, and licked his lips. "You've got no right to occupy this here domicile, Miss Stonewright, as I done told you, afore." He yanked on the hem of his jacket before buttoning the top two buttons.

"What kind of officer of the law enters a house without knocking?" Mrs. Granger asked with bristling eyebrows and a mouth twisted into a deep frown. "How dare you enter without knocking!"

"You've got no right!" he repeated, although the firmness of his statement was ruined by three more crablike steps toward the door. He stretched out a hand and grasped the doorknob.

Charity was still considering what Officer Carmichael had been doing in their cellar when Lady Hildegard moved around her.

"Miss Stonewright has every right to be here. This is her home," Lady Hildegard said.

"And who are you, Miss?" he asked, eyeing her insolently, his lips twisted into a sneer.

"Lady Hildegard Archer." Her chin tilted up. "My brother and I are here representing the Duchess of Peckham, the former Miss Haywood, in this matter. So you may rest assured that when I say this is Miss Stonewright's home, it is indeed her home."

Officer Carmichael's florid face paled and his grip on the doorknob tightened. "All right, well, um..." He was still mumbling disjointedly as he flung open the door and ran out, slamming the door shut after him.

"Idiot!" Mrs. Granger yelled after him. She turned and stared at Charity and Lady Hildegard. "I'm telling you right now, Miss Stonewright, if the law makes a habit of walking into this house, day or night, then I can't work here."

"No, Mrs. Granger—this was all a misunderstanding. Officer Carmichael has never done that before." She paused. *Or had he? He may have crept around this house dozens of times while I was out running errands.* She rubbed her arms, feeling the chill of vulnerability. "To my knowledge," she added. "We will change the locks. I'm sure he won't bother you again."

The cook eyed her doubtfully, turned back to the stove and set a kettle of water sharply in place. "I won't stay in a place in constant turmoil," she mumbled. "I've had enough of that." She looked over her shoulder at Charity. "Well? What are you doing in here? I told you I'd bring your tea to the parlor."

"Yes, Mrs. Granger," Charity replied as meekly as she could. She grasped Lady Hildegard's arm and dragged her out before they caused any further upset to Mrs. Granger's brittle nerves.

"What was that man doing here?" Lady Hildegard asked, stumbling after Charity. "You obviously know him."

"Yes." Charity released Lady Hildegard's wrist when they entered the main hallway. After a second's hesitation, she headed for the front siting room—what Mrs. Granger called the parlor. No point in making Mrs. Granger any angrier, and Charity really could use something to drink after the hot walk back from the market.

Lady Hildegard rubbed her wrist as she followed. "Why was he in the kitchen?"

The obvious answer seemed the easiest. Charity sighed and gestured for Lady Hildegard to precede her into the sparsely furnished sitting room. Two chairs, a couch, a side table and a low table in front of the couch remained, so at least there would be enough chairs to accommodate the two of them. The horsehair-covered couch was so stiff and uncomfortable that no one wanted to sit there unless forced to do so, but the chairs were all right.

"Last time, Officer Carmichael came to evict me," she said truthfully. "Perhaps he hoped he'd be more successful this time if he used the back door."

"Well at least you won't have to worry about that now that we are here." Lady Hildegard sat down and arranged her lovely dress over her lap. Then her hands moved restlessly in her lap, and she glanced around the room. "You must have sewing to do?" she asked, her brows lifting hopefully.

The never-ending sewing—the occupation of all ladies when they were not performing other work.

Charity gestured to the wicker basket sitting on the floor in the far corner of the room. A much-mended petticoat with a torn flounce rested inside. She'd been putting off repairing it because she feared the linen had grown so thin with washing that she was more likely to tear it than successfully mend it. She exhaled another long sigh.

"I was working on a new shirt for my brother. Do you mind if I go upstairs and get it?" Lady Hildegard asked as she rose.

"Not at all—that sounds like a wonderful notion." Charity got up and retrieved her basket. Perhaps she could get a few scraps of linen leftover from Mr. Archer's new shirt and use them to strengthen her repairs.

The thought made her feel more optimistic. But it couldn't vanquish her worries about what Officer Carmichael had been doing in her cellar while they'd all been out of the house that morning.

Had he somehow heard about the gold? Had he been searching for it?

How could that have happened?

No one was supposed to know except the eldest son of the eldest son. Her father had only told her because he had no sons. There was no one else left to tell.

So exactly what had Officer Carmichael been searching for in Oldwood's cellar?

Chapter Nine

Walking away from Mr. Tarte's offices, Edward's gaze was caught by movement in the thick branch of a tree, overhanging the walkway. A cat sprawled over the limb almost directly above him. As he watched, it rolled over luxuriously to rub its back against the bark, its head hanging upside down in the air, and its pale green eyes fixed on Edward. The cat had pale orange and cream-colored stripes and its left ear was a tattered mess. It was also slightly cross-eyed, and its long pink tongue lolled out of its mouth.

As he stared up at it, the animal stretched until its entire front end half draped over the edge of the branch, its head and shoulders hanging in midair. It stretched out its front paws at him, meowed meditatively, and overbalanced. It fell, making no effort to right itself, and landed in Edward's arms.

He couldn't help chuckling. The cat, as if taking umbrage, wrapped its paws around his left arm and proceeded to rabbit-kick him with its rear legs as it gently bit his wrist. Or gummed him. The cat seemed to lack teeth and after a minute, it started licking his wrist and the side of his left thumb before sprawling in his arms and purring loudly.

"Lovely," Edward murmured wryly as he set the cat on the ground. "Go home, sir." He brushed the orange and cream hairs off his sleeves.

The animal immediately began weaving through his legs, rubbing against his trousers.

Edward glanced around for an owner, or at least a house where the animal might have lived, but this particular block butted up against a tiny graveyard and an even smaller park with a few trees. The cat must have wandered away from its home and would undoubtedly wander back.

He set off again for Oldwood, but he hadn't even reached the corner of the block when he felt something grab his left leg. The orange cat was gripping his trousers and gumming the side of his knee. He gently removed the animal, walked a few steps, and once again felt the animal grab his leg—his right this time.

He released himself, petted the cat as it purred and writhed with pleasure, and strode forward. And stopped again as he felt the now-familiar grip on his leg.

The speed of his progress was considerably diminished as he repeatedly plucked the animal off his trousers, admonished it, and walked away.

His older sister, Lady Olivia, had dogs. Another sister, Lady Margaret, had rabbits. He was absolutely *not* going to be the Archer with cats, or even *a* cat.

Absolutely not.

But he couldn't help chuckling each time the cat ambushed him. The animal was so ridiculous and yet so gentle; it never even used its claws. He had a moment's concern when he released himself again and remembered the cat didn't have teeth.

How did it even survive?

When Edward finally arrived at the house, the inevitable happened. The cat followed him up the steps to the stoop and leaned against him, calmly waiting for him to open the door.

It seemed Edward *would* be the Archer with a cat. As he entered, the cat trotted inside, its head turning this way and that as it sniffed and glanced around.

"Very well," Edward said, closing the door. "I dub thee Nodcock, for obvious reasons. May your contests with the local rodents end in triumph, despite your lack of dentin."

The cat sat, licked one paw, and then stared at him with its crossed eyes.

Edward stooped to pet it once again, smiling as the animal rolled over and caught at his hand with its soft, warm paws.

When he finally stood and brushed off most of the cat hair, he heard the sound of voices and followed them to the sitting room on his right. His sister and Miss Stonewright were sipping tea and working industriously on their sewing, their chairs under the front window to make the most of the silvery winter light streaming through the panes.

Miss Stonewright's gaze caught his when he walked into the room. She blushed prettily and quickly bent her head over her work. A few stray locks of gently curling hair fell around her face, and a light draft from the hallway fluttered the golden-red strands curving over the nape of her neck.

Light from the window glinted over the mass of hair she'd braided and secured in a wreath at the back of her head, gently illuminating her creamy skin and rich hair. Even Aphrodite in Titian's painting, *Sacred and Profane Love*, paled in comparison to her radiance.

He didn't have a chance to speak before he felt Nodcock ease between his ankles and start rubbing against his shins.

"Edward!" Hildie exclaimed, looking up at him before she caught sight of the cat. Her eyes widened. "What's that? You have a cat? *You?*"

"Yes, even I, hard-hearted and cruel as I am, have discovered a soft spot for one of Nature's most wretched creatures," he said with a bland expression. He gestured at the cat, who had sprawled over his left foot. "This is the noble Nodcock, terror of rodents everywhere."

"Where did you get it?" Miss Stonewright asked, eyeing the animal.

"You are mistaken if you think any decision on the matter was mine, Miss Stonewright. Nodcock selected me by nearly falling on my head."

Miss Stonewright and Hildie giggled before Miss Stonewright bent to dangle her hand near the floor and twitch her fingers seductively. Nodcock remained as limp as an old rag draped over his shoe, idly swatting at the hem of his trouser leg with one paw.

"It does seem unaccountably attached to you," Miss Stonewright commented as she straightened.

A grin twitched in the corner of his mouth. "It is unaccountable. I hope it—" he bent and briefly examined the cat—"*he* doesn't present any difficulties? I did not mean to adopt a pet, but Nodcock allowed me no real choice."

Hildie laughed. "Nodcock? You didn't name him that, did you?"

"It seemed appropriate."

His sister shook her head and took another stitch in the half-completed shirt draped over her lap.

"It doesn't present any problems for me," Miss Stonewright said thoughtfully. "But I wonder if it will stay if it hears—" She cut herself off with a quick glance at Hildie.

He nodded at her, hoping his sister hadn't understood Miss Stonewright's reference to last night's sounds.

"Hears what?" Hildie lifted her head and stared at Miss Stonewright.

Miss Stonewright shrugged, keeping her gaze fixed on her sewing. "Noises. These old houses always have so many noises, particularly on windy nights. Cats are notoriously nervous."

Edward nudged the cat and lifted his foot. The cat slipped bonelessly off onto the floor, where it sprawled on its back, its paws folded over its creamy-white chest, staring up at him in complete relaxation.

"I don't think anything is going to bother Nodcock," Edward said.

"Maybe he won't stay, though." Hildie bit off a thread before picking up a spool and measuring out a fresh length. "He might belong to someone."

Edward frowned down at the cat. For some strange reason, he wanted the cat to stay. It wasn't even a particularly attractive cat with its tattered ear, lack of teeth, lolling tongue, and strange eyes, but he wanted it.

"He might at that," he said. "We shall discover the truth in time, I suppose." He changed the subject abruptly. "You ladies appear to be well-occupied."

"Yes. Oh—we hired a cook!" Hildie announced, her face glowing with pride at the accomplishment. She flicked a glance at Miss Stonewright. "And she is almost as temperamental as our old chef—so don't go in the kitchen." She giggled and covered her mouth with one hand. "She's very thin, though Miss Stonewright assures me that she can cook quite well."

"Then I'm sure we'll all be satisfied." Edward gazed at the curve of Miss Stonewright's long neck, shadowed by a delicate bit of lace decorating the neckline of her dress. Her skin had the radiant, creamy texture of a priceless pearl. His forehead wrinkled.

Miss Stonewright bent over her sewing more closely, her needle flashing in and out of the dingy linen draped over her lap.

"And we ordered a great deal of food to be delivered this afternoon, so I expect wonderful things at supper," Hildie said. When she saw the direction of his gaze, she looked at Miss Stonewright as well, and frowned critically. "We should have bought some fabric. Miss Stonewright would look beautiful in yellow, don't you agree?"

Although he couldn't see her face, a faint redness bloomed over her neck in a spreading blush.

"You are embarrassing our hostess," he chided his sister gently. "Though she would indeed look very elegant in yellow silk. Perhaps you could go out again this afternoon and do some more shopping."

Miss Stonewright's head snapped up, her blue eyes flaring with anger. "I don't need charity. I have a number of beautiful gowns," she stumbled over the last two words, and the crimson stain on her cheeks deepened.

Hildie laughed and leaned forward to touch Miss Stonewright's wrist. "Of course, but a new gown is always so nice. I'm not the best seamstress, but I do love sewing anyway, and I would never refuse an offer to obtain the material for a new gown. And I would hate to be the only one—it would make me feel quite selfish—so do go with me, and let us both have new dresses."

85

"We can hardly create new gowns in one afternoon," Miss Stonewright objected, although the anger was rapidly fading from her eyes.

"Of course not." Hildie giggled. "Even I am not that silly. So it is settled, then?" Her brows rose as she looked at Miss Stonewright.

"Yes," Miss Stonewright replied slowly before bending over her sewing again.

Edward caught Hildie's gaze and winked. He could trust his sister to buy what was required. He suspected that any *beautiful gowns* in Miss Stonewright's wardrobe were from the last century, if her current dress were any indication. She had obviously been scraping by on very little, and the thought both angered and saddened him. She was far too intelligent and beautiful to be reduced to such straightened circumstances.

"What will you do while we are gone?" Hildie asked, picking up her work again.

Edward grimaced. "Interview chaperones for you two ladies."

Hildie and Miss Stonewright's simultaneous sighs made him chuckle.

Hildie then rolled her eyes and shook her head. "In addition to the cook, Mrs. Granger, we have two girls coming—sisters. Are there not enough ladies in the house, now, to satisfy anyone?"

"No," Edward answered with a smile. "We require at least one mature, sensible lady in residence."

Both ladies raised their heads abruptly, and their angry expressions mirrored each other.

"We are both sensible!" Hildie protested. "And quite mature. How can you say such a ridiculous thing?"

The sound of a knock at the front door saved him from having to answer his sister. He grinned at them, his gaze lingering for a moment on Miss Stonewright's flushed face, before he nodded and turned around to answer the door. More like a dog than a cat, Nodcock trotted along after him, apparently afraid to let Edward out of his sight.

Which reminded him that while a butler might be too much to expect, a footman would be very helpful to answer the door and perform other duties that Edward's valet would consider beneath him.

By the time he opened the door, one middle-aged woman stood on the stoop and another was just turning onto the walkway, approaching the house. The clerk at Mr. Tarte's firm had obviously taken his task very seriously. The two ladies studying Edward through the doorway were just the first of a seemingly endless stream of genteel women, obviously in straightened circumstances, trying to hide their desperation and eagerness to find worthy employment.

By three in the afternoon, he was starting to think it was an impossible task. Despite his sympathy for the women he interviewed, with their repeatedly-mended gloves, rusty black dresses, and gaunt hollows under their eyes, most of them seemed barely able to hide the flashes of irritation in their eyes when they occasionally glanced up from staring at the floor.

They exuded sour bitterness and repressed anger. Most made it obvious that they felt it was beneath them to seek employment, even genteel employment, and their resentment of that necessity colored everything around them.

One elderly lady even kicked Nodcock away when he dared to sniff at the hem of her dark gray dress.

He picked up the cat and escorted the woman to the door.

None of these ladies would do. Miss Stonewright had enough challenges in front of her without saddling her with a chaperone seething with resentment.

When another knock sounded on the front door, he ran his hand through his hair and answered it, intending to inform whoever stood there that the position was no longer available.

"Mr. Archer?" a lady inquired as he opened the door. Her pale brows rose in query, and he stared at them for a moment. The thin, light brown hair formed sharp Vs with the point directly above her hazel eyes. The curiously formed brows gave her a permanently surprised look that almost made him laugh. "You are Mr. Archer, aren't you?"

"Yes, of course." He stood aside and waved her inside before he remembered he had intended to send her away.

Nodcock sat a yard away, watching her with interest.

"I'm Mrs. Maplethorpe, Mrs. *Doris* Maplethorpe," she said as if Charleston were rampant with other Mrs. Maplethorpes. "Mr. Tarte asked me to stop by. Personally."

"Would you care to sit down?" He gestured at the two chairs in the sitting room.

"No. I can only stay a few minutes," Mrs. Maplethorpe replied, her small, black-gloved hands gripping her reticule. When she saw Nodcock, she smiled at the cat and started to bend in its direction before she caught herself and straightened.

"Oh." He frowned. "You are here about the position, are you not?"

"Chaperone. Yes." She nodded and examined him.

Her round, broad-cheeked face was pleasant, with permanent laugh lines bracketing her generous mouth. The skin around her chin and neck hung in loose wrinkles, as if she had once been much plumper and had lost a great deal of weight, but she was not gaunt—at least not yet. He judged her to be in her mid to late forties and unlike the other ladies, she had an air of calm placidity and sensibleness that appealed to him.

Even Nodcock seemed to approve as he sprawled on the floor nearby and started purring as he licked one paw.

Edward smiled. "Excellent. Are you sure you do not wish to sit down? There is tea set out on the table in the sitting room if you wish for a cup."

"I'm sorry, but I have several other appointments this afternoon. I really only came as a favor to Mr. Tarte." She tilted her head to one side and continued her study of him with a pursed mouth, making him wonder if he somehow failed to live up to her expectations.

"Then you would not be interested in a position as chaperone to my sister, Lady Hildegard, and the lady who owns this house, Miss Stonewright?" Frustration made him sound harsher than he intended.

"I didn't say that." She laughed. "I am very interested— I simply don't have the time today to discuss the matter with you."

"I'm sorry. I had hoped to hire someone as soon as possible." Why had Tarte even sent the bloody woman if she didn't have sufficient time for an interview?

"Would this evening be soon enough?" Her hazel eyes twinkled. "Temporarily. I may not suit the young ladies, or they me."

"This evening?" he repeated.

"I can rearrange my schedule," she explained in a placid voice. "Eight o'clock? Everyone is always so much more relaxed after eating, that it is usually the best time to introduce new things. And people, of course." Her lips twitched, begging to grin.

"Of course. Eight o'clock. Yes, that would be excellent."

"Good. Oh, I am a widow, of course. Mr. Maplethorpe, my dear Martin, died two years ago. We had no children." A flicker of regret passed through her eyes, and her mouth drooped at the corners. "Mr. Maplethorpe was a lawyer and an old friend of Mr. Tarte's. This will be my first position of this kind—of any kind. I thought you might want to know my background. I do not have any references, although I'm sure you could discuss my character with Mr. Tarte."

He nodded, searching for a delicate way of asking about her living situation. "Would you be averse to living here?"

"Not at all. I have been a guest of Mrs. Tarte's long enough." She smiled. "I suppose that is what encouraged Mr. Tarte to suggest I look into this position."

He laughed. "I'm sure he will be sad to see you leave."

"Yes. I'm sure he will be overcome with grief," she said with a bland expression, although her hazel eyes danced with merriment. "Well, I must go. I shall return at eight, as agreed." She wasted no time on farewells and was gone before he had time to reconsider.

But as he watched her stride briskly down the sidewalk, he experienced no regret. In fact, all he felt was an enormous sense of relief.

Nodcock also appeared unconcerned about Edward's decision. The cat lay on its back, its bizarrely skewed gaze fixed on a small table standing against the wall, its tail flicking gently in the air.

Edward grinned and bent to scratch the cat's head. The only problem he had left to solve was the riddle of the ownership of Oldwood. Or Haywood Mansion. For some reason he couldn't quite fathom, he hoped Miss Stonewright was correct and that her family still owned the property.

She deserved a decent place to live, and the duchess didn't need the house. She would only sell it.

A frown settled onto his face as he considered the rambling history Mr. Tarte had rattled off. A small bit of information didn't fit in the picture, but it was more a vague sense of something *missing* rather than something out of place, and it wasn't just the missing bill of sale.

The thought troubled him as he reached down to stroke Nodcock's tattered ear again. Unfortunately, the cat had nothing useful to disclose and only purred more loudly.

Chapter Ten

Charity trailed after Lady Hildegard numbly, her arms filled with brown-wrapped packages. She didn't think that much fabric, in that many colors, existed in the entire world, much less Charleston, and she seemed to be carrying at least half of the available yards in her arms.

At first, she'd tried to protest when Lady Hildegard began ordering ten yards of this and thirteen of that, but the younger woman simply ignored her. If Charity grew too vehement, Lady Hildegard added another thirteen yards or so to the stack.

As the afternoon wore on, Charity's protests dwindled in both strenuousness and quantity until she just stood at Lady Hildegard's elbow each time she opened the purse her brother had refilled for her, and murmured weakly, "You shouldn't. Really."

"Do you think Edward has hired a chaperone?" Lady Hildegard's forehead wrinkled with thought as they turned a corner only two blocks away from Oldwood.

At the sight of the house, Charity sighed in relief and shifted the packages to the crook of her right arm. A sudden, sharp poke in her side made her glance at Lady Hildegard. "What? Why did you do that?"

"You are not paying the least attention. I was just wondering if Edward has hired a chaperone." She walked a little faster. "I was dreading it for fear that he might hire some sour-faced old dragon. But after due consideration, I wonder if it might not be a good thing, after all. If she can sew, she can help us make up your new wardrobe." She giggled. "And I might be able to make up my own gown, if there is any of that pale rose silk left."

"There ought to be more than enough left for you since I'm not sure it is precisely the best color for me." She flicked a glance at Lady Hildegard's smug face and under her breath, added, "As I mentioned when you purchased it."

Lady Hildegard unlinked her arm from Charity's and skipped ahead to run up the front steps to Oldwood's stoop. She glanced back over her shoulder at her with a smile. "I'm so pleased I brought the last few issues of Ackermann's Repository." When she caught Charity's gaze again, she said, "Or *La Belle Assemblée,* if you prefer. I have both volumes from last year and the last volume from the year before. Of course, the styles will be several months old, now, and I don't have the newest journal, but we ought to be able to make do." She thrust open the front door and entered. "Are you not excited?"

"So agog I'm unable to speak," Charity said, following her.

"Edward! Where are you?" Lady Hildegard called, cutting her off. "Edward!"

Letting her packages tumble onto the narrow table against the wall, Charity glanced up at the sound of a firm footstep. Mr. Archer walked toward them from the direction of the library. Her shoulders tightened as she thought about the mostly denuded shelves. Would he realize she'd sold all the books with any value?

Would he conclude that she was a thief as well as an intruder?

A relaxed smile curved his mouth, however, as he caught her glance. A strange feeling wriggled through her belly as she returned his smile. He must have been running his hand through his hair, as one thick curl hung over his brow while the rest curled wildly over his head making him look like a young boy returning from a day of mischief.

His gaze held hers.

She caught her breath, aware of how attractive he was with his warm brown eyes fringed with thick lashes and his wide shoulders. Her pulse thundered in her ears.

"Come, look—we bought all sorts of lovely fabric!" Lady Hildegard exclaimed, breaking the hushed tension stretching between them. "Did you find a chaperone?"

He nodded absently and walked forward. He flicked a glance at the packages on the table and his smile broadened. "Yes. We were both successful, it appears."

"Is she here?" Charity looked around, half afraid that they were already under observation by some stern-faced, disapproving woman.

"Not yet. She will arrive this evening around eight," Mr. Archer said, his brown eyes twinkling with amused awareness of her nervousness. "You have a few more hours of freedom."

As he spoke, his cat twisted around his shins and between his legs, leaving patches of pale orange and white hairs behind on the black wool of his trousers.

"Whatever possessed you to pick up that cat?" she asked, studying its tattered left ear, the rough pink tongue hanging out of its mouth, and its pale green eyes that seemed askew somehow. "That is the ugliest cat I've ever seen."

Nonetheless, although the animal was ugly, there was something very charming about its determination to remain as close to Mr. Archer as possible. She found herself grinning down at it.

"Nodcock chose me. I had little to do with it, I'm afraid," Mr. Archer replied. But his wry smile and the fondness in his eyes as he looked down at the cat showed that he'd already grown attached to the animal.

She smiled at the two of them, and then realized to her dismay that she liked Mr. Archer even better for the streak of illogical kindness running through him like a thread of gold through otherwise plain white linen cloth.

The cat fell abruptly over on its side next to Mr. Archer's feet and began grabbing at the hem of his trouser leg with its paws.

Grinning, she said, "Well, your cat doesn't seem to be in its right mind—it thinks your trousers are filled with mice."

"I was unaware that Nodcock ever had a right mind in which to be," he replied with mock surprise.

"No, I suppose not." She laughed and bent to scratch the cat's head between its ears.

Nodcock tolerated the caress but seemed to prefer rolling over Mr. Archer's shoe and batting at his trouser hem.

"Nodcock is very sweet, I'm sure," Lady Hildegard said impatiently. She picked up one of the bundles and untied the string keeping the brown paper in place. "But look at this lovely muslin. It will make a beautiful morning gown for Charity, do you not agree?" She unfolded the fabric and draped it over Charity's shoulder.

Flushing, Charity tried to move away, but Lady Hildegard gripped her arm to hold her in place.

"Very nice," Mr. Archer said in a disinterested tone, his gaze resting on Charity.

"The blue flowers in the design are the exact shade of Miss Stonewright's eyes, are they not?" Lady Hildegard asked persistently, her quick, slender fingers rearranging the muslin around Charity's neck.

Charity looked up and caught Mr. Archer's gaze. A breathless silence enclosed the two of them, making the hallway and Lady Hildegard fade for a few heartbeats. His firm mouth seemed so close, and his lips so soft.

"Close," Mr. Archer replied in a low voice. "But Miss Stonewright's eyes are a more vivid blue."

Heat flooded Charity's face. She stared down, her flustered gaze fixing on Nodcock in relief.

"Oh, pooh." Lady Hildegard snorted before staring at her brother. "Does this new chaperone sew?"

He shrugged. "I haven't the least notion."

"You don't know?" She dragged the muslin off Charity's shoulder and shook it out impatiently.

The flapping material caught Nodcock's attention. He sprang to his feet and leapt at the edge of the material, but Lady Hildegard swept it out of his reach before he could sink his claws into it. She refolded it quickly, keeping an eye on the cat.

"I didn't think to ask her," Mr. Archer admitted cheerfully.

"Well, you can hardly expect us to sew an entirely new wardrobe for Miss Stonewright on our own."

"You have Nettle—"

Lady Hildegard waved her hand and interrupted her brother impatiently. "Yes, yes. Nettle is all fine and well, if you wish to look like some old woman from the last century, but even *you* must admit that while she is competent, she is hardly an inspired needlewoman."

"I fail to see why I must admit anything of the sort," he replied with a bland, slightly bored expression.

"Oh, I don't know why I even *try* to hold a sensible conversation with you." Lady Hildegard punched her brother on the shoulder.

"I often wonder the same thing." He winked at Charity.

Her pulse fluttered again, as she grew intensely aware of him. She didn't want to like him—why did he have to be so attractive?

She went over and picked up the packages from the table to give her nervous hands something to do. "I should put these away." In the hallway upstairs, she heard the mellow chimes of the one clock that remained in the house. Six o'clock. "Mrs. Granger will have dinner ready in an hour." She glanced at the two siblings.

They looked back at her. The two were superficially quite different, with Mr. Archer's warm brown eyes and Lady Hildegard's gray, and yet they shared a sense of energy—a bold passion for life—that was irresistible and undeniably attractive. They made one feel that anything was possible; all one had to do was stretch out one's hand to grasp an exciting future.

What foolishness.

If things went the way Mr. Archer hoped, she would be destitute and homeless before the dogwoods bloomed. He might be happy to pick up stray cats, but she suspected it was only because they were just as easily abandoned.

She shifted from one foot to the other uneasily. She was being unfair and she knew it, but she *had* to think such things if she were to avoid swooning at his feet, overcome by his mere presence every time he entered the room. She snorted. She was too old to behave like a young girl in love with her brother's tutor.

When she glanced up, the two were still eyeing her. "Perhaps we should get ready?" she suggested.

"Yes." He nodded and escorted the women upstairs.

Despite her determination to be practical and show common sense, she pulled dress after dress out of her wardrobe that evening, searching for something—anything—that wasn't threadbare or pale gray from too much washing. If only they'd had time to do more than stack the new fabric on the long table in her sewing room. There was a beautiful sea green silk that would make the loveliest evening gown with soft, shimmering folds caressing her ankles. She could imagine Mr. Archer's warm gaze when he caught sight of her in it, standing at the top of the stairs.

Another ridiculous fantasy.

While she would soon have several fine dresses, it didn't matter if Mr. Archer admired her in them or not. He probably wouldn't even notice. Most men didn't know a fine dress from an old rag.

Her hands ran over the worn nap of an old, dark blue velvet gown she'd found a few months ago in a trunk in the attic. It was her one good dress. She'd spent hours carefully repairing small, black-edged holes in the skirt created when some past lady had stood too close to the fire. Fine lace she'd removed from another tattered dress encircled the graceful curve of the neck and crossed over the bodice.

A sapphire necklace had originally been wrapped in silk and placed with the gown, but she'd reluctantly sold that two months ago. She had no other jewelry except the small jet earrings she wore every day.

Well, what did it matter?

She wasn't going to some grand Charleston Society ball; she was eating dinner with Mr. Archer and his sister. They'd already seen her in all the glory of her daily dowdiness. The velvet dress was perfectly serviceable.

She folded the rest of her gowns and placed them back on the shelves of her wardrobe, thankful to close the doors on the sight of them. Feeling sorry for herself always irritated her—it was an awful habit—and she refused to indulge in it anymore.

The pantry downstairs was groaning under the weight of all the food, a warm fire crackled in the fireplace in the front parlor, and two charming dinner companions were awaiting her pleasure. There were even three servants performing all the tasks she had previously struggled to undertake. She looked at her calloused hands and short, torn nails. In a few weeks, her hands might be as beautiful and soft as Lady Hildegard's.

For the first time since her father passed away, she didn't have to remember to sweep the floors and fill her ewer with water before retiring for the night.

She was fortunate, even if she felt uneasy and a little resentful to have matters taken out of her hands so quickly. She smoothed her hair. When one of her fingernails caught in the fine strands, she bit it off and tried to thrust away her anxieties.

She ought to be happy. Her luck was finally changing, and she ought to take advantage of it, instead of worrying about everything so much.

Tonight, after the others went to bed, she'd continue her search for the lost Stonewright fortune. Perhaps her current streak of good luck would finally allow her to discover its hiding place.

Stepping out of her threadbare day gown, she lifted the velvet gown from the bed and drew it over her head. The folds felt warm and soft against her skin, and she was glad of the thickness. The sun had set two hours ago, and the room was growing drafty and chill.

When she finally entered the hallway, she heard the creak of a door and glanced around to see Lady Hildegard leaving her room, as well. Despite her determination to maintain a cheerful outlook, Charity's stomach dropped in sheer envy as her guest smiled and hurried toward her.

A lovely dress in creamy white silk shimmered with Lady Hildegard's movements, and a silvery ribbon threaded its way through her light brown curls. Her gray eyes sparkled merrily in her heart-shaped face, and her delicate arms were encased in beautiful, long white gloves. A simple, but obviously expensive, strand of pearls encircled her neck, framed by the embroidered scalloped edge of her gown. Small roses created from the same silk as her gown decorated the high waist, hem, and small, puffed sleeves. She'd draped a light cashmere shawl with a delicate gold and cream pattern over her shoulders as protection against drafts.

"You look beautiful," Charity said, her hand on her doorknob. "Your shawl reminds me—I forgot mine." She returned to her room quickly and grabbed her old gray knit shawl. It was a shame to hide her only good gown with the old thing, but it was better than shivering at the dining table so violently that she spilled food into her lap.

Lady Hildegard had followed her into her room. When she saw Charity pick up her shawl, she pulled off her own and held it out. "Oh, don't wear that—take mine. It will look so much better."

"But won't you be cold?" She hesitated, her own shawl hanging from her left hand.

Laughing, Lady Hildegard shook her head and thrust her shawl out further. "I have another one. In blue." When Charity didn't take the garment, she threw it onto the bed. Picking up her skirts, she dashed out the door, calling over her shoulder, "I shall only be a moment."

Despite her discomfort at Lady Hildegard's generous offer, she dropped her own shawl on a nearby chair and picked up the cashmere one. The garment felt so soft and light, and yet so much warmer than her old gray thing, that she couldn't resist draping it around her shoulders.

It looked beautiful with her deep blue gown when she glanced in the mirror. She sighed, running her fingers over the exquisite cashmere.

"There—doesn't that look better?" Lady Hildegard said breathlessly from the doorway. Her cheeks were flushed from running to her room and back. Another beautiful shawl, this one patterned with a deep blue, pale blue, and cream design, cascaded over her left arm.

"Yes, thank you."

"You should keep it. It looks so much better on you with your beautiful hair than it ever looked on me."

"No—I couldn't," Charity protested, although another quick glance in the mirror made her smile with pleasure. The gold and white design did look lovely, and it brought out the glints of reddish blond in her hair.

Laughing, Lady Hildegard gestured for her to join her in the hallway. "Don't be ridiculous. You should always bring your hostess a gift, so you can consider that our gift to you." She drew Charity's arm through hers and walked toward the staircase. "After all, we did descend on your house like a swarm of locusts. It is really the least we can do."

"You've already done a lot—too much." A rush of shame burned away her brief flash of pleasure. She felt like a poor relation, dependent upon others. The Archers had filled her pantry, hired servants, and purchased material to clothe her.

And they hadn't even tried to make her leave.

What was left of her pride felt battered and sensitive, waiting for the next painful insult.

"Nonsense. We are really more like sisters than mere friends, are we not?" Lady Hildegard shook her arm free long enough to give Charity a brief hug before descending the stairs. "You may borrow anything you like, and you *will* keep that shawl. I never cared for it—that is why I purchased this blue one. I much prefer blue."

Charity gave up with a small laugh. "Very well. Though if we are sisters, then you should be calling me by my given name, Charity."

"Charity—how nice! I wish you would call me Hildie, but Edward insists on using Lady Hildegard as if I were eighty instead of eighteen." Her small nose wrinkled. "Titles are so old fashioned and unnecessary—it is what a person *does* that matters, not what title one inherits. Don't you agree?"

"Well, titles do show respect. So perhaps you should not give up yours so hastily," she said with a smile. She stepped off the last stair and joined Lady Hildegard. "Do you think your brother is already in the dining room?"

"I suppose so," Lady Hildegard replied. She glanced around and laughed. "There is not much to entertain him in the library, and I doubt he would be sitting in that front drawing room, staring out the window into the darkness. It is rather lonely here, is it not?"

"It can be," Charity temporized. She hadn't really thought about it. Most evenings, she was occupied with searching the house for three things: anything she could wear, anything she could sell, and the elusive gold.

Or she was wearily completing the never-ending chores.

But if one were not so occupied, Lady Hildegard was correct: there was not much for a lady living alone to do in the evening.

When they entered the dining room, they discovered Mr. Archer already seated at the head of the table, requesting the names of the two girls carrying platters of food.

"Janet, sir," the girl closest to him said. She hesitated on Mr. Archer's left before placing the large plate of chicken on the table near his elbow. Large, black eyes on him, she curtsied as she wiped her hands on her apron. "This here's my sister, Kitty, sir."

The shorter, younger girl giggled nervously and then bit her plump lip, casting an uneasy glance at her sister.

Then she stared at the table with confusion before setting her platter of roasted potatoes, carrots, and onions next to the chicken. Flicking another quick glance at her sister, she dipped in a quick curtsy and then stepped back to stand partially behind Janet.

"This looks delicious. Send my compliments to the cook," Mr. Archer said, smiling at the two nervous maids, obviously trying to set them at their ease. "I'm relieved to see you here. We were in desperate need of your services, as I'm sure you've noticed."

A jerky, nervous giggle escaped from Kitty, who placed her hand over her mouth and moved even closer to her sister.

"Thank you, sir." Janet curtsied again. "We've got us some soup here, sir."

When he nodded, she turned and pushed her younger sister forward a step. The two hurried toward the kitchen.

When Lady Hildegard and Charity moved forward, Mr. Archer hurriedly stood and helped them to their chairs. "This Mrs. Granger of yours appears to be a decent chef after all, although it would have been more convenient to have everyone seated and the soup course served before the meat course."

"I'm sure Janet and Kitty are unaccustomed to serving and are too nervous to realize that. They won't make that mistake again," Charity said with a frown, feeling the need to defend the two girls. "They haven't had it easy since last summer."

A puzzled look crossed his face as he studied her, but before he could respond, the maids returned with the soup, a basket of fresh, still-steaming bread, and several small plates of butter. They silently placed one dish of fish soup in front of each of them, distributed the butter, and left the bread near Charity.

When the soft sounds of their footsteps faded down the hallway, Mr. Archer glanced at Charity with his dark brows raised in question. "Last summer?"

She sighed, regretting her reference to the ugly subject. The sad tragedy was still playing out in Charleston, and the topic wasn't pleasant for dinner conversation.

"There were some ... difficulties last June. Denmark Vesey, a free man, was accused of trying to start a slave uprising—like the one that succeeded in Haiti—and he was hanged last July. Close to thirty-five were hanged—it was appalling. There wasn't even evidence, just a lot of talk." Her voice rose with her frustration and anger at the situation. She swallowed before she could continue speaking more calmly, "So it hasn't been easy the last few months for blacks, particularly free ones." She shrugged and abruptly put her hands in her lap when she realized she'd picked up a piece of bread without thinking and had crumbled it into small bits on her plate. "They've been instituting all sorts of laws and making it next to impossible for anyone to buy their freedom. They even tried to keep free black sailors imprisoned on their ship as long as the ship was at dock. It's absolutely unspeakable."

"I take it you don't agree." Mr. Archer's brown eyes studied her.

"Do you?" she flung back.

"No. Of course not. As you said, it's unconscionable. We're supposed to be enlightened. Civilized." The quiet anger in his voice made him seem dangerous—hard.

She shifted uneasily, aware of a trickle of fear although his anger wasn't directed at her.

He was not a good man to cross.

A tightness in her chest made it difficult to breathe until he finally looked down and ate a spoonful of soup, his brow creased in thought.

"But mankind always seems to find ways to display barbarity, no matter how enlightened the age," he commented at last.

"I'm sorry. I shouldn't have brought it up," she said, sprinkling the breadcrumbs over her soup before picking up her spoon. A tight cramp in her stomach made her shift in her chair.

She couldn't solve the world's problems in one evening, and the atmosphere in Charleston was such that she would be a fool to pursue the subject too vocally. She might find herself under arrest as yet another conspirator, simply because of her feelings on the subject.

Gaze warm with sympathy, Mr. Archer said in a gentle voice, "You need not fear expressing your opinions to us. They do you credit." He paused to eat another spoonful of soup before asking, "I hope, then, this means that Janet and Kitty are quite free?"

"Yes," she replied shortly. "Of course."

Mr. Archer smiled. "We would have difficulties were that not so. I am relieved." He glanced down at his nearly empty bowl. "And Mrs. Granger?"

"Mrs. Granger immigrated here from Ireland," Charity explained with irritation before she realized Mr. Archer had never met their cook, and that he didn't know her situation.

"Excellent."

"Can we not talk about something else?" Lady Hildegard said, shifting uncomfortably. She pushed her half-full bowl away, her mouth downturned. "And just who is this woman you are foisting upon us as a chaperone?"

"Mrs. Maplethorpe. She is a friend of our lawyer, Mr. Tarte." He finished his soup and glanced at Charity. "Are you acquainted with her?"

"Mrs. Maplethorpe? You engaged Mrs. Maplethorpe?" Charity paused to look at him in surprise, spoon halfway to her mouth.

"Is she a friend of yours?" Lady Hildegard asked, her voice rising hopefully.

"Yes." She smiled, filled with a rush of relief. Suddenly, she was aware of her empty stomach and the delicious, spicy aroma rising from the soup. She swallowed a mouthful before adding, "I hadn't realized she was seeking employment."

If she had only known earlier.

Then she remembered there was nothing she could have done if she *had* known before the Archers arrived. She could barely afford to feed herself, much less another woman.

"I gather it was a rather recent decision," Mr. Archer said, eyeing the crisply browned chicken resting on a wide platter next to him.

"Is she nice?" Lady Hildegard rested her wrists against the edge of the table and leaned forward, her gaze fixed on Charity.

Charity laughed. "Very nice. You'll like her. I don't think I've ever seen Mrs. Maplethorpe flustered or angry. She is the most patient, good-hearted woman I know."

"You know her well, then?" Mr. Archer picked up a knife and began the delicate work of carving the chicken.

"Not very well, but I have met her at church a few times. She came to offer condolences after I arrived here from Philadelphia and she heard my father had died. She was very kind," she ended lamely. She had no wish to explain how Mrs. Maplethorpe had calmly ordered Officer Carmichael to get off the stoop and stop bothering innocent young women, when her visit coincided with the first time he'd tried to evict Charity.

"That is a relief," Mr. Archer said as he undertook to fill their plates with chicken.

The rich aromas of sage and butter wafted up from her plate. Charity's mouth watered as she took a generous helping of the herbed potatoes, carrots, and onions. The soup had only whetted her appetite, and for the first time in months, she intended to eat until she felt full, even if it was a very unladylike thing to do.

She flicked a glance at Mr. Archer, but his attention was focused on his own plate for the moment. Maybe he wouldn't notice her huge appetite, and if he did, well, too bad. He would be going back to England soon, anyway, where the pallid, thin ladies pecked at a few crumbs and considered themselves shamefully gluttonous.

"Don't you wish for any creamed celery?" he asked, gesturing to the serving dish on the table next to her. "I must say that I'm pleasantly surprised at the quality of Mrs. Granger's cooking."

She hadn't even noticed one of the maids placing the dish of celery there.

After serving herself a large helping, she passed the bowl to Mr. Archer, who took an even larger portion before handing it to Lady Hildegard.

"I'm famished," Lady Hildegard commented. "This is the first proper meal we've had in ages. Mrs. Granger is an absolute treasure, is she not?"

"Um, yes. Absolutely," Charity agreed.

She'd barely had time to finish the last bits of food on her plate before Janet and Kitty returned with trays to whisk away the dishes. The two girls appeared to have lost some of their shyness, and they exhibited a great deal of confidence in their swift, coordinated actions.

Charity glanced at Lady Hildegard and considered a more appropriate topic for conversation, only to be interrupted when the maids returned with dessert. The slices of apple pie, crowned with mounds of fluffy whipped cream, weren't particularly elegant, but the flaky pastry, cinnamon-spiced syrup, and warm bits of apple were so delicious that no one bothered to speak until their forks were scraping their plates clean.

"Miss Stonewright," Mr. Archer said, studying her, "may I ask a question concerning your family?"

She smiled. "I trust it will be neither impertinent nor too personal."

"You may be the judge of that." He chuckled and pushed his plate away. "What do you know of your grandmother?"

"My grandmother?" She stared at him in surprise. She'd expected him to ask about her father or grandfather and why she was so sure Oldwood was still theirs.

"Yes. Did anyone in your family ever speak of her?"

"My grandmother on my mother's side died years ago, long before I was born. Her grave is nearby, if you wish to visit it."

He shook his head. "Your father's mother—is her grave also nearby?"

A distant alarm bell gave a low, mellow ting in her mind—not quite a full peal, but enough to make her shift uneasily.

Her thoughts raced as she drew the tines of her fork through the crumbs remaining on her plate. "I don't remember anyone speaking of her."

"Surely she went with her husband when your father took him to Philadelphia when he grew ill?" he asked, his eyes fixed firmly on her face.

The heat of a blush prickled her face, though she had nothing to be embarrassed about. Nonetheless, she felt she'd done something wrong in failing to ask more questions about her grandmother. It made her look uncaring.

But it simply hadn't occurred to her before this moment.

Mr. Archer was correct: her grandmother *should* have been in Philadelphia with her husband when he was so gravely ill. But Charity couldn't remember anyone mentioning her, and there had been no headstone for her next to her husband's grave in Philadelphia. And there was no gravestone for her in the Stonewright section of the graveyard in Charleston because Charity had not seen it when she went to place flowers on her family's graves.

Of course, it was perfectly possible that she had been buried elsewhere in a plot with her own mother and father, even though that seemed unlikely.

Charity put her fork down and caught Mr. Archer's gaze. "I don't know. No one mentioned her, and I have never seen a gravestone for her."

"Interesting," Mr. Archer replied.

"Why do you ask?"

"There is no mention of her death in any of the family documents. You are probably already aware of this, but your family's bible is still in the library. I took the liberty of examining it to verify the chain of inheritance, and there was no date next to her name, indicating her death. All the others were noted."

So that explained his question. "I brought the bible back with me from Philadelphia when I returned last year."

"You entered the dates, then?"

"Those that I knew; my grandfather, my father, and my mother." Her voice softened. "She died when I was born—my father was heartbroken. First he lost his father, and then my mother. It must have been a difficult time for him, trying to cope with a new baby."

The years of grief had turned her father into an old man well before his time. Her first memories of him were of a tall, impossibly thin man with hair already turning gray and deep circles around his haunted, red-rimmed eyes.

He'd done his best, working as a clerk for a bank, but they'd never had much, although he kept talking about Oldwood and the treasure hidden somewhere in the house. He refused to return, though, wanting to stay near the graves of his beloved wife and his father. Every evening he visited them, some nights staying so long that she'd had to go searching for him to bring him home. If she hadn't, he'd simply have stayed there, forgetting to eat, oblivious to the cold and rain.

Over the years she'd watched him grow thinner and grayer until one morning, he simply didn't get out of bed.

"I'm sorry," Mr. Archer said softly.

Lady Hildegard echoed his words and gave her a sympathetic smile.

"Well, that was a long time ago." Charity took a deep breath and pushed the sad thoughts away before the lump in her throat choked her and released a flood of tears. "Is the date of my grandmother's death important?"

"No, in and of itself," Mr. Archer admitted with the wry smile that never failed to make her breathing flutter. "It wouldn't have affected the inheritance of the property in this case; it was just a minor detail."

"And you cannot abide any detail not accounted for, can you?" Lady Hildegard teased him.

"The law abides in details," he replied in a flippant tone. "Which reminds me, Miss Stonewright, did your father leave a will?"

Charity stared at him. "Yes, of course he did."

"Do you have it?"

"I thought you would have found it by now, since you work so often in the library." She grimaced and pressed the corner of her napkin against her mouth. "It is in the top drawer of the desk."

He smiled at her. "I seem to be remiss in performing a thorough search, so thank you for pointing that out."

"There is nothing unusual in it—I am the sole heir," she replied stiffly, crumpling the napkin in her hand.

"I am sure that is true. My only question is why you did not give the document to Mr. Tarte to go through probate?"

"What was the point?" she asked, wincing at the bitterness in her voice. "It doesn't change the fact that he thinks this house belongs to your duchess."

"Then it doesn't mention this property specifically?" His dark brows drew together.

She shook her head. "No. It was a very simple will—my father was ill when he made it. He didn't go into any details; he just named me as the heir of all goods and properties owned by him at the time of his death."

"I see," he said thoughtfully, before he pushed his chair back an inch. "Well, ladies, I don't propose to sit here alone while you two amuse yourselves in the sitting room. Unfortunately, Mr. Tarte gave me some papers to review, and I would like to read them again in light of Miss Stonewright's information. So if you will excuse me, I'll be in the library." He folded his napkin, placed it next to his plate, and stood. His long, elegant fingers rested on the edge of the table.

Charity glanced up at him and flushed, feeling silly and flustered. Lady Hildegard sighed heavily and got to her feet, eyeing Charity expectantly. She jerked to her feet, hitting her hip against the table.

What she really wanted was to excuse herself and return to her room to read until everyone went to bed so she could search the house. But she couldn't very well leave Lady Hildegard to her own devices.

"I bid you good night, then, Mr. Archer." She caught Lady Hildegard's gaze as they followed her brother to the door. "I'm afraid there is not much to entertain you. I have no pianoforte and no musical skill, even if I had an instrument to play."

"Do you have playing cards? We Archers are quite addicted to card games." Lady Hildegard laughed and hooked her arm through Charity's. Then she came to an abrupt halt in the hallway. "Oh! All that lovely fabric upstairs—I nearly forgot! Let us go up and get my *La Belle Assemblée* magazines and pick out designs. Does this Mrs. Maplethorpe sew?" She grimaced. "My dear brother claims he forgot to ask her."

"I haven't the faintest idea, either," Charity replied. The thought of arguing over necklines, hems, and embroidered decorations was daunting, particularly when her stomach was so full that it hurt to stand.

All that food had made her sleepy, and once again, she thought longingly of her bed and a book as they walked to the staircase.

"Well, even if she doesn't, I know you can sew," Lady Hildegard said as they approached the staircase. "And we can ask Janet and Kitty. They might know how to sew. My Nettle isn't much use except to repair a hem, I'm afraid. But she is very good with my hair."

"Yes, you always look so beautiful." Charity felt a light touch on her curls and glanced over her shoulder to see

Lady Hildegard pull her hand away and grip the banister. She ascended the stairs a little faster.

"You have lovely hair. You should let Nettle pin it up for you. She is quite good, you know, and I wouldn't mind in the least."

Charity's wistful thoughts went to Mr. Archer. While she had no need to impress him, a new gown and attractive hairstyle would be so nice.

Without thinking, she agreed and then winced, immediately regretting it when Lady Hildegard clapped and dashed past her up the stairs.

"Come to my bedchamber, Charity. We have all evening to ourselves to look at the fashion plates and gossip. Aren't you excited?"

"Thrilled," Charity replied dryly.

That was the end of her comfortable evening with a book. The Archers were clearly determined to change everything in her life, no matter how exhausted it left her.

Chapter Eleven

The elusive anomaly that Edward had sensed after visiting Mr. Tarte plagued him. The feeling of something not quite right had grown during dinner, and now it buzzed around him, tickling his neck like a fly.

Miss Stonewright's vague answers, her father's abbreviated will, and the documents the lawyer had given him only made the sensation worse.

What was it? What was missing besides the sales document?

Was it only some inconsistent fact hiding in the Stonewright family history and the pile of ancient legal papers? Several times, he came close to identifying it, but the idea never fully formed.

It was probably nothing except his desire to have all the facts neatly laid out in front of him.

There was the missing information about Miss Stonewright's grandmother, of course, but her grandfather's will clearly bequeathed Oldwood to his son, so the grandmother's fate didn't alter the unbroken line of inheritance, right down to Miss Stonewright's father.

And unlike the rest of the Stonewrights, who'd scrupulously avoided leaving the property to any female descendants, he'd had the foresight to write a will ensuring that his daughter inherited all the property he owned at the time of his death. Whether that included the house and all its contents was another matter.

As the clock chimed eight, he was interrupted briefly when Janet came in, curtsied, and announced that Mrs. Maplethorpe had arrived. The interruption was welcomed, and Edward rose to greet her.

"I'm relieved you didn't change your mind," he said with a smile.

Mrs. Maplethorpe laughed and shook her head, the black ribbons of her huge bonnet fluttering under her round chin. "If I'd been tempted to ignore them, Mrs. Tarte would have encouraged me to meet my obligations, I'm sure." She lifted her head, glancing up at the landing at the top of the stairs. "Where are the young ladies?"

"In their rooms, I imagine."

"Then we shouldn't bother them tonight. If you can show me my room, I'll just settle in. Tomorrow morning is soon enough for introductions."

"Miss Stonewright indicated at dinner that she knew you?" Edward asked, his brows rising.

"Oh, yes. We've met several times. But a few social calls are a far cry from assuming the role as chaperone, aren't they?" she asked, her round face dimpling. "So I daresay introducing her to the idea will be the first order of business tomorrow morning."

He grinned and glanced over his shoulder at the maid who stood near the front door, awaiting further instructions. "Janet, would you escort Mrs. Maplethorpe to one of the bedchambers near Lady Hildegard's? And see if she requires anything to eat."

Mrs. Maplethorpe nodded and flushed with pleasure. "Yes, a small bite to eat wouldn't be turned down. If it's no trouble."

"No trouble, Madame. There be some good fish soup still warm," Janet said with a quick smile. "And bread, too. If you'll follow me, please?" She picked up Mrs. Maplethorpe's two bags and headed for the staircase.

Mrs. Maplethorpe winked at Edward before she sedately followed the young girl up the staircase, disappearing into the shadows on the landing above.

When they gathered for breakfast the next morning, Edward was relieved to find Mrs. Maplethorpe fit in as smoothly as if she'd always lived there. During the following week, she spent a great deal of time working with the ladies on their new gowns and shaking her head with laughter over some of Lady Hildegard's more extravagant suggestions about the use of ribbons, furbelows, and ruffles.

While the ladies seemed perfectly happy, Edward was less so, particularly when he had nothing to look forward to after dinner except another evening of pouring over old documents. A growing sense of frustration at his lack of progress ate at him.

If he were forced to give his best judgment now, he'd have to admit that Miss Stonewright's claim appeared to be the strongest one. He could find nothing to indicate the house had been sold to Miss Elizabeth Haywood, the aunt of the duchess. She had taken possession of the empty house in 1799, shortly after the Stonewright family had gone to Philadelphia in search of a cure for the old patriarch, Henry Stonewright.

There was nothing to indicate she'd had the legal right to do so, other than the fact that she hadn't been evicted.

It made sense that Mr. Henry Stonewright, or his son, might have sold the house to finance his care in Philadelphia. However, Edward had nothing to prove it except the letter Mr. Tarte had given him from a supposedly disinterred friend of the Haywood family, which claimed that such a sale had occurred.

Where were the bloody documents pertaining to the sale?

And why did he feel he was missing some crucial point?

Sighing, he ran his hand through his hair and returned to the library once more, listening to the distant giggling of the ladies enjoying yet another of Mrs. Maplethorpe's stories. He should join them instead of relegating himself to this monk-like isolation and study.

After reading through the most recent documents again, he stopped and stretched. The fire had died down while he worked, and he no longer heard the ladies' laughter echoing down the hallway. Even Mrs. Maplethorpe's heavy tread, going back and forth in her bedchamber, had long since ceased.

He folded the scattered papers, and stood. The house was silent except for the occasional creak of wood as the night grew colder. He drew his watch out of his pocket.

Nearly one in the morning. His sister and Miss Stonewright must have gone to bed hours ago.

He prodded the remaining embers in the fireplace and replaced the screen. Time for him to retire, as well.

Without a secure place to store the documents in the almost barren library, he'd resorted to taking them to his bedchamber each night. He tucked them into his pocket and picked up the brass lamp from the table where he'd been working.

When he walked into his room, he placed the lamp on the highboy next to the door. After a moment's hesitation, he slipped the papers in the top drawer again. He never felt quite comfortable doing so, but it was as good a place as any. No matter what results his investigation yielded, he didn't believe Miss Stonewright would stoop to stealing or destroying them.

Although he didn't know her that well, she seemed to be honest.

The soft sound of the drawer closing woke Atwood, who had been sitting in the shadows of the far corner, fast asleep. He leapt to his feet and crossed the floor to Edward. "May I assist you, sir?" he asked, his hands already on the back of Edward's well-fitted jacket.

Edward nodded and continued mulling over what he'd read that evening while his valet assisted him to disrobe in respectful silence.

"Will there be anything else, sir?" Atwood asked at last as he carefully brushed and folded Edward's garments before placing them reverently in the old wardrobe.

"No. Go to bed, Atwood. I won't need you anymore tonight."

"Good night, sir," his valet said before bowing and easing out of the room. His footsteps faded away quickly as he headed for the servants' stairs at the end of the hallway.

A hush filled the house. The wooden floor creaked as he walked to the bed, noting that Atwood had thoughtfully drawn back the covers and placed a warming pan between the sheets, near the foot of the bed. He rested his hand on the warm lump for a moment, smiling tiredly. A chill draft swirled around his bare ankles. He was about to kick off his leather slippers and climb onto the high mattress when he stiffened.

The squeak of a stealthy footstep in the hallway made him lift his head. Were the horrifying sounds of his first night at Oldwood about to start again?

If they were, he was going to locate the source of the infernal noise and put an end to it. He remembered Miss Stonewright's wan face, and anger burned in his chest. If someone was trying to scare her out of the house, they were not going to succeed.

Easing toward his door, he listened, sure he'd heard the swish of silken skirts and rasp of a leather sole against the wooden floor. The soft noises neared his door, heading in the direction of the ladies' bedchambers.

He yanked open the door. A dark-clad figure stood a yard away. Reaching out, he quickly gripped the intruder's wrist and pulled him into his room.

Or rather, *her.*

"Hildie!" he exclaimed, taking in her plain, dark blue gown and the dark shawl draped over her head. "What are you doing wandering the halls at this time of night?"

She licked her lower lip and glanced around, wild-eyed as a cornered rabbit seeking a safe path to escape. "I—I was just in the kitchen. I was hungry."

"Really?" He closed the door firmly behind her and leaned a shoulder against it. He crossed his arms over his chest.

His sister was a terrible liar. Her eyes flashed this way and that, resting on anything except him. "Er, yes." She straightened, clinging to her excuse and saying more firmly, "I was hungry."

"You went to the kitchen dressed like that?"

"I, uh..." She glanced down at what appeared to be the oldest gown she owned. Oldest and ugliest. The muslin had obviously been inexpertly dyed a dark blue, and several lighter streaks ran down the skirts, giving it a threadbare appearance. And she had stout boots on her feet.

Boots that had a fresh crust of dirt around the edge of the soles and toes.

"You were outside—where did you go?" he asked, frowning at her. "What were you doing?" He gripped her upper arm and gave her a little shake. "Don't you realize it isn't safe for you to be out at night, alone? Didn't you hear what Miss Stonewright said at dinner? The city is unsettled—dangerous."

Under the veil of darkness, she could have been attacked, raped, or worse. Hildie had always been reckless, but he didn't think she was so careless as to walk around a strange city alone, at night. The thought of what could have happened to her made his hand tighten.

She shook her arm out of his grip and glared defiantly at him. "I heard her, and I know more about it than you do!"

"What do you mean by that?"

"I—" She broke off and glanced over her shoulder at the window. "Your lamp—I forgot—"

"What? What did you forget? What about my lamp?"

She pressed her fingers to her mouth and giggled as she shook her head. The sharp, high notes revealed her nervousness, and before he could get a reasonable answer out of her, he heard the scrape of wood over wood.

He looked at his window to see it slide open. A man's boot slipped over the sill, followed by a long leg. Then a tall, slender man, clad in a black jacket, black pantaloons, and black boots stood in front of the window. His gaze went straight to Hildie, and he grinned before noticing Edward.

The stranger's smile widened, and he nodded as he leaned back in a casual slouch against the wall next to the window. He crossed his arms over his chest, mirroring Edward, and looked at Hildie.

"Well, my sweet, are you going to introduce me to your dear brother?" he asked, clearly not the least surprised to see Edward standing in front of the door.

But he should have been surprised. And terrified.

Edward studied the stranger's handsome, amused face, noting his golden red hair and dancing blue eyes. When he glanced at his sister and saw her glowing face and the blatant admiration in her eyes, it was all Edward could do not to shoot the man where he stood.

And when the golden-haired stranger flicked another, longer glance at her, a brief softening in his face told its own story. A tenuous silver chain already bound the two together, despite the shortness of their acquaintance.

Love.

That treacherous emotion was easy to recognize even in this infant stage, and Edward's heart sank at the thought of the pain she faced in the future. The two of them wouldn't be staying here for long, and she would lose the object of her new-found desire when they returned home. Or when the amused scoundrel leaning against the wall grew bored and drifted away, as men of his stamp invariably did.

Edward could see at a glance that he wasn't reliable. And he certainly wasn't suitable for Edward's sister. Edward had vast knowledge of men like him from his university days. The rascals all charmed their laughing way into the hearts of young women, got what they wanted, and then abandoned them.

The existence of such rascals was precisely why institutions like Almack's existed, so the insincere and disreputable could be kept away from impressionable young women. All their fathers had to do was to pay a small subscription fee in exchange for the knowledge that their daughters would only meet eligible men with a serious interest in matrimony.

Edward's jaw tightened. As soon as they returned to England, Edward would make sure Hildie was approved for a subscription to Almack's, whether she liked it or not.

"Edward," Hildie touched his robe-clad arm. "This is Mr. Kevin Stonewright. He's Charity's cousin. Kevin—" She blushed and shifted her feet. "That is, Mr. Stonewright, this is my brother, Mr. Edward Archer."

"A pleasure," Stonewright said. He had the same air of insouciance Hildie exhibited far more often than she should.

That alone made Edward's temper rise.

"I'd like to say the same, but it's the middle of the night, and you are standing in my bedchamber," Edward replied in a dry voice.

As he spoke, his sister's comment about the lamp became clear. She must have intended to light the lamp in her own room to indicate the correct window for Stonewright to enter.

At least *that* had been prevented.

"Off to bed, are you? Well, don't let us stop you." Stonewright grinned. His gaze drifted to Hildie, and he raised his eyebrows.

She nodded before catching Edward's glance. A crimson wave colored her cheeks, and she dropped her gaze to the floor before shifting slightly towards the door.

Edward caught her wrist. "If you'll allow me, dear sister, I'll accompany you to your bedroom and then call Nettle to ensure your comfort."

Jerking her wrist, she cast another glance at Stonewright. "I—I cannot—please, release me! You don't understand."

"Hildie..." Stonewright's low voice whispered a warning. A slight frown puckered his brow.

"What do I not understand?" Edward asked, his grip on her tightening.

"I cannot—oh, *please*—she is pregnant! She needs my help." A tear trickled over her rounded cheek. "*Please!*"

"Pregnant?" he repeated before he studied Stonewright, coldness growing inside him.

Stonewright stared back, his face set in stone.

Hildie wiped her cheek and sniffed. "You don't understand."

"Unfortunately, I believe I do understand."

"It's not me—I am not the one who is with child." Hildie flashed a half-defiant, half-apologetic look at Stonewright. "You will help us, won't you? I told him you would."

"Who, then? Who is pregnant?" Edward asked, studying Stonewright.

"Nell—she's a runaway," Hildie gripped his forearm with her free hand, her gaze beseeching him to understand. "She barely escaped—oh, you must help us! Help *her!*"

He suddenly remembered the moaning noises and footsteps the first night, and Miss Stonewright's wan, exhausted face. Did she know about Mr. Stonewright and his activities?

And just who was Mr. Kevin Stonewright, anyway?

"When did she escape?" he asked in a low voice.

"A few days ago," Hildie said. Her gaze fixed on Stonewright, but he could have been a painting on the wall for all the impact her words had on his distant expression.

"We heard her footsteps and moans—" Edward began to say.

One of Stonewright's hands jerked. "Moans? What moans? Where?"

"In the hallway, late the first night we arrived. Miss Stonewright and I both heard the noises. How can you possibly expect to keep her hidden? We can practically hear her breathing—everyone in the house can," Edward replied in exasperation.

"But you couldn't have heard anything," Hildie protested. "Neither Toby nor Nell made a sound—I would swear to it!"

"There are two of them?" Edward asked sharply.

"Yes—they are married, and she is having a baby." Hildie twisted her arm free and caught his wrist, gazing up at him imploringly. "They have suffered so—you don't know what they've gone through—and they were going to be separated! Sold! Toby would never have seen his baby if they had not escaped."

"Does Miss Stonewright know?"

Hildie shook her head and looked at Stonewright.

"No. My charming Cousin Charity is in complete ignorance," Stonewright said, his mouth twisting into a wry grin. "No one here *should* have known."

"Except I saw their shadows behind the house and discovered them." Hildie smiled, her eyes glinting with excitement as she looked at Stonewright.

"You saw shadows outside and went to investigate? Alone?" Edward gripped her shoulder and gave her a little shake. "What if they had been footpads? Thieves?" His teeth ground together as images of all the terrible things that could have befallen her raced through his mind. She was no safer here than she'd have been in the worst parts of London. Worry fueled his anger, burning through his gut. "How could you be so irresponsible, Hildie?"

"I'm sorry, I—"

"You didn't think?" He interrupted her grimly. "That excuse is wearing thin. You are eighteen—you should have more sense." His voice grew low. "I trusted you."

Tears filled her eyes, and she sniffed again before saying brokenly, "I'm sorry—truly."

Stonewright stepped forward to pull her away from Edward. He looped his arm carelessly over her shoulder and studied Edward with an air of defiance. Although his face still wore the same, bland expression, his eyes blazed. "Leave her alone, Archer. If you want someone to blame, my back is strong enough to bear the weight."

"Very noble, I'm sure," Edward murmured, clenching his fists at his sides to keep from battering his charming face. "But have you considered what might happen to my sister if she were caught?"

Amusement curled Stonewright's mouth. "We won't be caught." He tilted his head to the side, his grin growing even more insolent. "However, much as we are all enjoying this conversation, we must return." His fingers tightened on Hildie's shoulder. "Did you get them?" he asked in her ear.

"Get what?" Edward asked, furious at the man dragging his sister into a situation that was likely to get her hanged. Get them all hanged if they were not careful.

"I—I came up to get my medicine bag." Hildie eyed him uncertainly.

"Why, surely—" he stared at his sister—"she's not giving birth? Now?"

"Yes, she is," Hildie replied, pale but firm.

"As I told you, no one can hear her in the house. It's impossible," Stonewright said.

"We heard something." Edward's words grated in his throat. "And a baby's cry—"

"It couldn't have been Toby or Nell," Hildie stated. "They have been absolutely silent."

There was no answer to that.

"How is it you are using this house, if Miss Stonewright is not aware of your activities?" Edward flung at Stonewright.

All he wanted was justification, one slim reason to beat the life out of the man. He'd dragged Hildie into an impossible situation, and even if she managed to escape the legal repercussions of her actions, there was that awful pain of a broken heart awaiting her in her future. He would do anything in his power to spare her that pain, but with a sense of rage eating away at him, he realized it was probably too late.

Stonewright shrugged. The long fingers of his hand resting upon Hildie's shoulder played with one of her dangling curls. "The house was empty for years, until my cousin returned after her father died. It seemed convenient." He shrugged again. "There's been no need to bother her."

So he did have some sense of chivalry in keeping his cousin well away from his illegal activities.

Illegal but strangely honorable. Edward felt his emotions writhe inside him.

He had studied law and meant to uphold it, but the laws here were cruelly unjust. Slavery was an intolerable horror. Part of him supported, even applauded, what Stonewright was doing, despite the fact that it exposed Hildie to an ugly reality of which she should have remained ignorant.

The thought of what could happen to her made his hands fist.

He studied the pair of them before walking over and throwing open the trunk at the foot of his bed. "Take my kit." He lifted out the leather bag containing his medical supplies. "Yours is more appropriate for fainting women. I should come with you—"

"No!" Hildie grabbed the bag and cut him off. Her chin tilted up, and a mutinous light hardened her eyes. "I will help her—I can do this. You would only scare her."

"I—"

"No!" she repeated in a harsh voice, leaning toward him.

"Very well, but if you need assistance—"

"No—I will do this."

Edward looked at her again. Her firm expression showed a strength she'd never displayed before. His respect for her rose. She was growing up—had grown up—into a woman; a competent woman, willing to accept responsibility under terrible circumstances.

"Be careful, Hildie. There are others in the house, now." He briefly considered asking Mrs. Maplethorpe for her assistance. She'd been so calm and capable since she arrived. But he quickly dismissed the notion. The fewer who knew about the small family, the better. "What are you doing regarding meals?"

"I took a few things from the pantry," Hildie admitted uneasily, glancing at Stonewright.

"Don't take anything more." His voice was sharper than he intended, and he deliberately gentled his tone when he poured a handful of coins out of his wallet and held them out to her. "Go to the market tomorrow morning—give any excuse you can think of—and get supplies. You'll only alert Mrs. Granger if you remove food from her kitchen, and she may be inclined to report the matter to the local constabulary. They are sure to connect the missing food to this Toby and Nell of yours. We don't need anyone asking questions." As she deposited the coins temporarily in the medical kit, he added, "And you will need extra linen, or whatever the baby will require—if it is indeed born here."

"But we just bought armfuls of fabric," Hildie protested.

"Which Miss Stonewright has seen. She will surely question it if any quantity of material goes missing." He ran his hand through his hair as his mind raced over what might be required if they were all to remain safe. "And if you have any gowns you can spare, and that Nettle won't miss, you may wish to donate them to the woman. I will see what I have in my chest for the man. They will need new, or at least different, clothing."

"Toby and Nell," she corrected sharply. Then she blinked a few times and added meekly, "Yes, Edward." She glanced up at Stonewright. "I told you he would help us. He may be stern, but he has the kindest heart of anyone I know."

Stonewright smiled down at her and tugged on the lock of her hair he'd twined around his fingers. "So you did, Hildie."

"Lady Hildegard," Edward corrected him sharply. Best the scoundrel realized now that he was aiming too high.

Grinning, Stonewright murmured, "Hildie." Then he pulled her curl harder, making her poke her elbow into his ribs. With a mocking smile at Edward, he lifted his hands as if in surrender and stepped away from Hildie. "Come, they've waited long enough, don't you think? The baby may already be here."

Hildie caught Edward's gaze and held it, a serious expression on her young face. "Thank you. This is so important—you must know—" She broke off and swallowed several times before nodding abruptly.

A new sense of urgency gripped Edward. "You have never seen a birth. I will go with you. It can be difficult."

"No! I told you I would do it. And I don't want to frighten Nell any further. She knows me—she does not know you," Hildie said, eyes burning and hands fisted at her sides, prepared for a fight.

"You have no experience—the process is..." Filled with blood and screams? Not something a young woman should see? What could he say to her?

"I know, Edward. But it will be better if it is just me. Truly," she said, her eyes huge with anxiety and understanding.

"Very well," he agreed grudgingly. "But send for me if you need me."

"I will, Edward." Hildie turned and smiled up at Stonewright, dismissing Edward as easily as that.

He caught his breath with a sense of loss at her casual movement.

After a glance at the window, Stonewright led the way through the door. The two of them disappeared at the shadowy end of the corridor, where the servants' stairs were located.

Edward took a step forward, wanting to follow his sister and protect her, but he stopped himself. She'd made her decision and had shown a great deal of courage in doing so. It would be a slap in the face were he to exhibit a lack of faith in her strength and resolution by following her.

He had to trust her. All he could do now was to ensure no one else guessed what a dangerous course they'd embarked upon.

Chapter Twelve

Footsteps scraped in the hallway, awakening Charity. She rolled over in bed, half-asleep, and listened. Nothing but silence.

A dream, nothing more. Relief eased her into grateful sleep.

It seemed but a few minutes later when loud knocks reverberated through the house. Charity sat up in bed. Her room was shrouded in darkness, and there was no hint of light seeping between the drapes. The last embers in her fireplace glowed a deep red, but provided no real light. She picked up the candle from her bedside table and padded over to the fireplace.

Carefully blowing on the embers, she managed to light the candle. The soft light glimmered off the small clock on the fireplace mantle. A little past four in the morning.

Another pounding knock echoed through the hallway.

Who could be at the door at this time of night?

She pulled on a thick, tattered wool robe, shoved her feet into her slippers and padded to the door. When she opened it, she glanced down the hallway.

To her surprise, Mr. Archer stood outside his bedchamber, closing the door. He held a lamp in his hand and like her, he was clad in a robe with leather slippers on his feet. Except his robe looked like it was made of thick, burgundy velvet with black silk lapels, cuffs, and belt.

"What is it?" she asked, before she realized the idiocy of her question.

"Someone is at the door." He studied her, but his expression was unreadable in the wavering light. "Go back to bed. I'll take care of whatever it is."

Another loud thump on the door interrupted him.

With an abrupt nod at her, Mr. Archer walked with a firm tread to the staircase and descended.

Charity hesitated less than a minute before she followed him. This was her house. Whatever, or rather whoever, was at the door, it was a matter of concern to her, too.

By the time she'd reached the bottom step, Mr. Archer had opened the front door. He held the lamp up at shoulder height and murmured something into the darkness beyond. Someone answered him in a harsh voice.

She blew out her candle and crept closer, keeping to the black shadows lining the hall.

Mr. Archer shrugged and stepped aside. To Charity's surprise, Officer Carmichael walked past him. He held a lantern in his meaty hand, and he scowled at Mr. Archer before looking around the hallway. Charity stepped into the gloom next to the staircase.

"To what do we owe this pleasure, Officer?" Mr. Archer asked in a voice that managed to sound bored and pleasantly disinterested in any answer the officer might offer.

"I'm here to search this here house, that's what!" the officer answered in a loud, demanding tone. His scowl deepened.

"In the middle of the night?" Mr. Archer placed his lamp on the narrow table next to him and leaned one broad shoulder against the wall. He crossed his arms and then raised one hand to cover a yawn.

"Yes, in the middle of the night," Officer Carmichael sneered. "There is fugitives—escaped slaves—in the area."

"Really? You imagine I am hiding these people in this house? Why, pray tell, would I do such a thing, keeping in mind that Lady Hildegard and I have been here only a few weeks." He cocked his head to one side. "Do you suppose I *know* these fugitives?"

"No," Officer Carmichael admitted grudgingly. "But they were seen in the area."

"Precisely where *in the area*?"

The officer flushed and shifted feet. "Nearby."

"And that is sufficient to persuade you to wake us up in the middle of the night to accuse us of this crime and search this residence?"

"Yes—it is." Officer Carmichael stared at Mr. Archer with a jutting jaw and compressed lips.

Mr. Archer stifled another yawn. Then he waved one hand through the air. "Then search away, Officer."

Officer Carmichael blinked at him. The lantern in his hand jerked. "I have your permission to search?"

"Since logic doesn't appear to be your greatest asset, I will clarify. You have my permission to do any idiotic thing you wish to do, as long as you allow me to return to bed."

"Logic!" the officer spat at him. "What logic?"

"What logic, indeed?" Mr. Archer smiled blandly. "There are a great many houses in this area. Docks are near, as well. One would assume that if someone wished to flee the area, they would either stowaway in one of the ships or escape into the surrounding countryside." He studied the fingernails of his right hand. "Just my initial thoughts, of course."

"Maybe so, but I'm going to search, anyway."

"Very well." Mr. Archer's smile widened. "And perhaps your visit was beneficial, after all. Your arrival has reminded me that the Duchess of Peckham requested me to present her regards to Governor Wilson. I will have to mention your diligence to him. I'm sure he will be very pleased to hear of it." There was no mistaking the steel core in his velvety voice.

Even Charity felt a moment of anxiety for the poor officer.

Officer Carmichael paled and shifted his feet, glancing through the open doorway to the safety of the darkness beyond. "I'm only doing my duty, sir," he said. He wiped his sleeve over his brow, sweating despite the chilly, predawn air pouring into the house around him.

"Indeed, you are. Very commendable," Mr. Archer agreed silkily. He made no move one way or the other, but the officer appeared to grow even more agitated.

Charity watched them, hoping Officer Carmichael would realize the foolishness of his position and decide to leave them alone for whatever remained of the night.

Although Janet and Kitty had done nothing wrong and were legally free, she had no doubt that Carmichael would take pleasure in terrifying them with questions.

"Well?" Mr. Archer prompted him.

The officer shifted a step toward the open door. "The docks, sir. Yes, the docks. Very sensible. As you said, you just arrived here—no reason to bother you," he mumbled, his words disintegrating into incoherence as he sidled out onto the stoop. "Good night, sir."

Just then, a faint wail arose from somewhere in the house. The distant noise sounded like the cry of a newborn baby. Charity lifted her head to listen, gripped by the urge to find the child and comfort it.

Officer Carmichael walked back into the hallway, an ugly smile on his mouth. "The woman was pregnant."

"Fascinating," Mr. Archer said languidly as he strolled over to the staircase.

Charity held her breath, but he passed her without appearing to see her in the shadows. An odd smile played over his face, an amused look she couldn't understand. How could he be so unconcerned with Officer Carmichael watching him with a smug expression on his nasty face?

Who had made that despairing cry?

Another wail erupted, louder this time, and seemingly above her head. She glanced up to see Mr. Archer raise his lamp to illuminate the stairs near the landing.

His ridiculous orange cat lay on its back near the top of the staircase. Its head and front paws hung over the edge of the stair, and as she watched, it wailed again, the cry ending in a curious up-note.

Then, as she watched, the weight of the cat's head and shoulders pulled it over the edge of the step. Fortunately, Mr. Archer caught it easily in one arm. The cat proceeded to grab his forearm, give him a few rabbit kicks with its hind legs, and nibble the side of his thumb. Then it started licking his hand. The raspy sound of its tongue filled the surprised silence.

Mr. Archer shook his head and carried the animal with him as he returned to Officer Carmichael. "Sounds remarkably like a baby, does he not? Disconcerting. Especially at night."

The officer flushed an ugly maroon. When Mr. Archer strolled a little closer to him, Officer Carmichael backed up to the door.

Mr. Archer sighed. "I cannot understand from whence came this myth about cats landing on their feet, assuming Nodcock here is an average specimen." He chuckled. "He has fallen on his head at least three times today. I'm convinced that what few brains he might once have had, have long since turned to soup." He looked at the officer. "I'm not sure my nerves can stand much more wailing and falling about the place. I don't suppose you are interested in a cat?"

"No, sir." Officer Carmichael sidled through the door. He stood on the stoop, his horrified gaze locked on the cat, now sprawled untidily in Mr. Archer's arm. "Good night, sir."

Before Mr. Archer could reply, the officer disappeared, his lantern bobbing in time to the fast pace he set through the darkness as he scurried away. Mr. Archer nudged the door closed with his slippered foot and gently placed the cat on the floor. He locked the door before turning to Charity.

A long sigh escaped her lungs, only to be caught in her throat. In a flash, she remembered Officer Carmichael climbing out of the cellar into the kitchen.

Maybe he hadn't been searching for the gold, after all. Perhaps he didn't know about it, and he'd been searching for escaped slaves.

Relief made her go limp. She leaned against the staircase, pleased to have that troubling mystery so easily resolved, until she gave it further consideration.

Why would he think there were escaped slaves in her house? Were Janet and Kitty in danger? Her pulse raced.

They had documents—her jaw clenched—she refused to let anything happen to them. They were nice, hard-working women. They didn't deserve to be harassed simply because their skin was a shade darker.

The sound of Mr. Archer's voice caught her attention. He murmured something unintelligible to the cat, scratched its muzzle, and headed for the staircase just as she slipped around the newel post.

"What are you doing down here?" he asked abruptly, holding the lamp up to stare at her.

His dark hair fell over his brow in wild curls, and the stubble on his chin gave him a rumpled appearance that made her long to step closer to him and straighten the twisted collar of his robe.

"I suppose you heard?" he asked when she remained silent.

She nodded, biting her lower lip to prevent a silly grin from spreading across her face as her heart thumped in her chest. "Yes."

"I hope that idiot didn't alarm you," Mr. Archer said, watching her reaction with such intensity in his dark eyes that she felt self-conscious. She pulled her robe more tightly around her, suddenly sensing that she was missing something. Although she couldn't account for the feeling, she thought that Mr. Archer knew something she did not.

"No, not at all." She sighed. "Ever since last July, the authorities have been frantic about repressing any possible uprising or escape. I've been worried about Janet and Kitty. Despite the fact that they are free, Officer Carmichael could take it into his head to arrest them anyway. Frankly, I wish they would simply free everyone and stop living in such a state of fear. But who am I—a mere woman—to suggest such a rational, sensible approach?"

"It is an ugly situation." His lips thinned, and his face grew stony. "The laws must change—if all men are created equal, then we must assume that *all* are equal—not just a few."

"Well, I sincerely wish you'd explain that to Officer Carmichael so he'd stop exploring my cellars when I'm not here," she murmured without thinking.

"Exploring your cellars?" he asked sharply. "Do you mean he's been here before, searching your house?"

"Yes. We surprised him that day your sister and I went to the market." She rubbed her eyes. They felt as dry and dusty as the attic.

He placed his lamp on the newel post and gently gripped her shoulders to turn her to face him. The dark stubble shadowing his square jaw gave him a dangerous, brooding air that made her pulse quicken again. She grew aware of the warmth radiating from him and seeping into her shoulders from his hands.

A thick lock of wavy hair fell over his brow as his intent gaze caught hers. "Why did you not tell me?"

"What was there to say?" She shrugged, though she almost hated to do so for fear that he'd take the movement as an invitation to remove his hands. His palms felt so comforting, and she stared at his chest, longing to rest her head against the muscled breadth. When she flicked one glance up at him, his gaze drifted briefly to her mouth.

A breathless tension filled the narrow gap between them.

"Did he show you a warrant?" he ground out with an effort.

"No," she whispered.

He drew her closer. One of his hands slipped up to cradle her head, tilting it up. The lamp's flame glimmered golden in his brown eyes before he pressed his mouth hungrily against hers. She gripped him, filled with an ache that surprised her with its deep need. She felt an answering desire in the taut muscles of his chest and arms as she clung to him, breathless with longing.

Too soon he lifted his head, released her, and stepped away.

After the heat of his body wrapped around her, the hallway felt cold. An icy draft caressed her bare ankles, and she wrapped her arms around herself, flushing with the realization that they were both clad only in nightclothes and robes.

"I beg your pardon," he said gruffly, picking up the lamp. "I took advantage—"

"No," she interrupted him and gripped his arm, her chilled fingers grateful for the heat of his muscled forearm. "Please, don't apologize. It's late." She tried to laugh but it sounded more like a sigh. "We are both tired. Distracted."

"Not so tired that I didn't know what I was doing," he murmured, his eyes glinting in the lamplight. His mouth grew tight, his face drawn with concern as he added, "You do know, don't you, that I would never leave you destitute and without a home, no matter what my investigation finds?"

For some unaccountable reason, tears stung her eyes. "I don't need your assurances, or assistance, and I'm not sure I like your suggestion."

Did he think she was willing to be his mistress? Is that what his kiss meant?

"Suggestion?" A brief flicker of confusion wrinkled his brow. Then he straightened his broad shoulders. "You misunderstand. I'm not suggesting anything improper."

"That almost makes it worse. And rather insulting," she cut him off with a short, bitter laugh.

His kiss had simply been a random impulse then. How he must despise her and her lack of social standing and money.

He took another step back. "Again, I apologize for my inability to make my meaning and intentions clearer," he said stiffly.

"You do yourself a disservice. I'd say your intentions were remarkably clear."

His jaw tightened. "I dislike disagreeing with a lady—"

"Oh, don't worry, Mr. Archer. I'm fairly sure we are in agreement when I admit that I'm not much of a lady." Pain welled up inside her, and she blinked her eyes rapidly.

She'd thought he was an honorable man who cared for her well-being, particularly after he hired Mrs. Maplethorpe. How wrong she'd been—how stupid! An honorable man would never have made such an improper suggestion. He'd shown himself to be perfectly content to take advantage of her situation for his own pleasure, and she wanted to hit him and weep with disappointment and rage at her gullibility.

"What you should be sure of is that you have indeed misunderstood the situation. Unfortunately, I see little purpose in arguing the matter in the middle of the night."

"In that, at least, we are in complete accord." She suppressed a yawn, pleased to show such evidence of her disinterest. "And you are correct, it's late, or rather, early—too early. I'm not sure I will get any further sleep tonight, but I would sincerely like to try."

"Miss Stonewright—"

She brushed past him and ascended the stairs, her head held high. Let him say whatever he wished to say if he wanted to persuade her; she knew his true nature now.

She would never be fooled by his kind eyes and sympathetic manner again.

Chapter Thirteen

Unable to sleep, Edward paced the length of his bedchamber and back. Women would be the death of him. First his sister and now Miss Stonewright.

How could she believe he harbored any intentions toward her except those of the most honorable sort? Hadn't he insisted they hire Mrs. Maplethorpe? Hadn't he been scrupulous—over-scrupulous, in fact—about taking advantage of her?

Except that kiss... He thrust the thought away.

Clearly, she had formed a prejudice against him and was determined to see him in the worst possible light, regardless of his actions. There was precious little he could do to alter such an opinion, and frankly, he wasn't interested in trying.

He needed to complete the task the duchess had laid on his shoulders and return to the sane society of London.

The decision did little to relax him, however. When his pocket watch showed six in the morning, he washed quickly in the cold water from the ewer and dressed. He was worried about his sister and the unknown, pregnant woman.

Had she given birth yet? Had she and the baby survived the ordeal?

Pregnancies often ended in tragedy in the best of circumstances, and no one could call this situation ideal.

I should have gone with Hildie—offered more help than simply my medical kit, her pride and determination be damned. She was his sister, and he frankly didn't trust Stonewright.

And that wail they'd heard earlier that morning might not necessarily have come from Nodcock, though his later cries were certainly providential. When he'd first heard the sound, he'd been certain it was the howl of a newborn babe.

Then there was Miss Stonewright's claim that Officer Carmichael had unofficially searched her cellar before. What did he know?

Exactly where were Toby and Nell hiding?

His uneasiness increased. The officer had been in the cellar, and that seemed like an excellent place to hide a runaway family. Perhaps Edward should conduct his own investigation while the rest of the house slept.

The cook, Mrs. Granger, might already be up to make the fresh bread for the day, but with luck, he could either slip past her unnoticed or quell her curiosity with the simple excuse of searching for Nodcock.

That cat had been making itself surprisingly useful of late. Edward smiled and pulled on his oldest jacket, not wanting to risk a better one in the unexplored area in the bowels of the house.

He picked up his lamp and made his way to the servants' hall and through it, to the kitchen. A dusting of flour on the large wooden table, along with a large bowl draped with a towel and a basket of eggs, stood as mute evidence of Mrs. Granger's early rising and industry. But the cook had apparently stepped away from her domain, at least for the moment. After pulling open both the pantry door and the outside door, he finally found a narrow little door in the far corner of the kitchen.

When he opened it, a well-worn, dusty wooden staircase stretched down into the darkness, clinging to the right-hand wall. He held the lamp aloft and descended. The stairs creaked under his weight and some of the narrow wooden steps bowed, ready to split in half at the least provocation.

The floor was simple packed dirt, and long pine shelves lined the wall in front of him and the wall on his left. The third wall was partially hidden by the staircase, and instead of shelves, there were large barrels lined up. Strolling over to them, he picked up the lid to one in the middle of the row and found it full of apples packed in straw. The others proved to be equally full of various supplies, including potatoes and onions. A few crates were stacked in front of them, and they contained cabbages and turnips, complete with their green tops.

The shelves directly facing the stairs supported a few dusty earthenware crocks, which he assumed were pickles and other preserved foods.

That was the extent of the cellar.

Edward looked around more slowly. While the room was large, most of it remained hidden in gloom, despite the glow of his lamp, and the dimensions appeared off. It was too small.

He ran a hand through his hair and sighed. Perhaps this was the wrong place to search, after all. It was very likely that while the house had been added to over the years, the cellar remained the same size as the original mansion. He raised the lamp again and walked over to the wall to the left of the rickety wooden stairs.

The well-made shelves were mostly vacant except for the crocks. After investigating two, he realized they were empty. However, it wasn't the jars and their lack of contents that interested him, it was the construction of the shelves holding them. An extra piece of long, thin wood, one inch in height and a quarter inch in width, had been nailed to the outer edge of each shelf. Unlike the shelves on the other walls, which showed the bricks lining the cellar, these shelves had a wooden backing.

In short, they look very much like the shelves in their cabin aboard the *Hercules*; shelves that were made with lips to keep anything placed upon them from falling off due to the movements of the ship.

Why would anyone bother to build such shelves in a cellar? There were no waves to move them or tumble their contents onto the floor.

He smiled.

A closer examination and careful prodding of the shelves finally revealed that the portion that ended in the far corner near the barrels could be swung outward, once he moved two of the barrels. Their hinges weren't completely noiseless, however, and disappointment stirred in him. He'd have expected Stonewright to keep the hinges oiled if the shelves hid a door that he used frequently.

A cobweb brushed his head and draped over his shoulder. His frown deepened. If he'd found the entrance to the room where the tiny family was hiding, it should have been free of such things. The webs were almost solid veils, thick with dust, and so ancient that even the spiders had long since abandoned them to the gray dirt.

He sighed. He had to be on the wrong track.

Still, the Stygian darkness tempted him with its gloomy mystery. Stepping past the corner of the shelves, he found himself in an earthen tunnel about four feet wide and six feet tall. He had to hunch to avoid hitting his head.

Every few feet, thick wooden beams supported the walls and ceiling. Repairs had been done on the arch directly in front of him. A brick arch had been built to replace the beams supporting the tunnel, and a few rotting wooden timbers sagged a foot away. He lifted his lamp and saw wooden planks above his head—perhaps the subfloor of the house.

The passageway only went ten feet before it made an abrupt right turn. Two more brick arches supported the walls and ceiling. Pale lichen covered some of the old, reddish bricks and fungus was growing on the ancient decaying beams. Edward came abruptly to a thick wooden door a few feet further along.

Perhaps this led to the hideaway Stonewright was using. He examined the door and found it bolted shut with a heavy, iron bar driven into the wooden supports surrounding it. When he tried to open it, the iron resisted him, completely rusted in place. He'd need a hammer to beat it open.

Frustrated, he kicked it. A hollow thunk answered him. The surrounding wood was rotten and riddled with termites, a fact which made him glance uneasily at the wooden support beams above his head. Gritty bits of wood and dirt drifted down to cover his shoulders.

Despite the danger of a cave-in, his curiosity won over common sense. He set his lamp down and hit the door with his shoulder.

Thunk.

The door gave slightly, the rotten wood cracking around the iron hinges and loops holding the bar in place. He hit it twice more with his shoulder, ignoring the bursts of pain. The wood finally splintered. Two planks in the center fell inward, disappearing into the darkness beyond. Heartened, he kicked at the remaining planks until he created a gap wide enough for him to slip sideways through the door.

He held the lamp aloft as he examined the small room. The air was musty, thick with the scents of muddy earth and decay.

Then he froze.

A musty, tangled pile of clothing huddled in the corner to the right of the door. The golden glow of his lamp played over it for a minute before he sucked in a breath and steadied his light.

Small animals had obviously found the corpse at some point. Small fragments of bone and clothing were scattered across the dirt-packed floor. The thin muslin outer dress was so rotted that only a few tatters remained as a ghostly pale layer above the coarser, yellowed linen petticoat.

Two gold rings glinted on the ground next to the body, the fingers they adorned dragged into a corner by rodents.

He approached the pathetic remains and held his lamp up. A tangled mass of pale hair curled under the tattered remains of a ruffled cap. The head was wedged in the corner. Empty eye sockets stared back at him.

He took a shallow breath of the moldy air and set his lamp down near the door. As gently as possible, he moved the fragile skeleton to lay it out on the floor. A small pair of earrings fell onto the ground. He picked them up, as well as the two rings, and gently removed a fragile gold chain and locket. After placing the jewelry in his pocket, he finished laying out the remains, carefully examining them for signs of the fate that had befallen her.

A few thin finger bones were tangled together between the body and the wall, and an industrious spider had apparently spun a web between the digits. He frowned and looked more closely. Not a spider web—hair. When he carefully removed the wispy strands and blew away the dust, the rich brown color surprised him. The hair of the corpse was silvery blond. He tucked the long strands into his pocket, as well.

The skull appeared to be undamaged, and there were no dark stains in the dusty curls pinned up at the back of the head. Much of the bodice of the dress was gone, however, including any chemise she may have worn. The fabric hadn't simply rotted; it was chewed away, based upon what remained of the tattered sleeves and skirts. He sat back on his heels for a moment, contemplating the absence of linen and muslin in the area covering the heart.

The animals that had carried off the small bones would also eat blood-soaked fabric. He picked up the lamp and nudged what remained of the brittle ribcage. Two of the fragile ribs appeared to be splintered. When he moved the remains again, something rattled softly against a bone. He pried away some of the rotting fabric from the back and found what he was seeking; a misshapen lead ball.

She had been shot, and her body hidden in the cellar.

Chapter Fourteen

Sleep was an impossible dream. Or perhaps it was just her dreams that were impossible. In any event, Charity could not go back to sleep, and she finally washed and dressed. Her spirits were as low as they'd been the night her father had died.

Why did Edward Archer have to prove himself to be the same sort of nasty-minded man as all the rest? Even Officer Carmichael had stooped to making lewd suggestions the first time he'd tried to evict her.

As if tolerating his company was better than starving.

Nonetheless, she felt ill when she thought about what Mr. Archer might be thinking about her.

A glance at the clock showed that it was barely twenty minutes past six. Mrs. Granger would be up by now, making bread. Even Janet and Kitty were probably awake, preparing to eat breakfast and start their daily chores.

Charity paced back and forth. The room felt smaller and smaller with each turn, until it seemed as if she barely walked three paces before she had to turn again.

The feeling of confinement was intolerable.

She grabbed her old shawl and left her room. She walked toward the staircase, pausing to stare at Mr. Archer's door.

It wasn't shut.

A slim, dark line showed at the edge of the door. She slipped over and peered inside his room, but it appeared to be vacant. While the sheets and quilt on his bed were rumpled, no one lay asleep under them, and the chair was empty. Even the embers in the fireplace had long since gone out, leaving only gray ash.

Where was he? A chill shook her, and she grabbed the edges of her shawl, pulling it more closely around her shoulders.

Had Officer Carmichael returned? Were they searching the house even now?

What would they do if they found the box of gold?

Nothing. She shook her head. She was being silly. They were searching for runaways, not the Stonewright fortune. They didn't know about it, and even if they did, what did it matter to them if her inheritance took the form of Spanish doubloons?

Mr. Archer had finally seen her father's will, which left everything to her. No one could deny her right to the fortune.

The only difficulty lay in her preventing them from stealing anything they found, and the only way she knew to prevent that was to oversee any search.

But where could they be?

Officer Carmichael was certainly interested in her cellars. Perhaps he would start there again, since they exerted such a strong attraction for him. She headed for the servants' passageway and slipped through it to the kitchen.

Mrs. Granger, Janet, and Kitty were all busy with some sort of argument, and flour was flying everywhere as Mrs. Granger slapped her bread dough with a vengeance, as if to punctuate the point she was making to the sisters.

Beyond them, the cellar door gaped, the space beyond black as pitch. She flicked a glance at the cook and two maids and eased along the wall to the opening. No sense in disrupting the domestic discussion, which all parties seemed to be enjoying, given their general excitement and the volume of their voices.

She descended halfway down the wooden staircase before she stopped.

I should have brought a lamp. The only light was that which seeped through the open cellar door.

Until someone slammed it shut behind her.

Charity was plunged into complete darkness. She gripped the rough wood of the handrail, chastising herself for forgetting even a candle.

But she'd expected to see Officer Carmichael and perhaps Mr. Archer here with their own lamps, obviating the need for her to carry one.

So she'd apparently been wrong.

A long, frustrated breath caressed her lips. Mr. Archer was probably in the library, reviewing the silly legal papers again. She should have checked there, first.

Honestly, sometimes she was as witless as a peahen.

She was about to turn around and return to the kitchen when she noticed a faint, golden glow emanating from the furthest corner of the wall on her left.

Officer Carmichael! He broke in, the disgusting oaf.... Her jaw tightened as she descended the creaking staircase.

The light in the corner flickered and then dimmed, as if someone had walked in front of it. But as she moved closer, she couldn't see anyone standing there, and something was wrong with the shelving. It seemed crooked or aslant. When she reached it, she realized that a narrow portion of shelves had been pulled away from the wall, and the light was cascading out from behind it.

A tunnel! Her pulse thundered in her ears as her breath caught in her chest. *That rotten cad is after the gold! He may be holding it in his greedy hands right now, counting every coin!*

She took a step toward the passageway before she realized the foolishness of confronting him alone. She was vulnerable, and she only had surprise and the power of anger on her side. Groping through the gritty dust on the shelves, she found a large earthenware jar. It smelled faintly of vinegar and dill, but the heft of it felt good in her hands.

Armed and breathing harshly with tension, she eased around the shelf and found herself standing in a narrow corridor. The light bounced fitfully off the walls and gleamed dully from the surface of small puddles of mud on the floor. A few patches of lichen glimmered damply, and the air smelled dank, leaving the earthy taste of dirt in her mouth.

She stepped forward cautiously until she reached the bend. The light dimmed abruptly again—someone had moved in front of the lamp. A huge, black shadow flared up the wall on her right before it vanished, and the golden glow returned more vigorously. She hefted the earthenware jar in both hands and slipped around the corner.

The hallway was empty! Then she noticed that the light was coming through the splintered remains of a wooden door several feet away. She paused to take a few deep breaths to calm herself, her gaze fixed on the gap. Movement caught her attention. A shoulder encased in a black jacket and an arm moved in a way that suggested he was picking something up.

Her temper flared.

Then he turned toward the door, but the light was at his back, leaving his face in shadows. A long leg encased in dark trousers stretched through the gap, then the rest of his body followed. Charity raised the jar in her hands, prepared to shatter it on his thick skull.

"Miss Stonewright!" he called, sounding startled.

"Mr. Archer?" She lowered the jar briefly before frowning. Her senses must have betrayed her. Why would Mr. Archer be down here instead of the library he loved so much?

Unless he'd found something in the papers he'd been studying so diligently.

He held out a hand, palm outward. "Miss Stonewright—I apologize for startling you." He gestured to the pickle jar.

Feeling idiotic, she lowered the jar and placed it on the floor next to her right ankle. "What are you doing here? How did you find this passageway?"

His gaze flickered away from her. He cast a quick look over his broad shoulder at the splintered door behind him. With a tired gesture, he rubbed his forehead in the crook of one arm.

The distinct impression that he didn't want to answer her questions came over her. He *must* have found something in those papers. She should have studied them, herself. He'd frequently left them in the library—she could have read through them at any time, and she'd been a fool to ignore the information they contained, even if their tangled legal words did leave her more frustrated and confused than enlightened.

"Well?" she prompted him, crossing her arms.

"I don't wish to lie to you," he murmured in a low voice. He flicked another glance at the door, his eyes shadowed by his frowning brows. "Honor—I thought I was an honorable man." He sounded angry—bitter—and the line of his jaw tightened.

The stony grating of his voice scared her a little. It seemed to hint at terrible things, hidden secrets she wasn't sure she wanted to know.

Uneasy, she remembered his questions and the reason for his presence in her house. Had he found some new horror? Some terrible betrayal, a crime that when exposed would only lead to more sorrow?

"What do you know of your cousin, Kevin Stonewright?" he asked abruptly, standing in front of the broken door.

"My cousin?" She blinked rapidly, confused by the sudden change in subject.

"His business—what he does," he explained impatiently. He brushed some cobwebs from his sleeve as he waited for her answer.

"Well, he's really only my cousin once removed. His grandfather was the younger brother of my grandfather—not that it matters. But I don't know much about him, other than that he owns a ship, the *Janus*." She smiled halfheartedly. "I saw it in port once; it has a unique figurehead."

A smile twitched his firm mouth. "Let me guess, two faces? That would be Janus, the god of transitions, passages, and endings. An unusual name for a ship."

"Yes." She nodded. "He's very proud of it, though." She wrinkled her brow. "But I don't really see what cousin Kevin's eccentricities have to do with you searching my house." She waved at the broken door. "Or destroying my property."

"No, well—are you sure you don't know anything more about your cousin?"

"I know he's completely unreliable, and I'd really rather not talk about him at the moment. Just what are you doing here?"

"As I said, I have no wish to lie to you—"

"So you are trying to change the subject to my idiotic cousin?"

A low chuckle rumbled in his chest. "Not precisely, no. I hope you will not misunderstand, Miss Stonewright—"

"Oh, please call me Charity. Your sense of honor is quite annoying enough without all those *Miss Stonewright* this and *Miss Stonewright* that," she said in exasperation.

"Very well." He smiled and leaned his shoulder against the wall before he remembered it was dirt. He straightened and dusted off his sleeve, his face growing serious. "I have no wish to betray any confidences, however, so I'm hoping we can leave the reason for my presence here unexplored— at least for the moment—and concentrate on other more important matters."

A chill shivered over her shoulders. She was suddenly conscious of the icy, stifling air in the narrow tunnel. She didn't want to talk about more important matters.

Her mind swirled back to the relative safety of Cousin Kevin and his ship, the *Janus*. Her knees shook. She reached out and pressed a hand against the damp wall. *Officer Carmichael—runaways. Janus, the god of passages. All those trips of Kevin's to the north ... New York ... even Maine. Carrying cotton—indigo—goods for the northern mills.*

And runaways.

That had to be what Mr. Archer was trying so hard not to talk about.

Cousin Kevin's odd schedule, leaving in the middle of the night at times, suddenly made sense. It wasn't the tides he was concerned about, it was the safety of those he'd stowed away on his ship.

And she couldn't fault him for his recklessness. If she owned a fast ship, she might have done the same. Except that she would never have given her ship such a provocative name—almost as if he were thumbing his nose at the authorities.

Which was so like him.

"I think I can guess," she said in a low voice. "Are they in there? Hiding from Officer Carmichael?" She nodded to the wooden door.

"What? No," he answered hurriedly, stepping forward as if to block the door. "I'm sorry—I had no wish to involve you—it is dangerous enough as it is."

"It is—but my cousin loves risk the way most people love their comfort. I should have realized it sooner." She studied him, her head tilted, uncertainty fluttering through her. "We are talking about the same thing, are we not? The run—" She cut herself off. What if he was referring to something else entirely, and she gave away Cousin Kevin's secret? An honorable man might be driven to inform the authorities.

He nodded, his smile twisting wryly. "Neither of us wish to put it into words, but yes. Officer Carmichael's runaways are here." He gestured vaguely at the walls. "Somewhere. But not in the room behind me."

"Then what is in there?" Her heart pounded in her chest. *He's found it—the Stonewright fortune!* She took a step closer and bent forward, trying to see past him into the black space beyond.

"Don't go in there!" He gripped her shoulder to draw her back. "Charity, please. It isn't pleasant."

She shook him off. "What is it?"

"Someone's remains," he said. "They seem to have been here for quite a while. I'm truly sorry."

Chapter Fifteen

When Charity leaned against the tunnel's wall, Edward moved to grip her shoulder. Even in the poor light from the lamp, she appeared pale and ill with shock.

"I beg your pardon," he said with a grimace. "I phrased that badly."

She stared at him with unseeing eyes before blinking and casting a quick, flinching glance at the ragged opening in the old door. She moved like someone who didn't want to see a gruesome sight, but was forcing herself to view it anyway.

"Who is it?" she asked in a low voice. She took one shaky step toward the doorway.

He thrust his arm across the opening, holding her back. There was no reason for her to see the pitiful remains that he'd laid out on the floor. They would only alarm her and give her nightmares.

She'd been through far too much already. He could only imagine how desperately alone she must have felt with a household of strangers, including a man she fully expected to demand she leave the only home she had.

No wonder she had been livid with him in the wee hours of the morning. He'd given in to temptation and taken advantage of her in that moment of relief after Officer Carmichael departed.

So much for his self-vaunted sense of honor. Frankly, it wouldn't have been surprising if she'd shot him on the spot.

"Ah ha!" A man stepped around the corner into the lamplight. "I knew you two was hiding something," Officer Carmichael announced with satisfaction. He lifted a battered tin lantern of his own to stare at them, a smile of grim triumph fattening his cheeks.

"What are you doing here?" Edward asked, stepping in front of Charity.

"What am I doing here?" Carmichael repeated with a sneer. "What do you think I'm doing here, my fine little lord?"

"What I think is that you had better have a warrant," he answered grimly.

"A warrant?" He laughed and nodded in Charity's direction. "She ought-a be glad I don't."

"How did you get past Mrs. Granger?" Charity asked, her hand on Edward's shoulder, her breath whispering past his neck.

He could feel the warm weight of her body pressing against his back and the slight tremble of her hand.

"Your cook? What's she got to say about it?" He took another step forward, his small eyes fixed on the door behind them. "Is that where they're hiding?" He studied Charity and licked his damp lips, his eyes filled with something like greed.

Edward's hands fisted at his side. "There is nothing here to interest you."

"Oh?" Carmichael chuckled. "So you've got yourself a few more treasures hidden down here, too. Well, well. Maybe we can strike a bargain, if you're so interested in these here fugitives."

Behind him, Charity was so close he felt her suck in a sharp breath and grow stiff. Her fingers bit into his shoulder.

"A bargain?" Edward frowned at the officer. If he thought Edward was going to offer him a bribe, he was sadly mistaken. Wherever Stonewright had hidden the tiny family, they were still safe, and Carmichael's impromptu search was illegal without a warrant.

Most of the laws of this country remained a mystery to Edward, but he was well aware of the few pertaining to illegal search and seizure, and he intended to make the most of them.

"Governor John Lyde Wilson will be very interested in this search, Officer, and repeated harassment," Edward drawled lazily. "I believe I may have mentioned him before?"

Carmichael chuckled. "Well, I doubt you're in any hurry to meet him, considering what you've got in that there room of yours. Can't imagine he'd be all fired up to shake your hand, knowing you've been giving aid to a couple of slaves."

Edward laughed. "You are obviously a man who only believes what he sees." He moved to the side of the passageway and held his arm out in front of Charity to protect her behind his body. "So perhaps you would like to see the contents of this room that has captured your attention to such a degree."

The officer snorted and eyed Edward, clearly suspicious. Edward smiled blandly.

Grumbling, Carmichael shoved his way past Edward and Charity and thrust one leg through the opening. He moved his tin lantern into the room and then hunched over to ease through the remaining rotten pieces of the door. A sharp intake of breath broke the silence. The glow from Carmichael's lantern dimmed as he strode around the small room, grumbling incoherently and apparently searching for his quarry.

The orange light grew brighter. Carmichael stuck his head back through the broken door. "What is this?"

Edward coughed into his hand, hiding his smile. "In my opinion, it is a corpse." He cleared his throat. "I apologize, Miss Stonewright for any outrage to your sensibilities. I had meant to spare you the details."

"No need." Her voice burbled over his shoulder, rich with suppressed laughter. A sharp edge to her words hinted at the tension underlying her amusement and barely controlled hysteria.

"Steady," he murmured, catching her cold hand in his.

She nodded, and her chin hit his back.

"Corpse!" Carmichael scrambled out of the room, red-faced and puffing. He cast uneasy glances over his shoulder at the tiny room, as if he expected the dead woman to rise and follow him.

"Yes. At least that is what it appears to be," Edward replied calmly.

Carmichael stabbed Edward in the chest with a meaty finger. "If that's a joke—"

"I assure you that this situation is not the least bit amusing."

"Then where's them slaves?" the officer yelled, his gaze flicking between Edward and the hole in the door.

"Who?" Edward crossed his arms over his chest and leaned against the wall, blocking Carmichael's view of Charity.

"Slaves! Them slaves! You've got 'em hidden—where is they?" Spittle collected in the corners of Carmichael's mouth, and his flushed face grew a deeper crimson.

"Your guess is as good as mine."

The officer took a deep breath and an ugly, crafty look passed over his face. "If they ain't here, why're you down here?"

"Frankly, I wish someone would remind me, as well. I'm afraid my discovery of that poor creature in the other room has wiped away any other concerns I may have had," he said, ignoring a soft, stifled snort coming from the corner behind him.

"It's the gold, ain't it?" Carmichael thrust his round head at Edward. "Where's it at?"

Edward stared at him. *Gold*? "I haven't the least notion to what you are referring."

"Gold, you blockhead. Ain't that what we're jawing about?"

"I don't know what *you're* talking about." Edward's clipped tones turned icy. "Or why you're here without a warrant, I might add. But I can assure you, there is nothing down here except that pitiful bundle of remains. If you wish to search for yourself, you are welcome to do so. However, Miss Stonewright and I are returning upstairs, as we have yet to have our breakfast."

Carmichael stared at him for a long minute, his wiry brows jutting out in an angry frown before he straightened. "I'm leaving. But you've got something hidden, and I don't know if it's them slaves or gold, but I'm gonna find it, you see if I don't. This ain't the end, no sir." He turned abruptly on one heel and started back down the corridor.

"Sadly, I agree. I'm sure it is not the end." Sighing, Edward stepped aside to let Charity go in front of him while he retrieved his lamp and held it up to light the passageway.

They walked into the kitchen just as Officer Carmichael was aiming a kick at Nodcock. The cat seemed intent on rubbing against the officer's leg and seemed unaware of the looming threat.

"Nodcock!" Edward called.

Carmichael's boot passed so close to Nodcock's tail that the fur ruffled in the wind. The cat ignored Edward, however, and twisted around to return to the officer.

Seeing the animal's movement, Carmichael's face contorted in an ugly combination of anger and horror. He almost ran to the back door.

Shaking her fist at him, Mrs. Granger yelled, "Scared of a little cat? Coward! How dare you sneak into a decent woman's house! Get out and don't return! Get *out!*"

The door slammed behind him.

Frowning savagely, Mrs. Granger sniffed, glanced at Nodcock, and stalked over to the ham on the kitchen table. She sliced off a piece and bent down, waving it in front of Nodcock's nose.

The cat's long white whiskers twitched, and he delicately took the piece in his mouth and walked away, tail up and tip waving in triumph.

With a jerk, Mrs. Granger straightened. She must have heard Charity and Edward, because as soon as the door closed behind Carmichael, she whirled around, scowling, and her face as red as an apple.

"Get out of my kitchen! All of you!" she yelled, her hands clenching around the edges of her apron.

"Mrs. Granger, I don't believe you've met Mr. Archer," Charity said calmly, stepping aside to allow Edward to walk into the kitchen.

He nodded at the cook. "Mrs. Granger."

"Mr. Archer," she said grudgingly. Her brows jutted over her deep-set eyes as she glanced from him to Charity.

"Officer Carmichael was afraid someone had broken into our cellar," Charity explained with a casual wave of her hand that suggested she found such fears ridiculous, if not utterly boring.

"He's an idiot," Mrs. Granger said, her firm voice indicating the uselessness of arguing the point, if anyone were so inclined.

Charity smiled and shrugged. "We will leave you to get back to..." Her words drifted off as she gestured toward the pans on the stove.

"Ten minutes." Mrs. Granger crossed her arms over her chest. "If I get some peace."

"We will be in the dining room." Charity avoided irritating Mrs. Granger further by deftly avoiding the words *thank you*. She touched Edward on the arm before she turned to walk out of the kitchen.

Edward nodded once more to Mrs. Granger, who continued to stare at them, obviously intending to watch the two of them until they'd fled from her domain. She was so gaunt and thin that her defense of her territory left him with the feeling that he'd been forcibly swept out of the kitchen by a bad-tempered broom.

There was no sign of Hildie or Stonewright in the dining room, and he noted Charity's quick glance around, as well, before she turned to study him. Sunlight streamed through the large window behind her, making her hair glow bright red and gold like the flames of a cheerful fire. Except the expression on her tired face was not happy. Her mouth drooped and a small V of worry had burrowed between her arched brows.

He placed his lamp on the sideboard and lifted the glass to blow out the flame.

"The remains... Who was it? Do you know?" she asked in a soft, hesitant voice.

"No." He could guess, but he didn't want to upset her if his notions should prove false. He dug through his pocket and pulled out the jewelry he'd collected. "Perhaps these can provide a few clues."

Damn. He'd forgotten he'd collected a bullet, as well. The lead ball rolled lopsidedly a short distance away from the rings and locket, despite its misshapen, flattened side. A sharp intake of breath made him lift his head to look at Charity. She pressed her fingers against her mouth, her eyes fixed on the spent bullet.

"Murder? Was he murdered?" she asked. Horror glazed her blue eyes, and her already pale cheeks grew gray.

"She—it appears she was a lady." He spoke as gently as he could.

"She—do you think...?" Her gaze fixed on his face.

"We shouldn't hurry to reach a conclusion." He picked up one of the rings. Letters were engraved on the inner surface, and grime filled the grooves, making the tiny words more obvious. "Her dress lacked the hooped panniers of the eighteenth century—it appeared to be more modern to me."

"More modern?" she echoed, her gaze growing distant as she considered his words. "So she could have died while the house was vacant?" She frowned, her brow wrinkling. "Or she could have been a servant. Servants never wore those ridiculous hoops under their gowns."

"Perhaps. But I didn't get the impression she was a servant." His hand passed over the small mound of jewelry. One of the rings was a large opal surrounded by what appeared to be small emeralds, rubies, and sapphires. Not the kind of ring one would expect a servant to wear. He held up the plain ring between his thumb and middle finger. "This one is engraved, *LIHBS and HBS.* It appears to be a wedding ring. Do the letters mean anything to you?"

She stretched out her hand, and he placed the ring on her palm. Her cheeks flushed and then paled before she drew a deep breath and examined the ring. Finally, she glanced up and gave a small laugh when she caught his gaze. "I don't wish to jump to conclusions." She tried to smile, but her mouth trembled until she pulled the bottom lip between her teeth. "My grandfather's initials were HBS—Henry Bartholomew Stonewright."

"Your grandmother?"

"Lenore," she whispered through pale lips. Her blue eyes were huge as she gazed at him, the ring clutched in her hand. "Do you think those are my grandmother's remains?"

"I don't know, but it appears that way." He closed the distance between them and took her in his arms, one hand gently pressing her head against his heart, feeling responsible for her grief. He would have done anything to spare her the pain of believing her grandmother had been murdered.

If it was her grandmother.

But whoever she was, she'd been brutally murdered and her body had been hidden in the cellar. Given the information he had, if it was Lenore Stonewright, she'd been killed at least twenty-four years ago. Most likely, whoever had murdered her was also dead.

But there was the distant chance that he—or she— might still be alive to face justice for their despicable actions.

He pressed his lips against the top of Charity's head and held her trembling body against him, wishing he could have spared her this on top of everything else that had happened. But part of him couldn't help but wonder if the answer to the question of ownership of Oldwood lay in the disintegrating hand of the corpse in the cellar.

He pulled a handkerchief out of his pocket and placed it in Charity's hand. She sniffed wetly and took a deep, shaky breath before she pushed him away.

"I'm sorry." Her voice quavered, and she took another juddering breath, holding his handkerchief against her mouth. "I never even met her. I don't know why I'm being so silly."

"It's understandable," he replied gently. "And remember, it may not be her."

"It has to be her!" she exclaimed, her words raw with pain. "Who else could it be? Where else could she have been all these years?"

The vulnerability and hurt exposed in her face made him glance down at the table and examine the remaining jewelry to give her time to regain her self-possession. "What do you know of your grandfather?" he asked at last, picking up the locket.

Inside, the tiny portrait of a white-wigged man occupied the left half, while an elaborately coiffed and powdered woman was on the right. Both done in the manner of the middle of the last century. He showed them to Charity, but she simply shook her head and refused to take the locket, her red-rimmed eyes filling with tears again.

"My grandfather loved her—he wouldn't have murdered her!" she rasped brokenly.

Love often turned to anger. From thence, it was but a short step to murder.

When he didn't speak, she flushed and swallowed, twisting his handkerchief between her hands. "He wouldn't have hurt her, I tell you!"

"He died before you were born," he pointed out gently. In truth, the most likely answer seemed to be that her grandfather had murdered his wife for some reason—most likely jealousy—and locked her body away in the cellar. Who else would have known about the secret room?

And then, overcome by guilt, or unable to stand living in the house any longer, knowing what lay beneath it, he'd taken his son's family with him to Philadelphia. And it seemed likely he'd sold the house to obtain the funds to move and be rid of it all.

155

It was sheer speculation, of course. Edward couldn't prove any of it, but it seemed to be the most logical answer.

"I don't care! He didn't do it, I'm sure of it." Despite her strong words, her blue eyes were stained with doubt. She looked at the jewelry on the table and flung the ring down next to the small pile. "Even if that is my grandmother, my grandfather had nothing to do with her death. He would have buried her in the family cemetery—no one would have questioned him."

"Perhaps. But who else would have known about that room?" he asked, hating himself for pointing out what seemed so obvious and increasing the burden bowing her slender shoulders.

"My father might have known—but he would not have murdered his own mother! He would have no reason."

"Would they have told anyone else?"

She stared at him, her face growing cold and her eyes hardening with anger increasingly focused on him. "You found it," she spat at him. As if suddenly realizing she still held his handkerchief, she threw the crumpled wad onto the table. "If you could find it, anyone could."

"Point granted." He smiled at her, trying to ease the tension tightening around them.

Her shoulders slumped. She looked away, her hands playing over the curved top edge of a chair back. "Will you promise me something?"

"Yes, if it is within my powers."

"Do not *assume* my grandfather is guilty." Her hands trembled and momentarily gripped the chair back before she slowly and deliberately released it, flexed her fingers, and dropped her hands to her sides. "It may be impossible." A smile flickered over her pale lips like a moth fluttering around a candle. "But I would have you at least consider other possibilities. Someone else." Her voice cracked. She pressed her lips together and swallowed. "It can't be too late, can it?" She looked up, her eyes searching his face, desperation shining in her unshed tears. "After all these years, there has to be some way to discover who did this terrible thing. Whoever it was, he killed my grandfather, too, you know. That's why my father took him to Philadelphia—because something was killing him." Her voice rose, and once again, she gripped the backs of the chairs. Her knuckles glimmered stark white in the grainy beams of morning sunlight streaming through the window at her back. "Father said something...." She broke off and glanced down, rubbing her forehead.

"That is an easy promise to make, for it is what I intended to do all along. The easy answer is rarely the right one." Edward moved closer and gently squeezed her left shoulder.

Her tense muscles felt hard as ice under his touch, and he slid his hand to the back of her neck and left it there for a minute to warm her cold skin. When he began to remove it, she reached up to hold his wrist, her left arm crossing her bosom to do so. She flicked a wan, tender smile over her shoulder before she sighed and released him.

His grip tightened as realization hit him. He loved her. Powerfully and with a deep need that made the breath catch in his throat. Tension gripped him. He forced himself to breathe and step away.

Now is not the time.

"And you must share what you find," she said at last. "Even if it is terrible."

"Of course," he agreed in a rough voice.

She glanced at him. "Where will you start?"

"I—" Something clicked in his mind, like the soft snick of a lock releasing as a door is opened. "I had planned to ask you this yesterday, but it slipped my mind. Do you know which room Miss Elizabeth Haywood used when she lived here with her niece?"

"Miss Haywood?"

"Yes. I assume the duchess, that is, the former Miss Charlotte Haywood, had one of the smaller rooms. She was only a child at the time."

"I haven't the slightest idea," Charity replied, looking at him askance, with a gleam in her blue eyes that suggested she thought the subject entirely irrelevant. "I wasn't here at the time—I only returned last June."

He shifted impatiently. "There might have been indications—a gown left in a chest, or something similar. Elizabeth Haywood died here, and her niece was sent to relatives in England. I doubt anyone bothered to give the house a thorough cleaning afterward. When you arrived, what was the condition of the bedchambers?"

A thoughtful frown creased her forehead. "Well, I wasn't even aware that the Haywoods had taken possession of my house and tried to sell it, until Mr. Bryant walked in, claiming he owned the property and accusing me of trespassing. That occurred just a week after I returned. And *he* swore he'd purchased it several years before, but had been concluding business in London and Paris and had just returned to take up residence."

"You must have explored all the rooms—what of the one you use? Was it the master bedchamber?"

She shrugged. "I liked it because it faces east and gets the morning sun. It wasn't the largest room, but it seemed the most pleasant."

"Were there any gowns left behind, anything to indicate a previous occupant?"

"A few jackets...." A tender, reminiscent smile lit her face. "I thought it might have been my father's bedchamber."

"What of the other rooms?"

"I did find some clothes—I sold a few and remade the others for myself." She flushed. "There were several gowns and shoes in the room Lady Hildegard uses, as well as your bedchamber. To be honest, though, I didn't pay much attention. I assumed they'd been left behind by my family. Why?"

"Were there any journals? Diaries or letters?" He ran a hand through his hair and glanced at the door to the hallway. "Would you object if I searched the house?"

"I have no objections, but I don't see the point. By the time that Haywood woman moved in, my grandmother was dead." She studied him. Suddenly her eyes flashed. "Oh, I see. You still wish to prove I don't belong here, that Oldwood isn't mine."

"Please, Charity, can we forget that for the moment? I am merely trying to paint a complete picture of that time—the turn of the century—and someone may have heard something. A rumor? Gossip?" He lifted his hands. "If there are any letters or a journal, anything that might give us a clue, we might be able to discover what happened."

"I don't know." She shook her head tiredly.

"There you are!" Hildie called from the doorway. She walked into the dining room, and her gaze drifted over the bare table before going to the equally bare sideboard. "I'm famished. Where is breakfast?"

No sooner had she asked then Janet and Kitty came into the room. The maids carried huge wooden trays, laden with all manner of delights, including a plate of mush cakes made of corn meal. Edward had never had them before, but he was rapidly becoming enamored of them drenched in honey and butter, their sweetness offset by a slice of salty ham.

Despite burning the candle at both ends, Hildie appeared rested and bursting with radiant energy like a miniature sun. She made him feel gray and almost elderly in comparison, and the wry twist to Charity's lips as she looked at his sister suggested that she felt precisely the same way.

He caught her glance and shook his head. She shrugged.

"Am I the only one interested in breakfast?" Hildie asked as she stood at the sideboard, heaping mush cakes onto her plate.

"No." Edward held the chair for Charity to be seated before he strode over to the sideboard. The dish containing the cornmeal cakes was half empty by the time he reached it. "You might have left a few for the rest of us."

"There are plenty for you, and Charity never eats more than one," Hildie replied jauntily. She poured a liberal amount of honey over the cakes on her plate and dribbled more over her ham, revealing her penchant for sweet things.

"You certainly seem cheerful this morning," Charity commented, staring down at the plate of eggs, ham, and a single mush cake that Edward placed in front of her. She pushed the eggs around with her fork listlessly.

"Yes. It's a beautiful day." Hildie shoved a forkful into her mouth and chewed hurriedly. "Let's go to the market! It is the perfect day for a walk."

Edward groaned as he took a seat at the head of the table. "Is it your intention to completely empty our coffers? You should thank Mr. Tarte that he had the foresight to open an account for us at the Second Bank of the United States, although the duchess may begin to wonder why we are requesting the transfer of such large sums of money so soon after arriving."

Laughing, Hildie scraped her fork over her plate to get the last few delicious crumbs. "I have no doubt she would understand completely. Have you seen the elegant dresses *she* wears? One doesn't get *those* for a few pence. She probably spends in a single day what we have spent our entire time here!"

"Perhaps. But I don't believe a young woman who hasn't even been presented to Society yet needs to dress like a duchess," he replied dryly.

Hildie snorted and pushed her plate away. "Shall we go, Charity?"

"I have to arrange—" Charity's gaze met Edward's. She clearly didn't want to talk about the remains in the cellar, but they couldn't be left there, either. "That is…"

He nodded. "I will be talking to Mr. Tarte this morning. I'll take care of it then." Tarte would be able to arrange for a proper funeral and take the burden off Charity's shoulders.

"Take care of what?" Hildie looked from him to Charity with suspicion.

"A small legal matter. I'd be happy to discuss it with you if you wish," he offered in an offhand manner. "I'm sure it wouldn't take longer than an hour—two at the most—to cover the essential details."

Hildie's face twisted with disgust, and she snorted. "You can take care of it, I'm sure. Charity and I are going to the market." She rose and held out her hand to Charity.

An exasperated sigh escaped Charity's lips, but she stood and joined his sister. The two ladies walked out, arm-in-arm, while he thoughtfully poured himself another cup of coffee.

With Charity and Hildie gone for several hours, he could talk to Mr. Tarte and perhaps even have time to search the bedchambers. And if he didn't find anything, there was the attic above.

The house seemed to be riddled with secrets, and it was about time to unravel a few of them.

After finishing his coffee, he made his way to the lawyer's office. Fortunately, Mr. Tarte was in and although his desk was still hidden under a barricade of paper, he seemed more than happy for an excuse to push them to one side. He clasped his hands on the clear spot in front of him and looked expectantly at Edward.

"I won't keep you very long, Mr. Tarte. I can see that you are busy," Edward said by way of a preamble.

Tarte smiled and removed his glasses to clean them with his handkerchief. "I am pleased to have the excuse to set these infernal contracts aside for a moment. Have you come to any conclusions regarding the Haywood property?"

"Not yet—that's not why I'm here." Edward cleared his throat and shifted on his hard wooden chair. "We've made an unfortunate discovery—"

"Concerning the property in question?" Tarte's pleasant expression faded. "I don't see how that situation can be any more unfortunate than it already is."

"It's only tangentially related to the property title and perhaps not even that. We have discovered some remains in the cellar."

"Remains?" Tarte sat up straighter and blinked, his mouth hanging open in surprise. He hurriedly put his glasses back on. "What kind of remains? Whose remains?"

"We believe them to be Mrs. Henry Stonewright's remains. There was jewelry which seemed to indicate that," Edward said carefully.

"Mrs. Henry Stonewright?" The lawyer seemed incapable of doing more than repeating Edward's statements. "*Lenore* Stonewright?"

"Yes. And we need your assistance to arrange a funeral—a small, private one." He studied the lawyer's shocked face. "There is evidence suggesting that she was murdered, and her body was hidden in the cellar. As you can imagine, we wish to avoid gossip and any scandal that might arise in the circumstances, so I trust you to consider this information privileged and confidential."

Tarte took off his spectacles again and fidgeted with the ear pieces, his gaze still fixed myopically on Edward. Then he picked up his handkerchief again and began rubbing the lenses of his glasses with nervous energy. "I see. Of course. This is very unfortunate."

"But you will arrange for a funeral?"

"Well, yes, of course. The Stonewrights have a plot in St. Michael's Churchyard. She can be interred there." He stared at Edward. "The church is on the corner of Broad and Meeting streets, surely you've heard the bells ringing?"

"Yes." Edward gestured impatiently. "We have attended services there. It should be quite suitable. Just a simple burial. Only Miss Stonewright will be attending. How quickly can it be arranged?"

After shoving his handkerchief into his pocket, he put his glasses on again, adjusting the wire frames with jerky fingers. "Tomorrow, perhaps." He nodded. "Yes, I can certainly arrange for her burial tomorrow morning in the family plot. Shall we say eleven?"

"Fine."

"Such a tragedy. Have you any idea who could have done such a thing?"

"No. I was hoping you could shed some light on that dark corner," Edward replied.

Tarte shook his head and seemed to grow calmer with the realization that he could not be held responsible for the situation. He clasped his hands in front of him. "Well before my time, I'm afraid. I heard the rumors, of course—"

"What rumors?"

"That old Henry Stonewright returned home from one of his trips to Philadelphia to find her gone. The assumption was that she'd run away with a lover." Tarte flushed and shook his head. "Terrible thing—my father said that she as good as killed old Henry, because he had a stroke that very week. Returned to Philadelphia for medical treatment and died soon thereafter."

"Your father—is he still alive?"

"No. He passed away last year," Tarte said, moisture gleaming in his close-set brown eyes. With shaky fingers, he adjusted his glasses again and fidgeted in his chair before firmly clasping his hands in front of him again.

"Did he say anything else?"

"No, I'm afraid not. Everyone always assumed Henry and Lenore were one of the few happily married couples in Charleston. It was quite a shock when she disappeared. I know my father never understood it."

"She didn't exactly disappear, though," Edward commented grimly. "She was murdered." He took a long breath. "Were the Haywoods and the Stonewrights friends at that time?"

"I beg your pardon?" Tarte's eyebrows rose with surprise.

"Were the two families friendly?"

163

"Surely, you don't suspect a member of the Haywood family?"

"Not precisely. I was simply wondering about the chain of events. If Henry Stonewright did sell his property before leaving, would he have sold it to the Haywood family?"

"It is possible, but I cannot say with any certainty. I was only a boy at the time. I didn't know either family very well."

"I see. Well, I suppose whoever is responsible for Mrs. Stonewright's death is long dead, but it would relieve Miss Stonewright's mind if she knew what happened to her grandmother. You mentioned a Mrs. Eggerton during our first interview—would it be possible for you to arrange a meeting with her?"

Tarte's hands remained clasped, but he rubbed his right thumb over the knuckle of his left. After a moment of consideration, he nodded. "Perhaps. She was certainly a friend of Mrs. Stonewright and may remember something helpful. She must be in her eighties, however, so you should not be too optimistic." He held up a hand when Edward opened his mouth. "Oh, she is still alive, and I believe she is still quite sensible, never fear." The lawyer picked up his pen, dipped it in the glass inkwell on his desk, and scratched out a few lines on a scrap of paper. Then he leaned forward to hand it to Edward. "Here is her address. You may wish to mention my name—I don't believe she sees anyone she doesn't know—assuming she accepts any visitors at all. At her age, she may not wish to do so."

"Of course." Edward waved the sheet to dry the ink before folding it and placing it in his breast pocket.

"Is there anything else?"

"No." Edward rose and shook the lawyer's thin, dry hand before leaving.

He waited until he was outside to glance at the paper. The address was not far from where he stood, but he hesitated. If he went back to the house now, he might still have the opportunity to search for letters and evidence that might shed light on what happened so many years ago.

Even if he found no answers, he might find information that would assist him in questioning Mrs. Eggerton. It would be a more productive course than a blind quest led only by his instincts.

With that in mind, he tucked the address into his pocket and headed back to Oldwood.

Chapter Sixteen

"Oh, Charity, you *must* buy that bonnet! You look absolutely fetching in it," Lady Hildegard said, clasping her hands together and pressing them against her bosom. Her gray eyes sparkled with mischief.

Charity jerked and realized that she'd been thinking terrible thoughts about Edward, instead of paying attention to his overly enthusiastic sister. The tips of her fingers touched the bonnet perched on her head as she glanced in the mirror on the counter.

She jerked again at the sight of the red velvet monstrosity, laden with so many feathers she looked like the rear end of a diseased peacock. The shopkeeper beamed, her round face wreathed in a wide smile.

No wonder the shopkeeper was pleased. No one in her right mind would even consider purchasing such a thing.

"Well? What do you think?" Lady Hildegard's voice shook with laughter. "The red velvet perfectly complements your hair."

If by *complements* Lady Hildegard meant *curses,* then she spoke the truth. Too bad Mrs. Maplethorpe had elected to stay at the house and work on one of their new gowns with Nettle. The cheerful widow would have supported Charity's view on the gaudy bonnet.

She suspected Lady Hildegard was taking advantage of her inattentiveness to play a small, but expensive, joke.

Charity took the hat off and handed it to the shopkeeper. "Lady Hildegard is so enamored of this bonnet that it would be cruel for me to take it." She turned and smiled at Lady Hildegard. "Why don't I buy it for you? As my gift."

"Oh, yes, it would look beautiful on the lovely young lady," the shopkeeper agreed breathlessly. "Very elegant."

"I couldn't possibly take it away from you, Charity," Lady Hildegard said smoothly.

"Perhaps you could share it—it would look so fashionable, so elegant on both of you!" the shopkeeper gushed. Her plump little hand ran over the velvet brim. "Red velvet is so unusual. Rare. Anyone who wears it will be unique."

"Very unique," Lady Hildegard agreed blandly.

"And stylish," the shopkeeper said. Her small, black eyes flashed hopefully from Lady Hildegard to Charity.

Charity hastily stifled a giggle at the woman's hopeful exaggeration of the hat's qualities, and she dropped her gaze to the edge of the wooden counter, afraid she would break into uncontrollable laughter if she caught Lady Hildegard's glance. She felt a little lightheaded, and she could feel the frothy pressure of hysteria building up inside her. Her lack of sleep was finally having a potentially embarrassing effect.

She was tempted to blame Edward for that, too. This entire situation was his fault. Why couldn't he have stayed in England? Why did he have to come here to disrupt her life and dig up skeletons?

Her grandfather couldn't have killed his wife, no matter what he said. He just *couldn't.*

She frowned. What was he going to say to Mr. Tarte? How could he explain why he suddenly needed to arrange for a funeral for her grandmother, who had been missing for the last twenty-four years?

The anger and a bitter feeling of betrayal coiled like a snake inside her, poisoning her with its venom. How could she ever have thought him attractive? How could she have enjoyed the warmth of his arms and his kiss? How could she have fallen in love with him?

The thought made her wince. *Love*? No, that couldn't be. She couldn't possibly have let him slip into her heart so easily, so quickly.

She thrust the idea aside, unwilling to let it fully form and grow into a deeper pain. He was just distracting her, playing with her, until he could gather enough of his precious evidence to toss her out into the street. She couldn't let him throw aside her affections, as well.

She glanced at Lady Hildegard, going rigid. Coldness seeped through the soles of her feet and streamed up her legs, freezing her in place with a terrible sense of vulnerability. The Archers both knew about her cousin and his activities. If they wished to do so, they could expose him and implicate her.

She'd be hanged along with her cousin.

That would resolve any awkward details with the property, once and for all, she thought bitterly.

When she glanced at Lady Hildegard again, the girl was studying her with warmly sympathetic eyes. Even though her eyes were gray and Edward's were brown, they held the same warmth and intelligence, and the same sympathy.

She hated the sympathy. It was simply another form of *pity*. She might not be rich, but she could take care of herself. She'd scrub floors if she had to in order to survive. She wasn't above honest work.

If the Archers didn't get her hanged, first. They seemed to hold all the power. Helpless rage tightened her chest, making it difficult to breathe.

When she looked around again, she found both Lady Hildegard and the shopkeeper staring at her. She glanced away to the shadow of a passerby, flashing through the large front window.

"Oh, there is, um, Mr. Brown. I beg your pardon, but I must have a word with him immediately," Charity said. She stepped toward the door.

"I'm sorry," Lady Hildegard said in a smiling voice. "Perhaps another lady will enjoy this bonnet." She rushed after Charity, catching her at the street corner and slipping her hand around her elbow to link arms. "You should not have abandoned me like that, Charity. I might have been tempted to buy that bonnet as a present for you."

Charity swallowed her bitterness and forced herself to smile. "You wouldn't dare." She looked at Lady Hildegard. "You didn't, did you?"

Lady Hildegard laughed. "Of course I didn't. I have never been privileged to see such a hideous thing in my entire life. You were so distracted, though, that I had to do *something* to catch your attention."

"I beg of you, don't ever do that again." Charity tried to lighten her tone. "I might have actually bought the thing."

"What is it, Charity?" Lady Hildegard pulled on Charity's arm to slow her rapid walk. "You look so worried. Edward hasn't done something foolish to upset you, has he?" She drew in a sharp breath and cast a quick, sidelong glance at Charity. "He hasn't discovered the property title or whatever he is searching for, has he? If he forces you to leave, I shall never forgive him. *Never!*" A mulish expression spread over her face. She tilted her chin up and compressed her lips into a hard line.

"I don't believe he's found anything about that, yet." Charity sighed. Her feet dragged over the sidewalk.

"Then what is it?" Lady Hildegard was quiet for a full minute before she continued in a lower voice. "Did he, um, tell you something? About, um, well something?"

"I did hear about something." She tried to smile but her lips felt stiff.

"About ... a certain matter?" Lady Hildegard seemed strangely reluctant to be the first to say the words.

Assuming they were talking about the same thing.

"My cousin? Mr. Kevin Stonewright?" Charity asked. She didn't exactly want to announce their secret, either. She glanced around, but none of the passersby were paying them the least attention.

"Yes, Kevin." Lady Hildegard's lovely face glowed.

Oh, no. Not Kevin.

Charity suddenly felt sorry for her. Her cousin was certainly charming, but he was a rogue if ever there was one, and Lady Hildegard was too young, too inexperienced to know how to protect her heart. She wouldn't understand that his flirtations meant nothing except an inability to control himself around a pretty woman.

169

"He has been busy of late, hasn't he?" Charity asked gently, trying to distract Lady Hildegard's attention away from the man who would no doubt hurt her as much as Edward was likely to hurt Charity.

"Yes. I'm so proud of him helping Toby and Nell. And little Henry. He is such a dear baby—you should see him!"

"A baby?" Charity asked. The danger of their situation took on an even more frightening aspect. How could they escape with a baby? One small cry...

That wailing ... had it really been Nodcock?

She went cold at the memory of how close they'd been to Officer Carmichael uncovering the truth. Thank goodness for Edward's idiot cat. A rush of affection filled her, and she found herself smiling.

Saved by a cat. Twice.

Perhaps she ought to get a few more of them to protect the house. The animals might serve to keep Officer Carmichael at bay. They could certainly reduce the number of rodents running around, chewing holes into her slippers.

"Yes. He is so dear." She sounded wistful. "I love him already."

"You are very kindhearted." Charity couldn't think of anything else to say.

Thankfully, Oldwood loomed ahead of them, and Lady Hildegard seemed to recall the inadvisability of discussing the runaways in public. She blithely changed the subject to the variable weather.

That morning, the sun had been shining brightly through a scattering of soft, fluffy clouds like balls of cotton floating in the sky. But a thick black line of thunderheads was moving in from the southeast, pushing the good weather inland and threatening a deluge. The wind had whipped up as well and blew through the streets, kicking up small swirls of dust and litter. The golden sunlight had turned to a strange, yellowish green that promised a gale.

A hint of pressure behind Charity's eyes warned that the impending storm was carrying a headache along with rain.

Good weather to spend searching for something to exonerate her grandfather. And maybe prove her family had never sold the property.

She'd been a fool to believe Edward's promise that he would continue his investigation. Why would he bother when his version of the story would support his family's claim that the duchess owned Oldwood?

It was all so neat and sensible—just like Edward himself.

For the first time in her life, she loathed anything that was neat and sensible.

As they removed their bonnets in the hallway and hung them, along with their shawls, on a line of wooden pegs to the left of the door, Charity glanced at Lady Hildegard. How could she possibly keep her out of her own bedchamber so that Charity could search it?

Lady Hildegard laughed as she brushed off her muslin skirt. "It sounds ridiculous after that long walk, but I still feel restless." She glanced up at Charity as she straightened. "I noticed a kitchen garden behind the house."

"That patch of weeds next to the kitchen door?" Charity grinned. "You are being charitable giving it the grand name of kitchen garden."

Lady Hildegard laughed again and touched her hair, pushing some of the soft brown curls off her brow. "Well, I recognized rosemary at the very least."

"And lemon verbena that seems determined to take over the entire plot."

"Would you mind terribly if I worked in the garden for a while?" Her hands passed over the sides of her dress as she stared at Charity with earnest eyes. "I have an old traveling gown, gloves, and a straw hat."

"But it is about to rain," Charity objected, even though her heart beat faster. Lady Hildegard was handing her the perfect opportunity to search her room.

She couldn't imagine what might be in there, but the more she thought about it, the more she believed that Miss Elizabeth Haywood might very well have selected that bedroom. It was the largest one, and it had a separate dressing room and windows on two sides.

"Rain?" Lady Hildegard wrinkled her nose. "It is not raining yet, and I prefer it overcast as it will be less warm. Please say I may go back outside," she pleaded.

Charity laughed. "I can hardly prevent you if you are so determined to do so."

"And you don't think Mrs. Granger will be angry, do you?"

"I don't believe Mrs. Granger will care one way or the other," Charity answered dryly. She touched Lady Hildegard's arm impulsively and smiled. "There is no harm in pulling a few weeds, and no one shall bother you. I promise."

Her face lit up with pleasure before she raced up the stairs to change her dress. Charity watched her go, realizing that Lady Hildegard was much more likely to visit the runaways than to try to bring order to the kitchen garden. Lifting her head to listen, she heard the creak of Lady Hildegard's door, but she realized with a start that she didn't hear Edward's firm tread moving around the house.

Where was he?

Perhaps he'd found something and gone to meet Mr. Tarte. Perhaps searching the house was useless, now.

No. She couldn't be discouraged before she even tried to do something to help herself. There might still be a clue he missed, something they all had missed.

She waited in the front sitting room for twenty minutes before she heard Lady Hildegard's light, rapid footsteps descend the staircase and head toward the kitchen. She waited five more minutes before she went up to Lady Hildegard's room and cautiously opened the door.

There was no sign of Nettle or Mrs. Maplethorpe. Most likely, they were still up in the large room they used for sewing on the second floor. The two women had formed an unlikely friendship and seemed perfectly content to sew and gossip for hours, leaving Charity and Lady Hildegard to do as they pleased.

Mrs. Maplethorpe might not be the sort of chaperone Edward had hoped she would be when he hired her, but her placid inattentiveness suited Charity perfectly.

The door to Lady Hildegard's room creaked as Charity opened it further. She stopped, hardly daring to breathe, but there were no new sounds, no running footsteps or accusing cries. A stifling hush had settled over the house that made it hard to move or even breathe for fear of breaking the spell.

When she forced herself to enter, she winced at the sound of the floorboards creaking under her weight. This room might be the largest bedchamber in the house, but it also had the noisiest floor. The oak planks seemed to clatter under even the lightest footstep, as if every nail had long since rusted into dust.

She stood next to the bed and looked around. When she'd first returned to Oldwood, she'd almost taken this room as her bedchamber. She didn't know why she hadn't, except that the silken gowns still folded in the wardrobe and the lingering scent of violets made her feel like an intruder. Even after she'd gotten rid of everything, that subtle perfume made her head ache when she came in here.

Just the memory of the sweet scent drove a spike of pain into her temple. She rubbed her forehead uneasily. She hadn't known Miss Elizabeth Haywood, but she felt her presence here, laughing mockingly at her. Elizabeth alone knew the truth about ownership of Oldwood, and she remained silent except for that ghostly echo of contempt.

Silly nonsense. The woman had been dead for years, and her belongings were gone.

So where should she search? She'd cleaned out the wardrobe and chest of drawers, but perhaps there was a secret drawer or panel somewhere. She gently removed Lady Hildegard's elegant gowns from the wardrobe and felt along the back and sides before she removed the drawers. *Nothing!* The chest of drawers was equally bare of hidden panels or secret caches.

After replacing the dresses and undergarments, she slid under the bed to search between the knotted ropes and mattress. Her efforts only yielded a new hairstyle, complete with fluffy balls of gray dangling from her curls. She brushed them off impatiently and started a slow walk around the room, pushing and tapping at the wainscoting and around the fireplace. She even risked a face full of soot by searching as far up the chimney as she could reach with the poker.

Frustrated, she returned to the center of the room, grimacing with annoyance at the creaking floor. If Elizabeth Haywood had left anything in this room other than her wardrobe and perfume, it was well hidden. She pressed the toes of her right foot against one of the bounciest floorboards between the bed and the window and let it push her up and down a few times. There was something satisfying in hearing it complain. The protesting creaks sounded just like she felt.

A tingle slipped up her spine as she bounced two more times. She held her breath for a moment.

The floorboard she was playing with was a short length, only three feet long, if that. The wood was slightly lighter than the rest, proclaiming it to be a more recent patch.

If it was newer than the rest, why was it so loose? It ought to have the freshest nails and be the firmest board in the bedchamber.

She grabbed the poker, but the pointed tip was too thick to slip into the crack between the boards, so she rifled through the small desk near the window.

A silver letter opener! That would do.

Slipping the thin edge between the planks, she was amazed at the ease with which she could lift the end of the new piece of wood. Dust and dirt cascaded down into the shadowy space beneath it as she yanked the board up and out. Holding her breath, she dusted off her hands and studied the complex geometry of joists and supports.

*Nothing! S*he sat back on her heels and let out a long sigh.

She'd been so sure. Her eyes burned with tears of frustration, and she wiped her cheek with a grimy hand.

Grasping the edge of the plank, she was about to replace it when she noticed a dusty, wood-colored corner of something wedged next to one of the joists. A scrap of wood left behind when the floor was patched? She leaned forward to touch it and pulled her hand back with a jerk when it gave slightly. Not wood. Something wrapped in tan oilcloth.

Her hands shook as she bent forward and gripped the bundle. It was wedged tightly between the joist and another piece of supporting wood. Her damp fingers slipped twice over the gritty dust of years before she managed to yank it free.

Sitting back on her heels, she could hardly breathe as she turned the package over in her hands. Elation surged like a tidal wave, making her shake with the force of excitement.

The package was larger than she'd initially thought, almost eight inches by six, and the oilcloth, tied with an old piece of twine, was cracking and filthy. A mouse had chewed through part of the twine, and as she turned it over with shaking hands, the string fell off. But the oilcloth had been folded so tightly for so long that it stayed in place, even without the string binding it.

Edward will want to see this. Her heart fluttered and then hardened. *So what? It's mine—I may not even show it to him.* Some of her excitement faded.

What if the book contained nothing but the petty gossip of the woman who'd lived here at the turn of the century?

Well, she wouldn't know until she opened it. In the meantime, she needed to straighten Lady Hildegard's room and wash some of the dirt and sweat off her face and hands.

A half hour later, she pulled a rocking chair over to the window in her own bedchamber and sat down with the package. She'd wiped off the dust, but the oilcloth still felt gritty to the touch. As she unwrapped the bundle, the outer cloth crumbled in patches, but it finally revealed a leather-bound book. With shaking fingers, she opened it.

Miss Elizabeth James

1798

Who the devil was Elizabeth *James*? And the year—it was too early. Her breathing faltered. Some guest had hidden it under the floor to keep it away from prying maids and forgot it when she'd left.

For whatever reason this little journal had been hidden in the house, it seemed unlikely to help her.

Her family hadn't left Oldwood until 1799. Her grandmother had still been alive, as far as Charity knew. And it wasn't even Elizabeth Haywood's journal. A diary written by some unknown woman in 1798 could contain nothing of relevance except details of a life that no longer mattered.

She almost threw the book across the room, but she took a deep breath instead. It might not provide information about ownership of Oldwood, but there remained the possibility that Miss James knew Charity's grandmother. She might have written something to hint at what had eventually happened to her.

Charity gently turned the book over and opened the back cover. Bold writing filled the pages almost to the end.

Only three blank sheets remained. Moving from back to front, she examined the flowing black cursive writing, searching for dates.

1801!

She read a few lines. The writer mentioned a few names unknown to Charity and then she saw it: *Charlotte.* She read more carefully. Elizabeth James referred carelessly to *that girl, Charlotte,* as if she were a pet cat or dog she didn't entirely like.

Her confusion deepened. Then her head lifted as she heard Edward's firm tread in the hallway and the creak of his door. The light was already fading into the pale gray of dusk.

Whoever the diarist was and whatever she had to say, she'd have to wait to say it to Charity until later.

Chapter Seventeen

Edward glanced at the clock as he entered his room, dusty and not completely satisfied with his search. True, he'd found several bundles of letters from Henry and Lenore Stonewright, but when he glanced over them, they didn't promise much. Most were dated from the middle of the last century, long before the critical years of 1798 through 1799.

"It is a bit early, sir, but will you be changing for dinner?" Atwood asked, holding a towel for him as he washed his face.

The soap stung his scraped knuckles and the scratches he'd gotten moving furniture and prying under loose boards in the attic. The refreshingly cool water felt bracing, though, and he took the jug from Atwood and sluiced it over his head, washing away the remains of cobwebs.

"Might as well." Edward wiped his face and hands before running the towel over his hair. "No point in changing again in less than an hour."

"Very good, sir." Atwood, anticipating Edward's decision, had already laid out his royal blue breeches, silver and blue waistcoat, and black jacket.

He helped Edward into the clothing before picking up the jacket he had been wearing between his thumb and forefinger. His eyes narrowed and his thin nose rose in the air with distaste, but after one reproving glance at Edward, he simply pressed his lips together and remained silent.

"Cleaning that should give you something to do, Atwood, besides eating Mrs. Granger's bread," Edward remarked, handing him his dusty-kneed trousers, as well. One leg had a tear just above the hem, and his valet stared at it with all the fascination of a mouse facing a cobra.

"Yes, sir," Atwood replied lugubriously. After a moment's hesitation, he draped the dirty clothing over his left forearm, holding the appendage well away from his own immaculate clothing to keep the dust from rubbing off onto him. "Will there be anything else?"

"No."

"Very good, sir," Atwood said with a shallow bow. He drifted over to the door and held it open for Edward.

On his way out, Edward picked up the bundles of letters again. They would give him something more interesting to read than the collections of sermons cluttering the shelves in the library. Apparently, Charity had sold any book that was even vaguely readable, leaving behind volumes which might be enticing to look at on the shelf, but were far less enticing to read.

Charity's door opened as he stepped into the hallway, and he waited as she closed her door gently behind her.

"Miss Stonewright," he greeted her, thrusting the bundles of letters into his pocket.

"Charity, please."

He smiled. "Charity, it is. You look very charming this evening." He fell in step beside her as she headed toward the staircase. "Is that a new gown?"

Her step faltered as she glanced down at her dress. Her gloved hands plucked the sides of her skirts and held the pale green silk out for a second as if to get a better view of her gown.

"Oh," she said. "Yes. Mrs. Maplethorpe finished it this afternoon and left it in my room." She smiled. "Just like the good fairy. She is an excellent needlewoman, is she not?"

"Excellent," Edward agreed as they descended. The slender gown was indeed flattering in its clean, simple lines. Charity looked very elegant in the shimmering, pale silk, and her thick hair seemed to gleam as softly as the fabric. "And I'm glad to see you overruled my sister's predilection for lace, ribbon knots, and ruffles. Her sense of fashion is nothing if not execrable."

Charity laughed. "Lady Hildegard's tastes are very, um, *exuberant*. But you can't fault her sense of color. I wasn't in favor of green, however she insisted, and I'm glad she did."

"You do look lovely, so I suppose I will have to agree."

She flushed and stared at the floor before he offered his elbow to escort her to the sitting room. "Too kind," she murmured, her lashes fluttering as she refused to meet his gaze. "You should let her know that you approve, though. She'd be delighted to hear it."

"It would only make her more conceited than she already is," he replied, his voice heavy with sarcasm.

"And you are opinionated." When she smiled up at him, a teasing gleam in her eyes, he felt an answering tug in his heart. She took a seat gracefully in front of the fireplace, arranging her silken skirts over her lap.

"So I am," he agreed blithely. He studied the floor for a minute, aware of her gaze on him as he sat in the chair opposite her. "Before my sister comes down, I wanted to tell you that I searched the house as thoroughly as I could in a few hours. I didn't find much—only a few letters."

Her head jerked up, and her gaze met his. For a second, he thought she was going to say something. Her mouth opened and then she shut it firmly, her lips forming a straight line.

She shrugged and dropped her gaze to stare at her clasped hands. "So you still believe my grandfather murdered his wife?" she asked in a low voice, refusing to meet his glance.

It was painfully clear that her trust in him had faltered, and that she fully expected him to break his word to her.

"I said I will reserve judgment until I find evidence one way or the other," he replied stiffly.

Her eyes hardened. "You are very kind. I'm sure the duchess will be very pleased with you when you return to London."

"I intend to ensure that she is satisfied that I performed my duty as promised. A man's worth is proportional to his sense of honor—"

"How reassuring," Charity interrupted. "I'm sure you will behave with perfect correctness then when you take my home away from me and accuse my family of harboring murderers. Among other things," she added bitterly.

"Perhaps we should discuss some other topic," he suggested gently. There was no point in arguing over something that had yet to happen and may never happen at all. "I neglected to tell you that I visited Mr. Tarte. He is arranging for your grandmother's burial in St. Michael's Churchyard at eleven tomorrow morning. I hope that you approve."

She nodded and relaxed her stiff shoulders, sighing. She didn't need to explain; he knew only too well what she must be thinking. There was the unspoken question lurking: *what had her grandmother done to be murdered?* It was the question every family of a murder victim eventually asked itself.

In her heart, Charity must have known that her grandmother was probably innocent of any wrongdoing. She was an innocent victim—but the ugly question always seemed to hover in the background, like the odor of smoke lingering long after a fire has died away.

"Thank you," she said softly. "I—well—I hope you and your sister will attend?"

"Of course." He touched her clasped hands, wanting to protect her and pull her into his arms and feel her soft hair brush his chin.

She looked so sad, so forlorn. She'd never known her grandmother, and suddenly, she was faced with the knowledge of her murder. Lenore had died and been hidden away in the dark while foul rumors had spread about her running away. The impact on the family had been terrible, and even now, Charity was facing the consequences.

Edward cleared his throat and gazed at the doorway of the sitting room. "After the funeral, I intend to speak to Mrs. Eggerton. I understand she knew your grandmother and grandfather. She may be able to shed light on what happened."

"I'll go with you." She gripped his arm. "I have a right to know."

"It may not be pleasant—"

181

"I *have* to go." Her fingers tightened on his sleeve. "Please!"

"Very well." A crooked smile twisted his mouth. He couldn't deny her that favor, and she did have the right to know, even if he wanted to shelter her from that knowledge. "She may feel more comfortable talking to you. I just hope it is not too painful."

"It won't be—and thank you," she said, smiling as she released his arm.

At that moment, Hildie and Mrs. Maplethorpe entered the sitting room together.

He studied his sister. A faint frown creased his brow. While no one could claim that his sister didn't look elegant, she didn't appear to be dressed in one of her fine evening gowns. The heavy brown fabric did have the bronze and gold gleams of silk, but she wore no jewelry except a gold chain around her neck. If there was a locket attached to the chain, the pendant was tucked under the modest edge of her bodice. There was only one row of small ruffles around her neckline, with wider ruffles running down the front of the dress and around the hem.

Brown leather shoes peeped out from beneath her dress.

His frown deepened.

She looked more prepared for a stroll in the dark than for supper.

Blast that Stonewright. She obviously intended to sneak out after eating and meet him somewhere.

Well tonight, he'd leave the dining room along with the ladies and have his coffee in the sitting room. That should put an effective end to any plans she harbored.

Mrs. Maplethorpe and Hildie had barely seated themselves and exchanged greetings with them before Janet entered with the news that supper was ready.

Beaming, Mrs. Maplethorpe stood with alacrity. Her round, rosy cheeks showed that she was regaining some of the weight she'd previously carried, and her hazel eyes gleamed with anticipation.

She rubbed her right hand over her left as she glanced around the room. "I must say Mrs. Granger is a treasure. I don't believe I've ever had so many excellent meals in my life." She patted Charity on the shoulder and made an encouraging gesture toward the door.

"Yes, and she is so thin! I would never have anticipated that she could cook. Her apple tarts are superb," Hildie said. Her unfocused gaze and the way she licked her lower lip suggested she was enjoying the memory of one of Granger's desserts very much.

Edward chuckled and winked at Charity.

She flushed and ignored the arm he held out to her. She hurried awkwardly through the door, following the other two women to the dining room.

Sighing, Edward trailed behind them.

Charity had every reason to be worried, but she might live up to her name a trifle more and actually be *charitable,* instead of giving him the cold shoulder.

As Janet and Kitty carried in groaning trays of food, Edward commented, "Mrs. Granger has outdone herself."

"Oh, I adore baked shad!" A wide grin dimpled Mrs. Maplethorpe's plump cheeks. Her hands fluttered to the table and then back to her lap as she watched Kitty serve the broth, while Janet held the platter of fish at Edward's elbow.

As he served himself, he had to bite the corners of his mouth to keep from laughing at Mrs. Maplethorpe's eager anticipation of the shad.

The second course consisted of spiced rounds of tenderloin with Jezebel sauce and small biscuits, a dish of beans Charity identified as hoppin' John, and a vegetable soufflé. Mrs. Maplethorpe seemed to be the only one inclined to talk, but she was mainly interested in which gowns the two young ladies would like made up next.

They'd just finished the delicious, tiny custard tarts for dessert when Janet rushed into the room.

"Mr. Archer, sir!" Janet called, pressing a hand against her chest. She gazed wildly around the room.

In the distance, Edward could hear the tramp of many feet and men's voices.

He stood, thrusting his chair away behind him. "What is it?"

"It's Officer Carmichael—he done returned and has him a bunch of papers—he says he can tear this house apart if he wants to!" Janet exclaimed in a panicked voice.

Edward caught Hildie's glance.

She gave one small, tight nod.

"Miss Stonewright and I shall speak to them," Mrs. Maplethorpe said. She rose majestically like a ship donning full sail.

Standing, Charity caught his gaze. "Go on. Mrs. Maplethorpe and I shall speak to him."

"Delay them. If you can," he said in a low voice.

Let Mrs. Maplethorpe make of that cryptic remark what she would. He didn't have time to question her about her willingness to throw herself at the authorities instead of hiding behind the only male in the household: him.

Hildie had already gone through the dining room door into the main hallway. He dashed after her, barely in time to see her disappear through an obscure door under the main staircase. His hand wavered over one of the lamps in the hallway, but he went on without picking it up.

No sense lighting the way for Carmichael to follow. Loud voices and Mrs. Granger's sharp, high tones echoed down the servants' corridor from the kitchen. Edward dived through the narrow door and let it slam shut behind him.

Complete darkness. He placed a hand against the wall and moved forward three steps. "Hildie?" he whispered.

A cold hand gripped his. "Here." Her words were barely audible. "Watch out—you are at the top of a narrow staircase. We must go down."

"Where does this lead?" Trusting his sister, he placed a hand on her shoulder and let her guide him down into the blackness. As his eyes adjusted, he could just make out a pale golden glow in the distance.

"The cellar," she whispered back. "We must be quiet—this runs underneath the servants' hallway to the cellar."

"Where in the cellar?"

A small, ghostly laugh answered him. Then she caught his wrist and pulled him forward. "Watch your head—we have to hurry now or they'll see us."

The narrow passageway opened through a small door under another set of stairs—the cellar stairs. Across the room, someone had taken an axe to the shelves hiding the corridor and room where he'd discovered the remains of Charity's grandmother. They could hear the rough voices of men beyond the gaping hole in the wall. Light from a lamp flared wildly, gilding the shattered shelving golden against deep black shadows.

Heavy footsteps clattered above their heads.

Was Charity all right? His gut tightened.

She had Mrs. Maplethorpe with her, but he didn't know how many men were in the house or what their mood was. It would be too easy for them to degenerate into a mob and do unspeakable things in the name of justice. He'd seen houses burned, people beaten or murdered over small things, simple misunderstandings. All manner of crimes were committed and then regretted later, but those regrets didn't help those whose lives had been shattered in the process.

Unfortunately, in this case, Carmichael's suspicions were well-founded. Nonetheless, he had to be stopped.

Edward caught Hildie's icy hand. "Where?" he whispered into her ear.

She was staring at the tunnel, her body tense. The light brightened for a moment, highlighting the dirt walls, and then faded. The rough voices grew more muffled as they moved deeper into the tunnel.

She didn't answer. Instead, she jerked her hand free and sprinted across the cellar to the corner at the far end of the broken shelves. He followed her, moving quietly through the darkness. They had to move now or risk being seen, and he realized that this was the only possible direction to go.

With a practiced movement, she pulled another section of the shelves away from the wall and slipped into the darkness beyond.

He followed and yanked the shelves back into place behind him, plunging them into musty darkness.

The passageway was less than three feet wide and only two yards in length. Hildie barely had room to open a plain wooden door and slip into the room beyond. A single candle lit the space, but its flame seemed as bright as day after the blackness of the narrow entryway.

He glanced around. *Of course!*

He should have been suspicious of the length of the first corridor he'd found and that odd right angle turn. There was space unaccounted for, nestled within that right angle, against the walls of the other earthen hallway.

This small room was cleverly hidden in that area, framed by the corridor and chamber beyond it. Unlike other parts of the cellar, old bricks lined three of the walls. The faint light barely reached the back wall, but the black surface appeared to be composed of long planks of time-darkened wood.

The candlelight flickered. The waxy stub of a candle was held in the hand of a man who was staring at him, his body hunched with tension. He faced Edward, took a deep breath, and steadied the candlestick as fear slipped around him and permeated the room.

As Edward studied him, his black eyes held his gaze, and a sense of inner strength flowed from him. This was a man who'd been tested by the forge of life and survived with his pride and backbone intact. His arms and neck were so thickly muscled that it gave him a hulking, bull-like appearance, but there was a sharp intelligence in his eyes and gentleness in his mouth and softly rounded chin. The bunched muscles in his shoulders and arms showed his steely determination, however, to pursue his chosen course and wrest his freedom, and that of his wife and child, by force if necessary.

Behind him, a woman wrapped in a shawl stood in the gloom, cradling a swaddled baby in her arms, her expression grim.

The man stepped in front of her when Edward's gaze dwelled on her beautiful, shadowed face and huge dark eyes.

"You have nothing to fear from me," Edward said, holding out his hand.

"This is my brother." Hildie edged around the man and went to the woman, putting an arm around her. "Edward, this is Toby and Nell." Her voice softened and she gently touched the baby. "And little Henry."

Relaxing, Toby slowly moved forward and shook his hand with dry, calloused fingers, all the time studying his face as if he could read their fate in his eyes.

Behind Hildie, the shadows in the far corner shifted. Edward stiffened and Toby turned, his hands fisted again.

Kevin Stonewright stepped into view. Then, another movement from the darkness on Nell's right caught his attention.

Nettle, his sister's personal maid stirred. She stared at him boldly with an upward tilt of her pointed chin.

"Nettle? What are you doing here?" he asked. Was the entire household involved in hiding the two runaways and their baby?

"I'm going, too," Nettle whispered with a quick glance over her shoulder. "It's my chance, and I'm taking it. There's nothing for me back home. I have a chance of a new life here—a future."

He nodded. If Nettle wanted to throw her lot in with Nell and Toby, all he could do was to wish her well. She had no family in England, no one left behind, so perhaps she'd find a better life here.

"Sounds like they're tearing the place apart," Stonewright said, his head tilted up, listening. "I thought they'd been following me. Couldn't shake them earlier.

Apparently, Carmichael isn't nearly the fool he appears to be." He flung an arm around Hildie's shoulder. "Hate to cut short the weather forecasts and introductions you British enjoy so much, but we've got to leave." His glance drifted past Edward's shoulder.

There was the sound of metal biting into wood. A thin trickle of dirt sparkled as it sifted through the light of Toby's candle. The authorities were getting closer.

Edward's shoulders tightened as he held out a hand to his sister. "We need to return upstairs with the others if we're going to avoid suspicion. We can keep Carmichael off the scent while the others leave."

Drawing closer to Stonewright, Hildie shook her head. "I'm sorry—I'm going, too."

"Going? Have you lost every shred of sense you ever had?" Edward asked sharply.

At the sound of his voice, the baby wailed.

Nell clutched him to her breast, nudging him to suckle to fill his mouth with something other than cries, but his small sniffles sounded like a scream in the heavy silence.

They all remained where they were, glancing at each other. Edward's jaw clenched as he listened for sounds indicating Carmichael had heard the infant. In the distance, he could make out a low murmur and then the muffled clatter of wood breaking.

When he caught his sister's gaze, she fumbled at her neckline and drew the golden chain that he'd noticed earlier into view. She unfastened the clasp and slid the chain out from the locket. Which she slipped over the ring finger on her left hand.

Not a locket, a *ring*.

Keeping his voice low, Edward's gaze fastened on Stonewright before sliding back to his sister. "Hildie—you can *not* go." When he studied her determined face, his stomach sank into his shoes. The maturity and stubbornness in her firm gaze and tight mouth said all too clearly that he no longer had any power—or right—to make decisions for her.

188

A sense of urgent desperation made him step forward. He couldn't let her do this. She was endangering her life and happiness, even if she didn't realize it.

"I'm sorry—I was going to tell you after dinner." She glanced up at Stonewright—her husband. "We intended to leave tonight. It's all planned."

"Planned?" he ground out. His right hand reached out to her briefly, before he deliberately dropped it to his side.

He knew that stubborn tilt of her chin so well.

But—how could he let her go? What would become of her? She was too young, too foolish to realize what she was doing—or what lay ahead of her. His desperation increased, raging on the fuel of frustration, turning his hands into tight fists.

She'd be caught and hung.

Even if she managed to elude the authorities, she had no idea what her life would be like here, without any of the comforts she'd known in England.

The little fool nodded as if she could read his thoughts.

"Sir," Toby stepped closer to him. "We done thought it out. My brother, Dixon, well, he's got him a place up in Erie. We's going there, and I've got me a job there, shipbuilding." He rubbed his callused hands against the hem of his dark jacket. "I'm a carpenter by trade—a good one. And Dixon, he done worked with that Daniel Dobbins of Erie." He dug into a pocket and held out a small bag, forcing it into Edward's hand. "We wanted our freedom— we was going to buy it until they changed the law. You find and give that there purse to Mr. Farnham. It's our price, last time he tried to sell us, and then some." He glanced back at his wife and baby, his face growing tender with pride.

There was no time to argue. Thuds on the walls made the dirt trickle faster, raising thick plumes. Hildie coughed into her fist and glanced at Stonewright. One way or the other, the authorities would find this small room soon.

Edward nodded, studying Toby as he put the bag in his pocket. "You can rely on me." He had to stop himself from asking the man to watch out for Hildie—Toby had the manner and character of the kind of man he'd hope his sister would marry one day.

A sober and serious man, so unlike the smiling insouciance of Stonewright.

A glance at Nell and the baby made Edward pull the bag out of his pocket again, though, as well as his own wallet. "I will give whatever sum necessary to this Farnham, but you must have some funds. The trip will be dangerous. And costly." The muscles in his jaw tightened. "You may need money for bribes, as well." He tensed and glanced over his shoulder, listening to the sounds of boots clattering up the staircase leading to the kitchen.

Were they sending for more men?

Stonewright laughed with a low, eerie snuffling sound. "Keep your money, Archer."

Toby backed away, clearly determined not to take anything from Edward, including his own money. He put an arm around his wife and drew her further into the shadows. Nettle followed, leaving just Hildie and Stonewright to face him.

"Kevin sold his ship, Edward. We have money," Hildie said in a soft, halting voice.

"For God's sake, Hildie, think about what you are doing!" Edward urged her, wanting to reach out and drag her back upstairs. He brushed some of the dirt off his jacket and hair and glanced over his shoulder. There was no time to argue. They had to get out of there. "You're used to servants—you aren't prepared for this country. It may sound romantic, but I assure you it will not be. Come with me—now!"

"No," Hildie said. "I'm not a child any longer. I know it will be hard."

"This country—" he broke off, choking on his words. He cocked his head to listen for the sound of more boots coming down the stairs. "You can *not* stay here. Come back to England with me. *Please*. Bring Stonewright, if you must, but return with me." He held out his right hand, his voice felt rough, hoarse with emotion. He couldn't lose her, not here—not like this. She was his little sister—little Hildie.

An image slashed through his mind. Hildie as a child, her smiling face and bubbling laughter as she dashed up the stairs ahead of him, turned around on the landing, and giggled at him before racing away.

Happily irresponsible—when had she turned into this courageous woman, ready to face the hazards of an unknown land?

"There are terrible things, that's true," Hildie said, her eyes shining in the flickering candlelight. "But there are good things, too. Freedom and possibility—a chance to achieve something wonderful. Oh, please understand and forgive me! I want to build a life here, with Kevin. I love him. You *must* understand!"

Those last simple words were like a molten sword tearing through his gut. He couldn't convince her, couldn't protect her any longer.

He had to try, though, one last time. "If you get into trouble, it will be months before I can return for you. You *must* reconsider."

Boots thudded down the cellar stairs, coming closer. They heard the sounds of men's voices, shouting, but the words were unclear.

"No." Her whispered reply was firm. Implacable.

"We've delayed too long," Stonewright said lightly, interrupting them. He stepped between them and eyed Edward lazily, but there was no mistaking the strength in the set of his shoulders and determination in his square chin.

Perhaps his sister hadn't made such a poor choice after all.

Although Edward's hands fisted again at his sides, wanting to break Stonewright's firm jaw and drag his sister away, he knew that his little sister had made her decision. She loved Stonewright. He could not stand in her way, no matter how desperately worried he was.

"If anything happens to her, I swear I'll hunt you down," he ground out in a low voice, thick with menace. "I'll hold you personally responsible."

Stonewright's gaze grew hard, but he grinned lopsidedly. "A bit rough, coming from my dear brother." He shrugged. "But if anything happens to Hildie, you won't have to search too hard to find me. Just look for the gravestone with my name on it."

So he intended to die for her, if necessary. Strong words, but perhaps, in this case, true.

Puffs of dirt writhed through the air. They exchanged glances, aware that they could not keep delaying. The search party was testing the wall again, and they'd gotten help. The authorities would break through at any minute and arrest all of them.

"Come," Stonewright swung Hildie around to face the far, dark corner where Nettle, Toby, and his wife and baby, stood in a tight group. "Wish us luck, Archer."

The candle's flame flickered wildly. Edward could just make out the dim outline of another narrow door before all of them ducked through it and disappeared into the night.

He stiffened, listening. A minute later, there was a yell and the sounds of feet trampling through the corridor on the other side of the wall. He started to follow and then forced himself to halt. He was more likely to lead the authorities to the fleeing group than help them if he walked out from behind the shelves.

"Good luck, Hildie. I love you," he whispered to the empty room. He ran his hand through his dusty hair, stifling the rush of hot emotion.

Silence descended once more. He picked up the candle Toby had left behind and moved to the door behind the shelving.

He had to do whatever he could to obfuscate their trail. His sister's life, and the lives of the others, depended upon it.

Chapter Eighteen

"Edward! Where have you been?" Charity leapt to her feet as Edward entered the sitting room. "Where is Lady Hildegard?"

He had dust all over his jacket, and his eyes blazed with some strong emotion that made her catch her breath.

What had happened? Something terrible—she rushed over to him and brushed the dirt off his broad shoulders and sleeves. Wherever he'd been, whatever had happened, there was no need for Officer Carmichael to see such evidence and grow even more suspicious. She looked into the hallway behind him, listening to the shrill sounds of Mrs. Maplethorpe's voice.

"She's gone," he said in a low voice.

"Gone? What do you mean, *gone*? Gone where?" She pressed a hand to her chest, feeling panic fluttering inside her.

"Gone." He ran a hand through his hair. The dark curls stood up as thickly as storm waves at sea. "She's married that bloody cousin of yours."

"Kevin?" A laugh almost escaped from her before she realized how angry he was. His jaw tightened at a pugnacious angle as she gazed at him, giving him a dangerous appearance, reinforced by the dark stubble shadowing his face. "I can't imagine—are you sure?"

"Of course I'm sure. Apparently, you were unaware of it, as well."

Charity placed a reassuring hand on his wrist, but he frowned and shook her off. She stepped in front of him, however, when he turned to stare at the darkness beyond her, his mouth a thin line.

"Cousin Kevin is a good man," she said, trying to ease the pain he was clearly feeling. She couldn't quite believe what he'd said, although she knew her cousin was impulsive. When had it happened? *How?* She focused on Edward. "He has a good heart."

"That I can well believe. The question is whether he can be relied upon when the adventure begins to pall."

"Yes, he can. I don't know him that well, but Mr. Tarte has often remarked to me that my cousin is a man one can rely on when difficulties arise." She gave him a tremulous smile. "If one can only forgive him for his flippancy." She gripped his arm, refusing to let him go, well aware of the irony of their situation.

Before dinner, she'd been furious with him, frantic with the fear that he was growing weary of untangling the mess surrounding Oldwood and that he would simply decide the Stonewrights had sold the property to the Haywoods to be done with it.

Where would she go? What would happen to her?

Now, he was the angry one, furious with the Stonewrights because her ridiculous cousin had run off with his sister.

Why did things get more complicated instead of less?

Edward took a deep breath, his square jaw tightening again before he finally glanced at her.

He smiled, though it looked a bit grim. "Well, there is nothing we can do to change matters now. Where is Officer Carmichael?" He looked around. "And Mrs. Maplethorpe?"

She released his arm and twisted her hands together. "She's in the hallway with Officer Carmichael." She gripped his forearm. "He won't listen to reason. He's arrested Kitty and Janet!"

Without a word he shook her off and stalked back into the hallway, glancing right and then left, toward the front door. "Carmichael!" he called.

Following him out, Charity kept to the shadows obscuring the walls, moving like a dark mist behind him. She castigated herself for behaving in such a cowardly fashion. But she'd tried to argue with Officer Carmichael before and had only stopped when he threatened to arrest her, as well, and let the judge decide the matter.

Mrs. Maplethorpe and Officer Carmichael both turned toward them with twin expressions of frustrated rage. Their scowls, flushed cheeks, and angry eyes made Charity cross her arms at her waist, her hands gripping her elbows. The officer looked as if just one more word would throw them all into a maelstrom of violence.

Before Edward could say anything, Mrs. Maplethorpe grabbed the officer's jacket. "I tell you, those girls are free women. This is an outrage! You have no right to arrest them, or anyone else in this house!"

"I've got the right to arrest anyone who interferes with the law," Officer Carmichael sneered. He shook her off roughly. "Get out of my way, you old harridan, or I'll arrest you, too!"

"You will speak to Mrs. Maplethorpe with respect," Edward said in a harsh voice, walking forward. He came to a stop in front of Officer Carmichael, paused, and then took one more deliberate step forward.

Trotting out of the shadows of the main staircase, Nodcock paused ten feet away from the men. His whiskers twitched before he eased over to Edward and began weaving around his master's ankles.

"Damn cat!" Carmichael glared down at the animal and then at Edward, his face twisted with loathing. He moved back a foot, glancing around uneasily. He was trapped in the corner next to the front door with very little room to spare. When his shoulder hit the wall, the officer took a deep breath, expanding his chest and staring at Edward in challenge.

A twisted, cynical smile crossed Edward's face.

That small retreat was enough to show Carmichael wasn't as sure of himself as he appeared.

"Now," Edward said. He clasped his hands behind his back, giving the impression of a thoughtful man, quite at ease. "What have you done with our servants?"

"Sent them back where they belong," the officer spat. His hands opened and shut repeatedly at his sides, and he thrust his head forward, spittle collecting at the corners of his rubbery lips.

"As Mrs. Maplethorpe indicated, they are free women. They work for us and belong *here*. I expect an immediate release and an apology," Edward said.

Charity held her breath, watching the officer.

Anger seethed over his face, and his lips worked silently as he clenched his hands, his knuckles whitening. The muscles in his shoulders tightened. Her gaze was drawn to the pistol and truncheon dangling from his broad, brown belt.

Oh, please! No! Edward had pushed him too far. He was going to kill him and then the rest of them.

She leaned against the wall, praying she was wrong, praying that the men in front of her would stop before it was too late.

She glanced at Mrs. Maplethorpe. The older woman caught her gaze and shook her head. Her previous angry flush was gone, washed away by the pallor of fear. The loose skin under her chin wobbled nervously.

In a low, grinding voice, Officer Carmichael said, "They abetted the theft of property—in fact, everyone in this house—"

Edward interrupted him with an exasperated flip of his hand and small snort. "There is no one in this house who should not be here." A small, tight smile twisted his mouth. "With the exception of you, of course. And your men."

The muscles in Officer Carmichael's jaw bulged. His face darkened. "We have a warrant."

"How delightfully refreshing of a change for you," Edward murmured. "Nonetheless, I feel obliged to point out that your search has gained you nothing. Or am I wrong?"

The officer stared at him, his mouth a white-rimmed, thin line.

"So perhaps this is all simply a misunderstanding," Edward said gently. "As I have endeavored to explain.

Those you seek were already found." He held up a hand when Officer Carmichael stepped forward. "And a new arrangement is desired. A purchase, in fact. While I have no knowledge or interest in this matter, I *have* been asked to act as an agent and undertake the purchase of two slaves. I have been given the purchase price." He eyed the officer. "Plus a finder's fee. I had assumed you had come to claim the finder's fee. Was I incorrect?"

So many conflicting emotions passed over Officer Carmichael's face that the skin twitched and tightened in waves for several seconds. The lamp on the hall table flared in a sudden draft, giving his expression a gruesome, contorted aspect. He blinked his gray eyes and licked his lips.

Charity moved closer to Edward.

"You can't just take another man's property. There weren't no sale arranged," Officer Carmichael said. "There was an escape—a theft of property that's got to be returned." He treated them to an ugly smile. "Property that we expect to recover any minute now."

"As I explained, they are not here." Edward sighed. "As you should have discovered already."

"The girls..." Mrs. Maplethorpe interjected in a hesitant voice. "They were *free*. You have no right—"

Edward nodded. "Let us not complicate matters. I'm sure Officer Carmichael will happily admit that he only took the girls into custody to *protect* them during the search and will release them as soon as the other matter is resolved. Is that not correct?"

"Free?" Officer Carmichael snorted. "Prove it."

"I believe they have manumission papers and certificates of freedom indicating that they were freed four years ago, after the death of their master. They have filed the papers attesting to their free status with the deeds office, as well. A very prudent action, I might add. You may visit the deeds office, or I will be happy to show you their freedom papers, once you are satisfied with the disposition of this other, so-called *stolen property*," Edward said mildly.

Charity moved again, brushing against Edward's arm. His body felt rigid with tension, despite his calm, almost disinterested, voice.

"There weren't no sale," Officer Carmichael repeated, although his words were less firm. His gray eyes flickered as he glanced at Charity and Mrs. Maplethorpe.

A clatter at the front door interrupted them, and Officer Carmichael had to step forward in order to open the door a crack. He blocked their view and whispered to someone outside in a low voice.

Stepping closer to Edward, Charity gave his arm a squeeze and stood on tiptoe to whisper, "Are they gone? Did they escape?"

She couldn't read the dark expression in his eyes when he glanced down at her and shrugged.

When Officer Carmichael closed the door and turned back, her fears returned in an icy wave. His mouth was compressed into a tight line. There was no hint of his intentions.

"Well?" Edward asked. "Will this matter be settled to everyone's satisfaction, or must we continue with this nonsense?"

"Mr. Farnham ain't interested in the money—he wants his property back," the officer said.

"I see."

Charity could feel the tension in Edward, burning off him like the steam from a kettle about to boil dry.

"One would think that a practical man would prefer to keep both his pride and fortune intact by selling his property, rather than facing the possible loss of it and subsequent humiliation." He smiled blandly at Officer Carmichael. "And then there is that finder's fee, of course. It is a shame to lose that, as well."

Officer Carmichael was silent for a full minute, eyeing Edward. "Mercer!" he yelled. Then he unhooked his truncheon from his belt and hit the door with it.

A rapid knock answered. The door edged open a foot. A gray-haired man thrust his head through the gap, his face a mass of wrinkles.

"Yes, sir?" the old man asked.

"Mercer, where are the prisoners?" the officer asked.

"Loaded in the wagon, sir," Mercer answered and hurriedly withdrew his head.

Apparently, the man knew Officer Carmichael very well. No sooner had he disappeared then the officer kicked the door shut.

Charity bit her lower lip as her heart sank.

Had they caught the fugitives, then? Was all lost?

The officer was just playing with them, then, teasing them with the possibility of escape when he knew it was impossible. Her muscles ached with the strain. She forced her hands to relax and took a deep breath.

The ugly notion that Carmichael was just as likely to take Edward's money, and then arrest them all, kept skittering through her mind like dry, dead leaves caught in an eddy of wind.

It was hopeless.

Even Edward appeared to hold the same concern. He partially turned to Charity and murmured, "Take Mrs. Maplethorpe and go for a stroll. It appears to be a fine night. Some fresh air will do you good. The officer and I have more important matters to discuss."

Part of her flared with anger—as if he were excluding women from a serious discussion between men—but deep inside she knew he was only trying to help her escape, and she was grateful. He'd deliberately couched his request in terms that Officer Carmichael would accept. He was trying to get Charity and Mrs. Maplethorpe away before the authorities decided to arrest them, as well.

And although it was cowardly, she *wanted* to go.

She glanced at Mrs. Maplethorpe. The older woman looked from her to Edward and back, clearly uncertain. They were both unwilling to abandon Edward, and yet if he were arrested, he would need someone to help him. She couldn't do that if she remained and were taken into custody, too.

"Perhaps we could retire to the sitting room," Mrs. Maplethorpe suggested.

If they did that, they could leave the door open a crack to listen. And if worse came to worst, they could blockade the door long enough to climb out of the window and escape.

The plan was weak, if not downright ridiculous, but it was better than a complete retreat.

"Yes, I would like to sit down." Charity held out her hand to Mrs. Maplethorpe. Gripping the woman's plump, reassuring fingers, Charity led her to the sitting room, but neither one sat down. They crowded together behind the door, keeping it open a crack.

As soon as the women left, the two men faced each other like a pair of dogs preparing to fight.

"If you're trying to bribe me, you're a damn fool," Officer Carmichael said. He kept his truncheon in his hand and tapped it against his thigh, watching Edward's face. "You can't buy me—I'm honest."

"That is a relief," Edward murmured in a voice so low that Charity could barely hear him. "If you are honest, then you know that Kitty and Janet are free women. A man of honor would not molest them. Whatever you think is occurring here, they are not a part of it."

"So you say," Carmichael sneered. Despite his words, the tapping of his stick against his leg had slowed.

"Let them return to work—Miss Stonewright has need of them—while we discuss this other matter. There is no need to involve women."

"Then you *do* know something!" he said, his voice ringing with triumph.

"I know nothing that will assist you, except what I have indicated. You may not be aware, but I have studied the law and am currently reviewing another matter with Mr. Tarte. I have been requested, in my capacity as a barrister—a lawyer—to handle this transaction with a Mr.

Farnham. I have never met the gentleman, of course, but I have been requested to serve on behalf of the purchaser. Again, as I mentioned, I have been authorized to provide a finder's fee, should one be required, as well as see that Mr. Farnham gets the fair market value for his property."

"And just who is this purchaser?"

"I am not at liberty to say. Do you really believe Mr. Farnham will be concerned over that trivial matter?" Edward sounded amused.

Officer Carmichael's truncheon stopped tapping his thigh. He stared at Edward, and Charity couldn't tell if he were persuaded or about to leap forward to beat him to a pulp.

She pressed cold fingers to her mouth, recognizing a flaw in her thinking. If he arrested Edward, what would she do? She didn't have any money—she couldn't get him out of jail—she couldn't do anything useful.

She moved her hand to the base of her neck and strained to listen.

When the officer didn't respond to Edward's question, he said, "Release the girls, Carmichael. You know they are innocent. You are a better man than this. Serve justice and do the right thing."

Officer Carmichael studied Edward for five long, tense seconds before he rapped the door again with his truncheon. His gaze never wavered from Edward's face. When the door opened a few inches, he tilted his head to speak a few quiet words over his shoulder, maintaining his stare.

The door closed.

"What is happening?" Mrs. Maplethorpe whispered in Charity's ear.

"Shush," Charity replied urgently through numb lips. She could barely move, even though the fingers of her other hand, clenched around the cold brass doorknob, ached.

Edward seemed content to wait in silence for the officer's response. Charity wanted to scream at them to come to a decision instead of waltzing around the point in endless circles.

Where were Kitty and Janet? The two women had to be terrified they would lose their precious freedom. She couldn't let that happen to them, but she'd felt helpless to stop the men. They swept the girls away and then tore apart her home and her life.

More than ever she needed to find the Stonewright fortune, if it still existed. Money could solve so many problems and provide so much freedom. If she were rich, none of this would be happening. The bitter, angry thought made her grip on the doorknob tighten.

The front door creaked again as it opened.

Officer Carmichael stepped toward Edward, forcing him back one yard, then two.

Charity's eyes widened. She let out a long breath when Janet slipped into the hallway, followed closely by Kitty. The two women were holding hands, and as soon as they stepped over the threshold, they halted. Janet wrapped an arm around her sister's waist and held her tightly, her beautiful, wide dark eyes glancing at the officer and then at Edward. Kitty trembled and kept her gaze fixed on the floor, but both women had been through enough in their short lives to keep their faces carefully expressionless.

Officer Carmichael barely gave them a sideways glance. "You claim these two women are free—"

"I *claim* nothing," Edward said curtly, interrupting him. "Kitty and Janet are free women, engaged by me as maids while I am in residence here. I have reviewed their papers. Everything is quite proper and in order. Mr. Tarte has also scrutinized the documents—we felt that was wise, given the recent issues in Charleston. He can attest to the fact that everything is as it should be. There should be no need to question either Kitty or Janet any further, or keep them from their work." He partially turned in the direction of the two women. "Please, prepare our bedchambers for the night, and lay a fire for Miss Stonewright. It has grown quite cool this evening. I do not wish for her to become ill."

"Yes, sir." Janet released her sister to drop a quick curtsy. As she straightened, she grabbed Kitty's hand and pulled her past Officer Carmichael without glancing his way.

Kitty never looked up. She walked hurriedly at her sister's heels, her right hand in Janet's and her left crossed over her waist in a white-knuckled grip on her sister's dark sleeve.

"Thank goodness," Mrs. Maplethorpe whispered before she took a step back. "Those poor girls..."

"They looked unharmed," Charity said. Should she go after the two women and make sure, or stay here?

"That Carmichael," Mrs. Maplethorpe said in a disgusted voice. "I'd like to box his big, wicked ears."

"So would I." She opened the door a bit wider and stood in the gap. They may have gotten Janet and Kitty back, but what about the small family hiding in her cellar? Had they escaped?

Her cousin and Lady Hildegard were with them. If they were caught... She swallowed. They would all pay the price if that were to happen. But her cousin was smart— clever. He knew what to do—he must have planned their escape, even if it seemed impossible to her that they could evade Officer Carmichael and his men.

Please, dear God, help them—let them escape! The words seemed so inadequate, but she felt hemmed in on every side. If she protested too much, or caused too much trouble, Officer Carmichael could decide to take Janet and Kitty into custody again and there was no doubt about what would happen then.

And if she asked about her cousin, the authorities might make the connection between him and the runaways, if they hadn't already done so. Her only recourse seemed to be to act as if she had no concerns now that Janet and Kitty were released and, by the sounds above her head, cleaning up the mess Officer Carmichael's men had made of their bedrooms. The men had conducted their search with obvious maliciousness, emptying

203

wardrobes and dressers as if they expected to find someone hiding in a space as small as a six-inch desk drawer.

"Thank you, Officer Carmichael," Edward said, his voice interrupting her desperate thoughts. He held out his hand. "You are indeed a man of integrity."

Officer Carmichael's mouth pinched in a frown, but he shook Edward's hand. "There's still the others. We can't have no fugitives."

"Of course not," Edward agreed. "However, I have explained the situation. There was a purchaser for Mr. Farnham's property." The stiffness in his voice told Charity that Edward was struggling to sound as unconcerned and callous about the runaways as Carmichael expected. She could only hope the officer didn't notice his disapproval.

"You can't hide an escape," Officer Carmichael said, his lower jaw jutting forward pugnaciously. "If Mr. Farnham didn't know about no purchase, then there weren't one."

"Perhaps we ought to arrange a meeting with him and discuss it. That would seem to be the reasonable thing to do."

"He won't agree. It's a matter of honor. And law. If we let them fugitives escape, others'll follow."

Edward sighed. "We seem to be repeating ourselves. Ask Mr. Farnham. I will be pleased to meet with both of you at any time that is convenient. Now, is that all?" Edward pulled out his pocket watch and stared at it. "It is growing late, and we are at an impasse until you speak with Mr. Farnham."

"I'll speak to him all right." Officer Carmichael hooked his truncheon onto his belt and gripped the doorknob of the front door. "And I'll return—you can be sure of that."

"I have no doubt," Edward said tiredly. "And we shall, unfortunately, be waiting."

Chapter Nineteen

Edward watched Officer Carmichael leave. Although he kept a relaxed smile on his face, he couldn't forget the sound of booted feet running after the small group as they'd left the cellar. Had they seen the fugitives? Caught them?

If they had, their situation would slip from inconvenient to wildly unfortunate very quickly. Nodcock leaned against his shin and peered up at him. The cat slowly blinked, gave a soft meow, and sauntered off into the shadows with tail held high.

Despite the cat's calm demeanor, Edward was tempted to pack up everyone in the household and leave on the next available ship bound for England. No doubt that action would only serve to convince the authorities of their guilt, however, and the main purpose of his visit would remain unfulfilled. Neither result was desirable.

"Thank goodness," Charity murmured after locking the front door behind Officer Carmichael. She cast an anxious glance at Edward, the corners of her lovely mouth drooping and her eyes dark with concern. "Did they...?" Her question drifted off as she flicked a quick look at Mrs. Maplethorpe.

"Everything appears fine—at least for the moment," he hastened to reassure her. He stepped closer and gave her shoulder a squeeze. "Don't worry. I don't believe Carmichael would have left so easily had he found anything—or anyone."

From the silence on the second floor, he heard the longcase clock toll the hour. They all lifted their heads to listen to the mellow knell. Two in the morning.

He looked at Charity, relieved she was safe and unharmed. Such a rush of tenderness filled him that he half-lifted his hand with the desire to touch her warm skin and feel the silkiness of her hair. She was such a mixture of softness and strength. Her eyes were shadowed with exhaustion and her skin was as pale as a pearl, despite the golden glow of the lamp on the hallway table next to her, but her shoulders were straight.

"I, for one, have had enough for one night," Mrs. Maplethorpe broke the silence. She moved closer to Charity and slipped an arm around her waist and gave her a squeeze. "You look tired, my dear. Let us retire. There is nothing more we can do tonight. And we should see if Lady Hildegard needs anything. She must be hiding in her room, terrified with all these terrible happenings."

Hildie ... Oh, dear God, let her be safe. He stared at the floor, remembering her departure into the darkness. She was so young—she had no idea what she was risking or what hardships she faced. He should never have allowed her to leave.

He picked up the lamp and cleared his throat. "Lady Hildegard is not here, Mrs. Maplethorpe. She is a married lady now."

Mrs. Maplethorpe stared at him. "I beg your pardon! *Married?*"

"Yes. She married Miss Stonewright's cousin earlier in the week. I should have informed you." He forced a smile. "I humbly beg your pardon."

"Married," Mrs. Maplethorpe repeated. "Well, we certainly have had an exciting day, haven't we?" She grinned at Charity. "It is a good thing, then, that I'm here, isn't it, my dear? With just you and Mr. Archer..." She clicked her tongue, her eyes sparkling with mischief. "Well, there is no need to worry. I'm not leaving you alone, Miss Stonewright, you don't have to worry about that."

Charity flushed and glanced sideways at Edward. Her blush deepened as his smile twisted ruefully. He shrugged, nearly chuckling at the aggravated expression wrinkling her face.

Holding the lamp aloft, Edward nodded and gestured toward the stairs. "You are remarkably reassuring, Mrs. Maplethorpe."

"Yes," Charity murmured in accord, although he noticed she winced as she said it.

Mrs. Maplethorpe smiled and pressed her left hand against Charity's back to encourage her to ascend the staircase ahead of her. With one foot on the bottom step, Mrs. Maplethorpe snapped the fingers of her free hand once and paused. A soft meow sounded, and Nodcock came at a swift trot. He curled around the newel post, eyed Mrs. Maplethorpe, and ran up the staircase ahead of both the women.

"So that is where he spends his nights," Edward commented as he followed behind Mrs. Maplethorpe.

She cast a quick glance over her ample, rounded shoulder. "I hope you don't mind, but I like having him in my room at night." She grinned, her eyes glinting with laughter in the lamplight. "He keeps my feet warm."

He laughed. "Then by all means you must continue to enjoy his company."

Even Charity had a soft smile curving her lips when they finally parted at the landing, Mrs. Maplethorpe taking the lamp from Edward since she had the furthest distance to walk down the corridor. She saw her sole charge safely to her room before she snapped her fingers again and trundled down the hallway, with Nodcock following along docilely at her heels, his tail held high.

He waited until she closed her door before he entered his own room.

Once again, Atwood was sitting in the chair by the window, his head nodding, snoring gently. The creak of the door made him jerk upright.

"Sir!" Atwood leapt to his feet and glanced around the room, blinking.

"Atwood," Edward greeted him, loosening his neckcloth. "I'm surprised our good constable, Officer Carmichael, allowed you to remain."

Atwood drew himself up, a look of distaste making his brows bristle and mouth thin. "He desired me to remove myself, sir, but I refused. I could not allow him to rifle through our clothing and accoutrements. It was unthinkable."

"Your dedication does you credit," Edward replied dryly, stifling a laugh. He could well imagine Atwood's indignant response to Carmichael's search. He just wished his valet had felt inclined to be as protective of the rest of the bedchambers.

"May I assist you?" Atwood moved around to Edward's back to gently remove Edward's jacket.

"Were you aware of Nettle's plans?" he asked as he untied his neckcloth and removed it, handing the long strip of linen to Atwood.

"Nettle, sir?" Atwood's forehead wrinkled in puzzlement as he folded the neckcloth and set it aside for laundering. "Miss Nettle does not see fit to confide in me, sir. Surely, she has done nothing untoward?"

Edward laughed, though there was a note of bitterness slicing through the amusement. "Not untoward, just awkward. It seems my sister has married Miss Stonewright's cousin, and Nettle is following her mistress to her new home. It was quite a surprise."

"I can well imagine, sir!" Atwood stopped to stare at Edward, open-mouthed. Horror widened his eyes until the whites gleamed. "I can only offer my sympathy—er—congratulations." He flushed in confusion and busied himself with brushing off Edward's jacket.

"Sympathy and congratulations are both in order." Edward's laughter drifted into a low chuckle. "We were all surprised." He studied his valet. "You are not harboring a similar desire to remain here, are you?"

"Here?" Atwood's voice squeaked. "Surely, you're not—that is—you are not intending on *staying*?" He sounded so scandalized that Edward couldn't help laughing again.

"No. In fact, I believe another week or so should be sufficient to bring my work on behalf of the duchess to a conclusion." A bitter sadness crept through him like the dark mists that occasionally swirled around the mansion. He had to make his final determination on the disposition of Oldwood. It did no one any good to delay the inevitable.

And there was still the matter of Lenore Stonewright's murder and her funeral. *Tomorrow—actually today.* It seemed incredible that so much had happened in one day.

He poured water into the basin, washed his face, and rinsed the dust out of his hair. Atwood handed him a linen towel, and he vigorously rubbed his head and neck.

Charity would not forgive him—he was not a fool—and once she was settled elsewhere, he had no reason to stay. He had a duty to return to England, even if he didn't already long to do so. The cool, green sweep of the lawn surrounding his country estate beckoned him.

Home. Without Hildie. The thought was bittersweet, but he still ached to return where he belonged.

"Very good, sir." Atwood breathed a sigh of relief. "Do you require anything else?"

"No—that is all for the night."

Atwood bowed, and after straightening a few more items to his satisfaction, he slipped out of the room.

Staring at the bed, Edward realized sleep was but a distant possibility. Tension made his shoulders and neck ache. He strode to the window. Outside, the darkness revealed nothing but the even blacker silhouettes of shaggy oaks and buildings. No sign of Hildie, no way to know if they had all escaped. He could only hope she'd eventually send word that she was safe.

A glance at his pocket watch reminded him of the late hour. The time and days were slipping away. They were already well into February. The Red Star Line's packet service to Liverpool left New York on the twenty-fourth of each month. He'd have to leave soon if he wished to make that sailing. Although the duchess was patient, there were limits to even her tolerance.

Charity. He knew what he *wanted* and what most women in her position would be relieved to accept. But Charity was too independent to view marriage as a solution to her problems, particularly if it meant she would have to leave Charleston and travel to London as his wife. Her heart was here, just as his was in England.

This was *her* home, even if the evidence was not in her favor.

He paced back and forth in the narrow space of his bedchamber until he paused once again by the window.

The bundle of old letters he'd found sat forlornly on the small writing desk next to him. With a deep sigh, he moved to pick up the lamp and walked back to the desk. Perhaps if he read through them once again, he'd find something to settle the matter in Charity's favor and solve the mystery of the death of the poor woman in the cellar.

At the very least, if they failed to clarify those matters, maybe they would finally lull him to sleep.

The first few letters were intensely personal communications between Henry Stonewright, Charity's grandfather, and his wife, Lenore. It was clear the two loved each other deeply and viewed any separation as a severe trial. After five or six, he began to scan them, regretting the necessity of intruding into their privacy. The letters were not meant for any other eyes and held very few details about their social life and acquaintances.

The only mention of the Haywoods had been written by Lenore in an offhand comment about the child, Charlotte Haywood.

... I visited little Miss Haywood the other day. I am so sorry to relate that she seems quite sick with worry about her dear papa, Captain Haywood. He is gone again, and Heaven knows when the child will see him again. The poor little thing is surrounded by strangers; even her governess is new and doesn't seem the least bit sympathetic to the girl's plight. It was all I could do not to wrap my arms around her and drag her home with me.

If only her aunt hadn't disappeared so many years ago. I often think about her and pray she didn't jump into the river, as so many claimed. What a terrible fate to contemplate, and the tragedy has left dear little Miss Charlotte with no one to care for her when the Captain is at sea....

While Lenore was obviously concerned about Charlotte's happiness, she wasn't concerned enough to mention her again in any of the later missives. Family matters and intimate vows of love were the main topics of those, and it wasn't until he was nearing the bottom of the packet that the tone of the correspondence became more troubling.

With increasing frustration, he discovered that many of Lenore's last letters were missing from the bundle, so he couldn't read the words that had triggered Henry's replies. He had only a few shorter missives from Henry, suggesting that his wife was unhappy at his absence and having difficulties with one of their friends.

Or perhaps not so much a friend as an acquaintance. The second to last letter had an urgent tone that made Edward frown as he reread the most disquieting sections.

My dear Lenore,

Is that sour little person still bothering you? I cannot rest, thinking about it. God, how I wish I were there to hold you in my arms and protect you....

Do not allow such visitors in the house if you can avoid it. Say the word, and I will return to you; no business is worth risking your peace of mind....

All my love,

Your Henry

The letter was dated in the fall of 1798. The name of the person annoying Lenore was not mentioned in the letter, leaving Edward to sit back and rub his eyes, considering the implications.

Where was Lenore's original letter? What had she said? Her other letters had revealed a spirited woman with a lively sense of humor and deep concern about the health and welfare of her family. Her very human irritation with her son's wife made Edward smile as Lenore took pains to mention the details of their son's life and the myriad ways his wife failed in her duty to him. So typical of many mothers, she felt the girl was not quite good enough for her son.

But he could find no mention of anyone, male or female, in the letters from her to indicate she was afraid of anyone.

So what had she written to Henry to arouse his concern?

The last letter in the bundle was short, simply stating that he was leaving Philadelphia and would be home as soon as humanly possible.

The chair creaked as Edward sat back. He rotated his stiff shoulders and flipped through the old bundle one last time.

What happened when Henry Stonewright returned home? His arrival must have been around the time Lenore's body was locked in the cellar because the remaining members of the family had departed for Philadelphia shortly thereafter, never to return to Oldwood.

By the middle of 1799, Miss Haywood had miraculously reappeared after having disappeared many years before. She and her niece, Charlotte Haywood, moved into Oldwood. Miss Haywood had claimed the Stonewrights sold the property to the Haywoods, and to prove her claim, Charles Cooper had written his statement, supporting her.

The vague whispers of something wrong, someone bothering Lenore while her husband was gone, suggested that the matter had come to a head around the time of Henry's return.

It wasn't hard to guess what had happened, and Edward's theory saddened him. Lenore's letters had given him the feeling that he knew her, and he'd liked her. Surely she was not the type of woman who would try to hide an affair through the subterfuge of complaining about a man to her husband, throwing the blame on her lover as a way of explaining his presence during her husband's absence.

And Henry's letters showed him to be an honorable man concerned about his family and still very much in love with his wife. However, love was a two-edged sword. If he returned home to find his wife in another man's arms, what would he do? Would he kill her in a jealous rage and hide her body?

Who else would know about the secret room in the cellar?

It had to be Henry. He'd returned home and something had happened, that much was certain.

Whatever had happened, Henry hadn't wanted anyone to discover it. He'd hidden Lenore's body, and then stricken by a stroke—perhaps brought on by guilt over what he'd done—he'd gone to Philadelphia.

Oldwood had been closed up and most likely sold to finance his family's trip.

He stood and stretched. While the sky outside was still dark, the chill in the air hinted that dawn was near. There were no absolutely clear answers. Tomorrow they would attend the funeral and then talk to Mrs. Eggerton, hoping she could shed some light on the situation.

But after that, he'd have to make a decision. He'd have to tell Charity what he'd discovered and come to what seemed an inevitable conclusion.

Then, he would have to make arrangements to return home. It was time.

Past time.

Chapter Twenty

When sleep failed to wrap her in its healing embrace, Charity picked up the old, tattered diary again, plumped the pillows behind her back, and settled into bed to read. Her lamp was almost out of oil, and the sky outside her window was glowing rose, gold, and celestial blue when she finally closed the book and lay it on her bedside table.

Her eyes ached, and she rubbed them tiredly. A wide yawn made her jaw crackle. She stared at the window, too tired to make sense of what she'd read, and afraid to try. She slipped further under the covers. A little sleep—that's what she needed.

A small, brown Carolina Wren flew up to her window and perched on the ledge before hopping back and forth and peering through the window with a beady black eye. It gave a few tentative chirps and then sang, *rattle-pate, rattle-pate, rattle-pate.* A sleepy smile curved her lips as she watched it until the heaviness of sleep claimed her.

Bright sunshine streamed over her face when Charity finally woke up. The wren was gone from her windowsill, but a few tangled stalks of brown grass in one corner suggested that it would be back. She laughed and shook her head at the bird's optimistic insistence on starting nests at all times of the year and in the oddest places it could find. Nothing ever seemed to deter the little brown bundle of feathers or dull its energy.

She splashed water over her face and neck, washing quickly before dressing in an old black silk gown. Today was her grandmother's funeral.

The thought sent a chill down her spine, but she straightened. No matter what they discovered from Mrs. Eggerton, nothing could hurt Lenore Stonewright any further. She deserved both respect and her final peaceful rest.

When she went to close the wardrobe, her hand lingered, however, over one of the new sprigged muslin gowns Mrs. Maplethorpe had made up for her. Her old gowns, laundered to pale gray and still folded neatly on the lowest shelf, seemed to rebuke her for abandoning them. She shut the door sharply, resolving to tell Janet to tear them up and use them for rags.

The past was done.

Even just the few hours of sleep she'd obtained had settled a few things in her mind. She had an idea, now, about where she might find the Stonewright fortune, and she would force Edward to see that he'd been wrong all along. Oldwood was hers. It didn't really matter what Mrs. Eggerton had to say about Lenore Stonewright.

Charity picked up the old journal and moved toward the door.

Odd though, how that thought seemed to turn the golden sunshine to gray.

If she could prove the Stonewrights owned Oldwood, then Edward would be able to return to England. She'd be victorious. And alone.

Would there be any reason to celebrate such an ending?

She gripped the diary, holding it against her chest, wishing she held Edward's warm hand instead.

Then realization hit her like a shaft of sunlight after a storm. She loved him. She loved the twinkle in his eyes that sent butterflies fluttering through her belly, his warmth, and his wry sense of humor. She loved the way he cared about his sister, and the apologetic, half-ashamed look on his face when he brought Nodcock home with him. He was far from perfect—his interest in the law was frankly inexplicable and irritating—but he also showed rare insight and a sense of honor she had to admire.

And although she'd always prided herself in being a strong woman, sometimes, she just wanted to feel his strong arms around her and let go of her worries for a few minutes. She was tired of being alone, tired of always having to display a strength she was far from feeling.

Oldwood would feel empty without his firm tread in the hallway or coming down the stairs. She'd miss his smile, and the way he made her feel challenged and alive.

Sighing, she left her room and was surprised to see Edward stepping into the hallway.

He glanced her way and grinned, his brown eyes twinkling. "I was sure I would have to choke down my coffee alone." He waited for her to join him before turning toward the staircase. "Or have you already breakfasted?"

"No. We are both late. Janet will be furious, I'm sure." Intensely aware of the breadth of his shoulders and warmth, she fixed her gaze on the stairs, descending carefully. Feeling foolish, she kept seeing herself tumbling down the steps because he'd distracted her.

"We'll just have to brave her fury and pray she's left something on the sideboard." His voice was rich with amusement, although he almost instantly sobered. "We have a little time, however, before the funeral."

"Yes." She let out a breath when she reached the hallway without embarrassing herself.

Flicking a glance in his direction, she flushed again when his gaze caught hers. The morning light bronzed his dark hair and revealed a small shaving nick on the side of his square chin. His dark blue jacket and white cravat highlighted the tan he'd somehow acquired, and he seemed to exude a calm strength that made her long to lean against him and feel his arm heavy across her shoulders.

She swallowed, her heart thundering and her mind empty of sensible thoughts. The feel of the diary in her hand made her hold it out.

"What are you holding in your arms?" he asked, gesturing for her to precede him into the dining room.

"What?" she repeated. "Oh—I found it upstairs. It's a diary. A woman's journal."

"Oh?" He seated her before moving around to his own chair as she picked up the coffee pot and poured them each a cup. "Have you read it?"

"Yes." She sipped the tepid coffee, praying that it would help her stop feeling like a babbling idiot.

One of his dark brows rose in a mild, silent question. He took a sip of his coffee and grimaced, but he managed to drain the cup before he put it down.

"Miss Haywood—that is, the duchess—that wasn't her aunt," Charity said. She refilled her cup and gulped it down. Her stomach gurgled in protest.

Edward handed her the basket of fragrant yeast buns, a bland expression on his face.

When he caught her staring at him, he nodded. A light flashed in the depths of his dark eyes and for a moment, she thought he already knew what she was trying to say. "You are going to explain that somewhat surprising statement, aren't you?"

"Yes. That is, I found a diary in the bedroom at the end of the hall."

"A diary?" His gaze grew intent, pinning her in place. "Your grandmother left a diary?"

"No." She shook her head. "Not my grandmother's. It was written by someone else, a woman called Elizabeth James."

"James." He frowned thoughtfully and rubbed his napkin over his lips.

Her gaze followed his gesture. For a breathless moment, she felt his mouth pressed against hers again, and the deep warmth of his body.

He shook his head and placed his napkin next to his plate. "I don't recognize the name. Was she a guest here?"

"No—that's what I'm trying to tell you. She *pretended* to be Charlotte Haywood's aunt, but she wasn't."

Knowledge lit up his eyes. "Ah, yes. That makes a great deal of sense."

"What makes sense?" she asked impatiently. How could he possibly know anything about it, when she hadn't told him and had just read about it last night?

"I found a letter from your grandmother Lenore. She was worried about Charlotte because her father was at sea so much. She mentioned that Charlotte's aunt had gone missing some years before." He gave her a wry, self-deprecating smile that made her heart thunder in her chest with longing. "I *assumed* that the aunt had been found around the time when Charlotte lost her father and had agreed to care for the young girl. Apparently, the rumors about the aunt's death were more accurate. It would have been simple enough for an adventuress to pretend to be the long-lost woman, particularly when she offered to care for her little niece." He grinned at her. "So Charlotte's *aunt* was not actually who she said she was."

"Yes—that is, no, she was not," Charity said, sitting straighter. "She was an imposter, and if she could lie about that, then isn't it likely that she lied about owning Oldwood? She wasn't even a Haywood."

"There is that letter from Cooper, however," he said, his gaze growing distant. "But..."

"But what?" she prompted impatiently, studying his face. "Do you know how annoying it is when you do that?"

His brows rose, and his mouth quirked in a near-smile. "When I do what? Think?"

"Yes," she said, even though she felt increasingly silly. "It's as if you know something that no one else does—as if you have some secret knowledge."

His grin widened. "You have a great deal in common with my sister. She used to say precisely the same thing." A shadow crossed over his face at the mention of his sister, though he kept his tone light.

She reached out and touched his wrist briefly, her heart twisting in her chest. He had to be worried about Lady Hildegard—she was, as well. If only they would get word about their fate, one way or the other.

"Nonetheless," he took a deep breath, "I do have some additional information to share with you. That letter from your grandmother was part of a packet of correspondence between your grandparents."

"There were more? What did they say?" She leaned forward, the edge of the table pressing against her ribs. She fisted her hands on either side of her plate to keep from reaching out and grasping his wrist.

"There was no mention of a sale of this property," he replied slowly, his brows drawing together in a thoughtful frown.

"You see! I told you Grandfather never sold Oldwood—he wouldn't!"

He held up a hand briefly. "I'm afraid the letters were dated well before your family left this house, so it is not conclusive. But in the absence of any document pertaining to the sale, well..." He studied her, his eyes warm with sympathy. "And given—" He broke off abruptly. "What else did this James woman's journal say? Was there anything about a Mr. Cooper?"

"Cooper? Why do you ask?" She studied him uneasily as she recalled what she'd read. The journal had been so vague about most things, most likely because the author knew what she was talking about and saw fit to explain very little.

"I have some thoughts on the matter. Was that the diary you had in your hand? Perhaps you would allow me to glance through it?"

Her right hand dropped to her lap where she'd hidden the journal beneath her napkin. "Yes, I suppose so." She sighed. "She did mention him. But she mentioned several other men, as well." Her brow wrinkled, and she frowned in an effort to recall the names—she was always so bad with names. "She wrote about a Mr. Ben Harris and Mr. George Sloane, as well. She seemed to enjoy collecting secrets and using them to her advantage."

"So Mr. Cooper wasn't her only victim?"

She shook her head. "No. But she was particularly pleased with the power she wielded over him. In fact, she was gloating—it was quite awful, really—that she knew some foul secret of his. He must have done something truly terrible."

"And she used that secret to convince him to write that letter stating that the Haywoods owned this property."

"Yes. How did you know? You *did* see the journal, didn't you?"

"No—mere conjecture on my part." Amusement glinted in his dark eyes.

A fluttery feeling drifted through her when she caught his gaze. She glanced down at the table and managed to ask, "But you see, don't you? We never sold this house. I've been right all along."

He shook his head. "Perhaps."

"This is my *home!*" She half-stood, wincing when she heard the sharp note of desperation in her voice. "Elizabeth James had no *right* to claim she owned this house—she just used that Haywood child and the Haywood name to obtain entrance here so she could search for the gold." She pressed her fingers against her mouth and stared at Edward, hoping he didn't hear her mention the Stonewright fortune again. She didn't want to remind him and prayed he didn't catch her remark.

But comprehension flashed over his face. "Gold," he repeated. "Ah, yes. I'd forgotten."

"It's not the only reason I'm here—this *is* my home!" Charity said, sitting down with a thump. Everything was falling apart, and she felt helpless to halt the downward spiral.

"Precisely what mythological treasure are you and Officer Carmichael seeking?"

"The Stonewright fortune," she replied dully, staring at her plate. "It's here ... somewhere. My grandfather's father died before he told him its location, so it has been lost for a very long time." She raised her gaze to his. "That's how I know we didn't sell this house—Grandfather would never have done that, knowing that the gold was still here somewhere."

"Perhaps he no longer cared," Edward said in a soft voice. He reached over and clasped her cold hand. His fingers felt warm and strong around hers, but she pulled away nonetheless. "You should read the letters I found— he loved your grandmother very much."

"Then how could you think he killed her?"

"Jealousy... In the last letters, he mentioned that someone was annoying your grandmother while your grandfather was gone. Her side of the correspondence was missing, but it is possible that when he returned, he found your grandmother in the arms of another man."

"How can you say that?" She quivered, almost inarticulate with anger. "If she was being annoyed by someone, she would not suddenly decide to—to have an *affair* with him! That is absurd."

"I'm sorry—this is difficult, but you must realize that her annoyance may have been feigned. It may have been her way of trying to maintain the appearance of innocence and excusing the man's presence in their house." Although his gaze remained locked on her face, she could sense that he was no longer seeing her. He paused for nearly a minute before he blinked and his dark eyes regained their focus. "And that may have been Cooper's secret that Miss James exploited to gain access to this house.

"According to Mr. Tarte, your family left this house to go to Philadelphia just a few weeks after the last letter in that bundle was written; a letter from your grandfather stating that he was on his way home. Given that none of Lenore's letters from around that period were included in the bundle—only those she'd received from your grandfather and had had time to place in her packet—I fear you may be correct." His eyes burned with a feverish light that seemed to see into the distant past. "Your grandfather surely kept the letters she wrote to him, but she never received them back from him to add to the bundle. The most likely explanation was that she was already dead."

"And grandfather must have thought she'd run away!" Charity exclaimed, grabbing his hand in her excitement. Thoughts and possibilities whirled through her mind, floating over the deep sadness she felt for her grandfather. What had he thought, what had he *felt* when he returned home to find his adored wife missing?

She couldn't imagine the pain he must have experienced.

"Mr. Tarte indicated your grandfather had a stroke around that time, probably caused by the shock of returning home and finding his wife gone." He stopped suddenly, though he gave her fingers a squeeze. "I'm sorry—I just realized—we are back to the initial problem. Who else but your grandfather would have known about that secret room? He may have returned home to find her in the arms of Mr. Cooper and killed her in his rage."

"No—you're wrong. Others knew about the room. Miss James—*she* knew, just like Officer Carmichael did. Somehow, she found out about the gold and tried to get Mr. Cooper to help her find it. He must have been the man my grandmother said was annoying her—he must have been trying to get into the house to search for it." Her grip on his hand tightened. "Grandmother may have caught him in the cellar—he must have found the passage. You guessed it, why couldn't he? And he killed her and hid her body in that room. When Grandfather returned home, she was gone."

"And Mr. Cooper may have found the gold—he was a very rich and influential man, according to Mr. Tarte."

She shook her head. "No, his family was always wealthy, anyone will tell you that. If he had found the gold, Miss James would never have had to pretend to be the missing Haywood woman to gain entrance to the house— she'd have known there was nothing here."

"The question remains, however: why would she believe being a Haywood would grant her rights over the property? The house had to have been sold for her to believe that."

"Not if she blackmailed Mr. Cooper to state that the property was hers!"

"He could have done that for Miss James—she didn't have to assume the identity of Miss Elizabeth Haywood and take on the care of an orphaned girl."

"I don't know—but I do know I'm right somehow." She rubbed her temple tiredly and listened to the chimes of the distant clock. "It's late—we need to leave for the funeral and talk to Mrs. Eggerton. Maybe she can tell us why my grandmother was murdered and why Miss James wanted to be Elizabeth Haywood." She stood and moved to the door, waiting for Edward to follow her.

"What color was your grandfather's hair?" he asked, seemingly out of nowhere as he followed her. At the door, he placed his hat on his head and ushered her outside.

"Color?" She laughed out of sheer confusion and touched a curl that had escaped from her bonnet at the nape of her neck. Her hair felt damp, and she glanced up. Clouds had moved in, obscuring the sun and casting a uniform gray pall over the streets. "Red—when he was young." She smiled sadly at an errant memory. "My father said he was as bald as a cuckoo's egg by the time he was forty, though. Father used to laugh about the fact that he was the first male to retain his hair in a very long line of bald men. Why?"

"I see. Perhaps the task is not so impossible after all."

"What do you mean?" she asked, hardly daring to hope for a solution as she slipped her hand through the crook of Edward's arm.

"There were some dark hairs caught in your grandmother's hand."

"Her hair?"

He shook his head. "No, she was already turning gray, but it appeared she originally had pale hair—not dark brown." He gazed down at her. "I believe she may have fought to save her life and tore the hair off her assailant. I don't suppose that diary in your lap mentions anyone's hair color, does it?"

"Miss James had red hair—it was one of the ways she was able to convince everyone that she was the missing Miss Elizabeth Haywood. Apparently, Miss Haywood also had that particular shade of reddish-gold hair."

"I don't suppose she mentioned Mr. Cooper's appearance?"

"No—yes!" She almost stumbled in her excitement. *"Dark as the devil himself* is how she described him. He was always staring in mirrors and fussing with his hair—she was very contemptuous of his vanity. Not that it matters," she said, letting out a long breath. All their speculation was so useless. None of it could prove that Oldwood was hers, and the gold was still lost, perhaps found and spent long ago by Miss James. "As I mentioned, she also wrote about other men—Mr. Harris and Mr. Sloane—and I don't remember anything about their hair color. Besides, Mr. Cooper has been dead for years. If he killed my grandmother, it doesn't matter anymore."

"It does matter—to you." He placed his hand over hers. "So it is important."

She couldn't stand to see the compassion in his eyes. She stared at the tall clock tower of St. Michael's Church, coming into view. A sick headache throbbed in time to her heartbeat.

"You are right." She rubbed her temple with her free hand. "You've been right all along. There is no proof that I still own Oldwood, and a great deal of circumstances that suggest I don't. Miss James had no reason to become Miss Haywood, unless doing so meant she could live here. And from what you said, my family and the Haywood family knew each other. Apparently, they were friends. It would have made sense for grandfather to sell Oldwood to Mr. Haywood after he had his first stroke. This place probably filled him with pain after his wife disappeared."

"That's true," Edward said slowly. He rubbed his square chin thoughtfully. "Precisely. That may be precisely why she became Miss Haywood and took in the orphaned Charlotte. Who would suspect her of being a fraud if she was caring for a small girl? And it would make sense to everyone that Henry Stonewright might have sold his property to Mr. Haywood, since they were friends. Miss James took advantage of the fact that Mr. Haywood was lost at sea shortly thereafter, and your family never returned from Philadelphia to claim the house."

"Then—are you saying you believe I *do* own the house?" She pressed a cold hand against her chest. Her heart pounded against her ribs, threatening to break free.

"Well, the diary you have indicates that Mr. Cooper's letter may have been written under duress and was therefore false. Failing more information regarding that aspect, there is no document supporting the sale of this property. So I cannot trace the title. But let us forget this subject for now. We must still interview Mrs. Eggerton, and we are at the churchyard."

He guided her through the gate, and she was both relieved and saddened to see only the pastor standing next to an open grave. A few feet away, a lone man dressed in faded blue trousers and a brown jacket leaned on a shovel, clearly waiting to complete his work.

After a brief greeting, the pastor mumbled through the proper words while periodically glancing up at the heavens, which were rapidly growing darker. A heavy drop of rain landed on his narrow, pointed nose as he said the final words and gently closed his bible.

Charity nodded to him when he turned to her, her throat closed with sudden grief. She hadn't known her grandmother, but it hurt to think of her final desperate moments and her grandfather's despair when she vanished without a word. In a husky voice, she thanked him, and let Edward lead her away.

"Do you wish to return to the house?" Edward asked, pausing to unroll an umbrella.

"No. We have an appointment with Mrs. Eggerton, do we not? I want an end to this, one way or the other."

"Very well," Edward replied, moving forward.

A heavy, cold rain beat down upon the black folds as he held the umbrella above their heads. Within a few seconds, puddles had already formed on the walkways, and the hem of her black dress was wet. It slapped her ankles with each step and dripped water into the tops of her short boots. She could feel the moisture sliding down her instep and pooling around her toes.

They had only walked a block before she was regretting her decision to visit Mrs. Eggerton. She was cold, wet, and entirely miserable. But the Eggerton house was not far, and they were standing on the stoop before she had the chance to tell Edward she wanted to return home, instead.

Edward knocked and the door was opened by a blank-faced man who took Edward's dripping umbrella with a frown of distaste and ushered them into a sitting room just off the main hallway.

"A Mr. Archer and Miss Stonewright, madam," he intoned before closing the door behind them.

Charity glanced around the pleasant sitting room. A cheerful fire burned in the massive brick hearth, and heavy, pale yellow draperies were drawn over the windows, shutting out the dreary weather. A tiny figure wrapped in several blue and green shawls sat in a wing chair in front of the fire. Her lap was covered with a fluffy red blanket, and her feet must have been propped up on a footstool beneath the blanket because Charity could just see two of the elegantly curved legs of the stool peeping out from under the blanket's hem.

"Stonewright?" a high, quavering voice called. "Miss Stonewright?"

"Yes, Mrs. Eggerton." Charity moved closer.

The lady waved a small, heavily veined hand, and Charity caught it, giving it a gentle squeeze. "Sit—no, ring for tea, if you please. Then sit."

Charity caught Edward's gaze. He nodded and strode over to the bell pull in the corner and gave it several sharp tugs. Before he could join them again, the wide, double door opened. The butler stood aside as a maid hurried in, carrying a large silver tray. She placed it on a low, round table next to Mrs. Eggerton, curtsied, and left, all without glancing up at any of them.

226

"Will you pour, my dear?" Mrs. Eggerton asked. She peered up at Charity, her round face framed by a cap frothy with lace and a few wispy gray curls. Although her skin was as wrinkled as a withered apple, her cheeks held a trace of rosy color, and her cloudy blue eyes still retained a sharpness that surprised her. "I cannot manage so well anymore." She raised her twisted hands briefly and clicked her tongue. "I am pleased to have guests, however. Not many come to visit, though that nice Mr. Tarte comes once a week." She laughed abruptly. "To see if I still live, I suppose."

Wet hem slapping her ankles with each step, Charity poured them each a cup of tea, handed them around, and took a seat on the wing chair opposite from Mrs. Eggerton. Edward sat on a small, brown silk settee nearby.

"I'm so glad to meet you," Charity said politely. "It was kind of you to grant us some of your time."

Another harsh laugh interrupted Charity. "I have nothing *but* time."

"Did Mr. Tarte tell you why we wanted to speak to you?" she asked, holding her teacup between her hands. The tea had warmed the fragile china, and the heat felt good against her damp fingers.

"Something about your house—I must admit—I didn't particularly care. I enjoy visitors too much to turn any away, regardless of their reason for coming."

Charity exchanged a relieved smile with Edward. "I understand you knew my grandfather and grandmother?"

Mrs. Eggerton nodded, nearly upsetting her cup of tea. She lifted the cup with shaking fingers and took a small sip, her blue eyes watching them over the rim.

"Would you mind if I asked a few questions concerning them? You see, I never knew my grandmother, and well, I'm trying to understand what happened to her," Charity explained hesitantly. She hadn't expected it to be so difficult to broach the subject without betraying the fact that she knew her grandmother had been murdered.

She didn't want to shock Mrs. Eggerton or make her regret agreeing to see them.

"Lenore?" The wrinkles in Mrs. Eggerton's face grew deeper as she frowned. "She's gone."

"I know, Mrs. Eggerton." Charity glanced at Edward, but he was watching their hostess. "Do you remember when she disappeared?"

"Of course." She nodded so vigorously, her tea sloshed in its cup. "1799, wasn't it? Or was it 1798?" The grooves in her forehead tightened.

"1798," Charity said. "My grandfather was in Philadelphia, I believe."

"Yes, yes. I remember." Mrs. Eggerton nodded. "Philadelphia. So he was. My dear Mr. Stonewright liked to travel there. Friends or business—always something to take him away." She took another delicate sip.

"Do you know if my grandmother had any friends who visited her while my grandfather was gone?"

"Gone? Oh, yes, gone. Well, I visited Lenore—many times. We were friends, you know, and she was always so lonely."

"I'm glad she had your company, then." Charity leaned forward and touched Mrs. Eggerton's hands. "Did she have any others to rely upon? I had heard—"

Mrs. Eggerton's blue eyes flashed, and her thin mouth trembled. "I don't care what you heard—she loved Henry—they were devoted! He loved her so much he had a stroke when she disappeared! There was nothing any of us could do for him, *nothing*!" Her hands shook, and she clasped them together in her lap as her lips worked. Tears filmed her faded eyes, and then a single drop spilled over to drip down her cheek. "I never realized.... Well. That is what happened to the best of my recollection. It was so long ago."

Alarmed at her paleness, Charity got up and knelt by her chair to put an arm around her. Mrs. Eggerton felt even smaller and more fragile than she appeared, the bones of her shoulders as thin as a wren's.

"I'm sorry—I didn't mean to upset you." Charity caught Edward's concerned gaze. Should she tell her that Lenore hadn't really gone, hadn't run away without telling her?

Apparently divining the direction of her thoughts, Edward gave her a nod.

"Please don't be alarmed, Mrs. Eggerton, but I do have news," Charity said.

"News? Of Lenore?" Mrs. Eggerton wiped her cheek with one of her gnarled hands. "Tell me." She gave a small, harsh laugh. "I will not die just yet—tell me what you know."

"My grandmother—" She paused to glance at Edward, unsure how to relate the truth.

"We have discovered that Mrs. Stonewright never left Charleston," Edward said in a low voice.

"She is alive?" Mrs. Eggerton clutched the red blanket and stared at Edward.

"No, I'm afraid not," he replied. "She died. In 1798, we believe. Around the time she went missing."

One of her little hands covered Charity's left hand where it rested on the arm of her chair. Her fingers were warmer than Charity expected, and she gave her a reassuring smile.

"So you found her in the cellar. You do not believe your grandfather...?" Mrs. Eggerton rubbed her hand over Charity's fingers. "You can *not* believe that, my dear. He would never hurt her." She caught the edge of the blanket and drew it up over her chest as if feeling a draft. "How did she die? Could you tell what happened?"

"She was shot," Edward said.

Charity glanced at him, startled by his abrupt statement.

"Shot?" Mrs. Eggerton actually sounded pleased at the news. "Shot? Then that proves it. Your grandfather was afraid of weapons of that sort." She laughed and patted the blanket over her lap. "He was afraid it made him less of a man, but there it was. He refused to have any such weapons in his house. If your grandmother was shot, then someone else did it, my dear, not your grandfather. And he would have had to bring his weapon with him, for Henry never could abide the thought of firearms." She laughed again and shook her head. "He feared they would blow up and burn the house down. Such nonsense. Even *I* have firearms, though I doubt any of them can be safely used. It has been many years since I last saw them." A frown deepened her wrinkles, and she glanced at the door. "If they are still here and not stolen or sold. These servants..."

"I'm sure they are still here," Charity assured her, touching one of her small, fluttering hands.

"We found some letters, Mrs. Eggerton," Edward said. "Apparently, Mr. Stonewright thought someone in Charleston was annoying his wife. Did she ever mention anything to you about this?"

"Annoying her? *Annoying*?" Mrs. Eggerton laughed, her wrinkled hands clutching her blanket. "The question might be what did *not* annoy her, young man. I suppose even I annoyed her at times, though I was simply trying to alleviate her loneliness." Her gaze drifted to the fire, and she blinked sleepily.

Charity looked at Edward. He nodded, and she sat back in her chair before asking, "Do you remember a Mr. Cooper?"

"Cooper?" Mrs. Eggerton hid a yawn behind one hand. "Charles Cooper?"

"Yes. He wrote a letter to Mr. Tarte, stating that my grandfather sold his house to the Haywoods around that time. Do you remember anything about that?"

"That time?" Mrs. Eggerton looked at her, the corners of her mouth pulled down in confusion.

"Around the time my grandmother disappeared— before my grandfather left." Frustration made Charity's voice louder than she wanted, but Mrs. Eggerton didn't seem to notice.

The older lady nodded. For a moment, Charity thought she was falling asleep until she glanced over to Charity and said, "You must be mistaken."

"Mistaken?" Charity glanced at Edward.

He shook his head and lifted his broad shoulders.

"No, we are not mistaken. Why would you think so?" she asked.

"Why, he wasn't even here—in Charleston. He'd been gone at least a month before—to his estate in Georgia. Some problem—I can not remember precisely—but he was gone for six months, at least."

Charity's heart raced. So Charles Cooper couldn't have direct knowledge of such a sale, and more importantly, he couldn't have shot her grandmother. Her thoughts whirled.

If he didn't do it and her grandfather was afraid of firearms, then who had shot her?

"Did she have other visitors, then, around that time? What about Mr. Sloane and Mr. Harris?" Charity asked.

"Those two nitwits?" Mrs. Eggerton laughed again and picked up her teacup to take another sip. "I suppose they may have visited her, though they were more my friends than hers." She took another sip, her cloudy gaze fixed on Charity's face. "I was younger, you see." She giggled and placed her cup on the table beside her. "Though she was still beautiful, of course. She held back the hands of time well for a woman her age."

"Were either of them dark like Mr. Cooper?" Charity asked uncomfortably.

Mrs. Eggerton was blinking at the fire and appeared to be tiring quickly. She snuggled down further within the embrace of her armchair and tucked the blanket more firmly around her, as if settling in for a nap.

"Dark?" she repeated drowsily, her voice fading. She wriggled as if to wake herself and rubbed her eyes with the back of one hand. "They both wore wigs—old fashioned." She shrugged. "I could not say if they were fair or as dark as I was, once." She smiled at Charity. "Day and night—

that's what Henry once called Lenore and me. He was always a bit of a poet, was dear Henry, though Lenore was too sensible to pay his words much mind." She sighed and slumped again, staring at the fire.

"Perhaps we should go," Edward said in a soft voice. He looked at Charity as he placed his teacup on the silver tray.

Charity rose and went back to kneel next to Mrs. Eggerton. She pressed her palm over one of Mrs. Eggerton's small hands. "Thank you for allowing us to visit."

"You will come again?" Mrs. Eggerton's hand twisted under Charity's so she could give her fingers a squeeze. "I get so few visitors."

Charity smiled and gently clasped her hand. "Oh, yes. I will most assuredly return. Thank you."

Edward took her elbow and assisted her to stand, murmuring, "It was a pleasure to make your acquaintance, Mrs. Eggerton. Thank you for your time."

By the time they reached the wide doorway and Charity turned to glance back at Mrs. Eggerton, the older woman's chin was already resting on her chest. Her gnarled hands were relaxed on top of the blanket, and she was clearly napping.

The butler was waiting for them on a chair just outside the door, and he escorted them silently to the door.

The rain had stopped, and the sun was struggling to escape the embrace of thick banks of heavy, gray clouds. A chilly breeze rifled through the branches of a Live Oak standing at the corner, and the damp air carried the odors of wet dirt, horse dung, and the tang of salt from the ocean.

They departed in thoughtful silence, and they'd almost reached Oldwood before Edward glanced at her, his eyes dark and enigmatic.

"What are your thoughts?" he asked as he held the front door open and waited for her to enter in front of him.

"I don't know," she answered ruefully. Discovering what had happened to her grandmother seemed impossible. However, instead of discouraging her, she felt her determination to find the truth growing. "I feel as if we've taken a step back—I was so sure it was Mr. Cooper." She smiled at him. "At least we know one thing; my grandfather was not responsible."

He took her elbow and guided her into the sitting room. Glancing at him several times, she felt uncertainty fill her, making her stumble over the edge of the worn rug in the center of the room. She couldn't read the expression on his face, but a hardness in his square chin and a shadow in his eyes made her feel nervous. And a little afraid.

Had he come to a different conclusion?

She sat on the edge of a worn, brocade chair and clasped her hands in her lap.

Pacing to the window and back, he looked at her and then dragged one of the other chairs over to face her.

He sat down and leaned forward, resting his elbows on his knees and clasping his hands in front of him. "I need some time to consider matters." He straightened and sat back. Then he smiled at her. "However, we can resolve some questions in relatively short order. We have the wills your grandfather and father left, do we not?"

She nodded. The rhetorical question should have filled her with hope, but instead, her nervousness increased. Something loomed in front of her—something she didn't want to face.

Oldwood was hers, she was sure. But that fact didn't fill her with the joy she'd always anticipated. And she didn't want to examine why too closely.

"We shall have to review those to ascertain if all property was left in your favor, of course. However, I believe we can conclude that Oldwood does belong to you." His brown eyes grew darker before a flash of amusement lightened them. He grinned. "And if you are not too tired, we may be able to solve another mystery."

"Which mystery?" She eyed him suspiciously.

"The mystery of the Stonewright fortune." He stood and held out his hand.

She rose and grabbed his hand as she stumbled over her hem. "You found it?"

His grin widened. "Not yet, but I do have some notion of where we might look."

"Then lead on." Her lips trembled, but she managed to smile. "I am right behind you."

Chapter Twenty-One

The visit to Mrs. Eggerton left Edward thoughtful—too thoughtful to discuss the death of Lenore Stonewright with Charity. Since there was also the question of the Stonewright fortune, there was no better time to address that than now.

"Where is it? Where are we going?" Questions tumbled out of Charity's mouth as she clung to his hand with cold fingers.

He rubbed her hand before letting her go and opening the door to the servants' corridor. "The cellars."

"Cellars?" She halted abruptly and half-turned to stare at him. "We have already searched the cellars, as have Officer Carmichael and his men."

"Yes, but they never discovered the extent of the rooms down there." He smiled at her and gestured for her to move forward.

She increased her pace and was almost running when she entered the kitchen. Standing at the table, kneading dough, Mrs. Granger glanced up, scowled, and opened her mouth to order them out, but Charity waved at her and headed for the far corner.

Mrs. Granger's mouth snapped shut, and she glared at Edward in silence. She sniffed and pounded a fist into the dough before folding it over and kneading it roughly with flour-dusted hands, flicking angry glances at them for their unwanted intrusion into her domain.

He smiled at her and strode after Charity. Pausing at the sideboard, he picked up a lamp and lighted it from the coals in the stove with a bit of tinder. Then he followed Charity through the door and down the narrow wooden staircase to the cellars.

She stood in the center of the room, staring at the broken crockery and splintered remains of the shelves hiding the hidden passageway. When he joined her, she waved at the destruction. "Officer Carmichael knew it opened, why did he have to destroy everything?"

"I imagine it was faster than trying to figure out the trick," Edward commented dryly. He held the lamp aloft and strode past her to the opposite end of the shelving. "I should have realized when I found the first corridor that there might be another one." He grinned at her over his shoulder. "The measurements were all off."

She returned his smile, although it looked uncertain in the wavering light. Her eyes looked tired. "So there is another corridor? Another room?"

"Yes." He nodded and gripped the shelving to pull it away from the wall. It swung out smoothly. The hinges had been well-oiled by Kevin Stonewright to keep his movements secret. "Your cousin knew about it, and used it to hide the runaways he was assisting."

"But how did he know?" She edged over to him and peered around his shoulder into the space revealed behind the hidden door. Her hand gripped the sleeve of his jacket. "If he knew about this room, then..." She peered up at him, the corners of her mouth drooping. "Did he find the gold?"

"I can only speculate," he admitted. "However, it is worth searching, isn't it?"

"I suppose so." She sounded unsure and a little disappointed. She stepped back and looked at him. "Are you sure?"

"No," he answered cheerfully, edging around her to place his palm against her lower back. "However, we won't know until we look." He guided her forward, holding the lamp above them to light the way.

She entered the short hallway, and after an uncertain glance at him over her shoulder, she walked into the room where Toby, Nell, and their baby had stayed hidden.

When she stopped in the center of the room, he moved past her to the far wall. The lantern revealed the long, heavy planks of old wood that he'd noticed before. He ran his fingers over the cracks indicating the door the small group had escaped through. A knothole served as the doorknob. When he stuck his index finger into the hole, he was able to pull the door open, revealing a dank, narrow passageway beyond. The odor of damp earth was strong.

"What is that?" Charity asked. She stepped forward and peered past his shoulder into the darkness, her body pressing against his back.

"A passageway leading out." He shrugged. "I'm not sure where it goes."

"Is that where the gold is?" She stepped around him and halted a foot into the passageway.

"I don't think so." He drew her back into the room, closing the door. "Would you hold this, please?" He handed her the lamp.

She grimaced, but accepted the lamp and held it up. "If it's not in there, then where is it? Why do you think it's here?"

"Just a hunch." He ran his hands over the wooden wall.

The rough planks had many knotholes and gaps, making it difficult to determine if there was another door or compartment hidden behind it. He poked and pried until he reached the dirt floor and then sat back on his heels, studying the barrier.

As soon as he'd seen his sister slip through the hidden door, he'd been sure that the wooden wall hid other secrets as well.

Had he been wrong?

Charity placed the lamp on the floor behind him and began rapping on the wood. Years of dampness had rotted some sections, and her knocking thudded mushily in those areas. A few dislodged pieces fell to the dirt floor in a shower of splinters.

She stepped back, as well, a frown of disappointment flickering over her beautiful face. "Nothing. So it isn't here, either."

"Perhaps." He stood and dusted his hands off on his thighs. He moved forward to examine the area nearest the wall where the wood was darker and disintegrating badly.

He pulled out a knife and probed the blackest portion where Charity's raps had dislodged some of the wood. An old, rusted hinge fell to the ground at his feet. Above that, his knife met only more wood. But below it, he felt the bite of metal upon metal. Another hinge.

Yanking out large chunks of rotten planking revealed a large space in the wall, lined with bricks.

"Charity, perhaps you would like to step over here while I hold the lamp." He moved back and picked up the light, holding it at shoulder height.

Charity chewed on her lower lip and moved forward. She wiped her nervous fingers against the black skirt of her dress before she slipped her hands into the exposed hollow.

"I feel something!" she exclaimed. She cast an excited glance over her shoulder. "It's square—wood and metal!" She struggled for a minute, twisting this way and that before she stepped back. "I can't shift it. Can you bring it out?"

He handed her the lamp and stepped over to the wall. Sure enough, wedged inside was what felt like a wooden box, the corners reinforced with metal. He could feel the sharp edges and round heads of the nails holding the box together. Hands on either edge of the side facing him, he tried to pull it out. It was firmly wedged in place. Moving around for better leverage, he squeezed his right arm into the small gap between the box and the wall and shoved the container against the opposite side.

There was no sense of movement. Taking a deep breath, he leaned against the wall and shoved again. This time, the box shifted. He gripped it with both hands and yanked, finally pulling it free from the small space.

"You found it!" Charity exclaimed. The lamp's light wavered in crazy beams against the walls, and she placed the lamp on the floor before she moved closer to him.

He placed the chest next to the lamp and stood back. The golden light revealed a chest about twenty-four inches long, with a rounded lid reinforced with metal strips. The remains of two leather handles were nailed to each side, but the leather had rotted long ago, just leaving a few crumbling bits affixed to the chest with rusted nails. An old, corroded lock hung from a hasp at the front.

"Can you open it?" Charity knelt beside it and brushed her hands over the rounded lid and lock.

The metal was so rusted it hardly presented any difficulty at all when he slid his knife under the metal hasp and pried the mess away from the chest. The entire assemblage, including the still-closed lock, fell into the dirt at their feet.

Charity took a deep breath, her hands clasped in her lap as if she were too nervous to open it.

"Go ahead," he said, placing a hand on her warm shoulder.

"What if it's empty, after all?" she whispered.

"You won't know until you open it." He gave her shoulder a reassuring squeeze.

With trembling hands, she lifted the lid.

At first glance, there appeared to be nothing inside but clumps of dirt, and he felt a sudden stab of disappointment. He'd so wanted to give Charity something that she could accept without feeling a slight to her dignity and independence. But as he watched, she reached out and touched one of the lumps. The brown crumbled away under her fingers—dry, old leather. Then, amidst the dirt-colored flakes, came a golden gleam.

She picked up one of the coins and rubbed away the bits of moldering leather. Holding it up, she looked at Edward.

A Spanish doubloon.

"You appear to be a very wealthy woman, Miss Stonewright," he said, a crooked smile twisting his lips. "Congratulations."

"Wealthy," she whispered. A breathy giggle escaped her. She dug into the box, brushing away the old leather to reveal several small piles of the gold coins.

"Well," he said, brushing off his hands once again on his trousers. "You now have Oldwood and the means to maintain it."

"Once you and Mr. Tarte review the wills and title," Charity reminded him quickly, although her gaze was still fixed on the contents of the box.

"A minor matter that can be completed within a few days," he said heavily. He strode to the door. "I will borrow a bowl from Mrs. Granger. That chest is too rotten to hold the coins."

"Wait!" She glanced up at him. Her eyes were shadowed in the flickering light, but she looked pale. Troubled.

Looking over his shoulder at her, he raised a brow instead of striding back and sweeping her into his arms as he longed to do.

"I—" She broke off. Her hands twisted in her lap as she stared down again at the gleaming gold.

"We can discuss it upstairs," he replied gently as he returned to help her to her feet.

A laugh choked her. She placed her hand over her mouth, her gaze moving from his face to the box of gold at her feet. "I never expected to find it." Another short, sharp laugh escaped her. "Wishful thinking—it is so odd to think it was here all the time, and my grandfather never knew where."

"Yes." He smiled, his gaze running over her beautiful face. "Well, the Stonewright fortune has been restored at last, and you no longer need worry. Let me get that bowl— you can adjust to your new position as a wealthy heiress after we return upstairs." He gave one of her hands a squeeze before he turned and walked away into the darkness.

Chapter Twenty-Two

Staring down at the crumbling leather fragments scattered over small piles of gold, Charity felt something akin to revulsion. *A wealthy heiress...* Edward's words burned like hot ash from a fire.

He could leave now without worrying about his promise to ensure she had a home. There was no reason for him to stay, no reason for concern about her or her future.

But she *wanted* him to stay. She kicked the side of the box, cracking the old wood. A few slivers fell onto the dirt floor. She ought to be ecstatic, not filled with despair.

A nasty little voice whispered that the gold might tempt Edward to stay. Every man wanted a rich heiress for a bride, didn't he? There was more than enough here to tempt any man.

The ugly thought sickened her.

How contrary she was. Before she found the gold, she feared that Edward was only kind to her because he viewed her as a destitute woman in need of his assistance. Now, she was worried that he might only be interested in her—if he showed any interest at all—because she was wealthy. Why could she not be pleased and confident that if he showed affection, it was because he admired her for herself? Why was the state of her finances so important?

She rubbed the spot between her brows and nudged the box again with the toe of her boot. When one had grown up straining to find sufficient funds to clothe oneself decently and put food in the larder, one tended to place a great deal of importance on wealth. In fact, the state of one's finances was the single most important quality that determined one's social status and even attractiveness.

Homely girls were never really homely if they were wealthy.

But Edward had never seemed to place a great deal of importance on such things, her heart wailed. However, she'd be a naïve fool to assume he would discount it entirely. He'd seemed to find her attractive—she flushed thinking about his one tender kiss and her longing for another—but she couldn't help thinking that he might show even more interest in her now.

She might desperately want that interest, but she was too proud to accept it if his interest were tainted with avarice. He had never struck her as an acquisitive man, but most men in his position knew it was their duty to marry well for the sake of their family and social position. Very few would choose a poor girl over a rich one.

A dull ache thrummed in her temples, and she rubbed her eyes. The dank smell of wet earth, rotting wood, and the faint smoke from the lamp made her feel as if she were suffocating.

She felt irritated and confused. Rich or poor, she loved Edward Archer. She wanted to see the warmth of love in his brown eyes and know that he wanted her for herself, not because she was either so poor that she needed his assistance, or so rich that she was appropriate as a potential wife.

She wanted him to love her for herself alone.

If that were even possible.

"Here we are," Edward said, striding into the dingy room. He held out a large wooden bowl. "Mrs. Granger was none too happy to have any of her cookware leave her kitchen, but Janet overruled her and thought this might do."

She took the bowl and knelt, filling it with the coins from the chest. At the very bottom were three silk bags. When she tried to pick up one of them, the fabric ripped, releasing a cascade of stones that flashed green, blue, and gold in the shifting light. *Jewels*. She picked up a handful and held them closer to the light.

"What are those?" Edward asked, squatting next to her.

"I don't know. Jewels, I suppose." She prodded the stones in the palm of her hand. Some were cut into rectangles, but most were uncut rocks that glowed dully when held up to the flame of the lamp.

"May I?" he asked.

She nodded.

His long fingers sorted through the stones at the bottom of the chest and selected several samples. After examining them, a boyish grin crooked his mouth. "You are fortunate, indeed. If I am not mistaken, you have several excellent emeralds here, as well as aquamarine, topaz, amethyst, and a few other gems. A treasure, indeed."

She let the stones in her hand dribble through her fingers into the bowl. "Yes. Fortunate."

His curiosity made her hate the stones. A hot pulse of anger flashed through her, and her jaw tightened.

Then deflating, she sighed and brushed the back of her hand over her forehead to push an errant curl away. When she looked up, Edward was studying her with an intensity that made her pulse race. She stilled for a moment, and then forced herself to look away.

"You don't sound pleased—is there something wrong?"

"No. What could possibly be wrong?" She shook her head, took another breath, and began moving the remaining jewels from the chest into the bowl.

"Come, let us return upstairs and have some tea. You must be exhausted, though you hide it well." He dug into the pile of jewels and began transferring them by the handful to the wooden bowl.

"Thank you," she replied dryly, aware that her black dress was still damp, and she most likely had smudges of dirt on her face. No wonder Edward had been staring at her so intently. She probably looked like some poor, homeless waif, dressed in rags.

Except that she wasn't. She was a rich woman, as he had reminded her several times already.

They soon emptied the chest, and Edward picked up the bowl before helping her to her feet. She lifted the lamp and moved ahead of him, lighting their way up the creaking wooden stairs.

In the kitchen, Mrs. Granger was bending over the stove, staring into a pot as she stirred something. They managed to slip into the room without earning more than a sidelong glance and a grunt from her. Charity blew out the lamp and replaced it on the sideboard.

"Miss Stonewright is in need of refreshment, Mrs. Granger," Edward stated as she moved through the doorway to the servants' hall. "Please send a tea tray to the sitting room."

"I'll bring it," Janet replied as she came into the kitchen from the pantry. "We got us some of them cakes Miss Charity likes, fresh from the oven."

"Perfect," Edward said.

When Charity glanced over her shoulder, Edward grinned and gave her a wink. An answering tingle sizzled down into her belly, and she smiled before hurrying down the corridor to the sitting room.

Placing the bowl of riches on a narrow table against the wall, Edward caught her gaze. "Are you sure you are well?" He frowned. "Did you catch a chill in the rain?"

"I am not so weak as all that." She forced a laugh and gestured to the chairs by the fireplace. "Would you care to sit? I'm sure Janet will be here with the tea at any moment."

He strode over and knelt in front of the fireplace, filling the gaps between the logs with tinder and using a phosphorous box to start a fire. The flames were slow to catch, and he prodded the smallest sticks until the red and gold fire took hold. Charity watched the play of his muscles under his jacket, wishing it didn't hurt so much just to be near him, knowing he would be gone soon.

By the time he stood, wiping his hands on his trousers, Janet had entered the room.

She set the tea tray next to the chair where Charity was sitting and curtseyed. "Do you need anything else, Miss Charity?"

"No. Thank you, Janet." Charity fluffed her skirts out to let them dry faster in the warmth radiating from the fireplace and tried to appear placid—content with her lot in life.

After the maid left, Edward sat down in the chair opposite hers and studied her face. "Are you still worried about your grandmother's fate?"

"Grandmother?" She glanced up from the task of pouring their cups of tea.

"Or is it simply the surprise of finding your inheritance at last?" He leaned forward and placed a warm hand briefly over hers. "Something is worrying you."

She smiled and handed him a cup before pouring cream and adding a spoonful of sugar to her tea. Delay failed to help her find the words she was seeking. "So much has happened so quickly." She paused and took a sip, grateful for the warmth of the drink. "I am still astonished, I suppose, by it all."

He nodded. "It will take a while to accustom yourself to it." He sipped his tea thoughtfully. After a moment, he placed his cup and saucer on the table and gazed at her, his brows wrinkling. "What was your impression of Mrs. Eggerton?"

"Mrs. Eggerton?" She looked at him, surprised by the question. "I liked her—she seemed very sweet." Charity sighed and set her cup down. "I just wish she hadn't torn all our nice, neat theories asunder."

"Yes," Edward said. "However, it was an enlightening interview."

"Enlightening?"

He nodded. "I wonder if she realized...."

"Realized what?"

"Realized what she was saying—or admitting." He gazed at her, his brown eyes darkening. "Or hadn't you noticed?"

"Noticed what?" she asked impatiently. "Speak plainly—what is it you believe she admitted?"

"We did not say where we found your grandmother, did we?" He countered her question with one of his own.

Irritation flashed through Charity, but she took a deep breath and tried to remember their conversation. She couldn't remember precisely. However, she knew she hadn't mentioned where they'd found her grandmother's body. She shook her head.

"And yet she knew where your grandmother was." He leaned forward. "She could only have known that if she had something to do with her death."

"But—she was my grandmother's friend! Why would she do anything to harm her?"

Concern puckered Edward's brow and tightened his mouth. He studied her as if weighing his choice of words. "I believe she was more your grandfather's friend than your grandmother's. That hair I found—it was quite long." His lips twisted. "I am loath to say this, but men, particularly men who wore wigs at that time, often had very short hair. Some shaved their heads, in fact. And women, well, I'm sure you know that some women will pull the hair of their opponent in a fight."

"Are you insinuating that my grandmother was the sort who would indulge in a low fight and pull hair?"

"If she were fighting for her life—yes. I'm sorry, Charity."

"You believe Mrs. Eggerton fought with my grandmother and shot her out of jealousy over my *grandfather*?" The very notion was ludicrous.

"Your grandfather, or the treasure. It seems that the Stonewright fortune was a secret that was shared by a greater proportion of the Charleston populace than you realized. She may have persuaded your grandmother to search for it, argued with her, and..." He shrugged and leaned back, his gaze fixed on her face.

"I can't believe it!" She was staggered by the suggestion. How could tiny Mrs. Eggerton have done such an evil thing? And yet, when she considered it, several of

Mrs. Eggerton's statements showed a knowledge that she would not have had if she were completely innocent.

With shaking hands, Charity refilled her cup of tea and took a sip, trying to make sense of her whirling thoughts.

"I'm afraid her comments got us as close to the truth as we are likely to come at this late date," Edward said at last. "I am sorry. For what it is worth, I also liked her. She had a great deal of charm."

She sipped her tea and offered him the plate of cakes before taking one herself. Eating granted her time to consider his words and review their visit to Mrs. Eggerton. Small snatches of their conversation suddenly changed, growing darker with hidden meaning.

"I don't know," she said, feeling wretched. "It is so terrible to think about it."

"And terrible to live with," Edward commented. "She has kept that secret for a very long time. Her words may have been a sort of confession—she may have been unburdening herself at last."

Charity lifted her head. "Then we must visit her again. I want to ask her directly. If it is weighing on her conscience, she may admit it."

"Perhaps." He took a bite of the sweet almond cake and wiped his lips with a napkin.

"We should go tomorrow," she said with sudden decisiveness. "I want to know. If you are correct, she will surely say so."

"And what then?" he asked in a gentle voice.

She shrugged. The almond cake seemed dry and crumbly in her mouth, and she had to take a sip of tea to choke it down. "I just want to *know*. I don't wish to have her arrested—she has so little time left—and we've already given my grandmother a decent funeral. Is it so terrible to simply want to know?"

"No." He smiled, and she felt her heart expand joyfully in her chest from the understanding in his eyes.

Her gaze roved over his features, dwelling on the thick, black lashes surrounding his deep brown eyes, the strength of his square chin, and the dark shadow of the stubble already starting to grow back, although it was barely four in the afternoon.

"Will you go with me?"

"Of course." A thoughtful frown crumpled his brow. "However, I do have another task to complete. I must see Mr. Tarte again regarding a small matter." His gaze caught hers, and he smiled with easy, warm charm. "A debt that must be paid to ensure there will be no issues with your cousin's abrupt departure from Charleston. Once I have placed the issue in Mr. Tarte's capable hands, I will return, and we can visit Mrs. Eggerton again."

The words had barely left his mouth before Mrs. Maplethorpe sailed into the room, Nodcock trotting along after her. "Janet said there was tea...." Her gaze fastened on the tray at Charity's elbow.

Nodcock meowed, rubbed against one of the table's legs, and jumped into Edward's lap. Edward absently scratched his head and massaged the cat's tattered ear as the cat made biscuits on his knee and purred loudly.

"Join us," Charity said, waving to a nearby chair.

Mrs. Maplethorpe pulled the chair closer to the fire and held out a hand, waiting patiently for Charity to pour a cup of tea and hand it to her. "That is quite an interesting bowl of odds and ends over there, is it not?" she asked in an elaborately innocent voice. She watched Charity with twinkling eyes as she accepted her cup and took a sip.

Charity exchanged glances with Edward and let out a long sigh. "Yes. The Stonewright fortune has been found at last."

"Indeed. So I had assumed." Mrs. Maplethorpe nodded, an annoyingly placid look on her face as if it was exactly what she had expected. "That should make matters much more comfortable. You should be very pleased." She smiled and raised a plump hand to touch a bit of lace at her neck. "You are an heiress, now. I'm sure the best of Charleston Society will be delighted to invite you to wonderful events—balls, soirees; oh, it shall all be very exciting."

"Yes, I suppose so," Charity said. The thought of attending the social functions that apparently thrilled Mrs. Maplethorpe just made her feel very tired. She caught Edward's gaze and thought she saw a flash of sympathy in his eyes.

He wouldn't be there, though, to suffer with her. And eventually, she'd have to settle on someone. Make the best of it. Pretend to be a good wife. The gray, dull future she saw ahead made her feel as if she were gasping for breath under the grinding weight of a millstone.

Mrs. Maplethorpe gave her a sharp glance. "You shall be invited everywhere, my dear. The Stonewrights have always been a very respectable family." She clasped her hands with evident satisfaction in her lap. "Never fear, my dear, by this time next year, your biggest problem will be deciding which offer you wish to accept."

She glanced at Edward, but he was gazing out the window, his expression unreadable. The rain had started again, pattering against the panes and smearing the glass with rivulets of chilly water. Did the weather remind him of England? Home? A touch of longing seemed to pass over his features, making the corners of his mouth turn down ever so slightly, barely perceptible to anyone who wasn't so aware of him.

Did he miss his friends? His family?

Her hands twisted so tightly together that her fingers ached. Loneliness had been her only companion for so long that she recognized it easily in others, or so she thought. She'd grown accustomed to it, but it must be new to Edward. With his sister gone, he must be aching to return home and be done with the irritating mess the duchess had handed him.

The sense of an ending, of an unwanted change, seemed to linger in the damp air like an icy mist. Even the crackling flames of gold and red in the hearth couldn't dispel her black mood.

"Oh, Mr. Archer!" Janet called, rushing into the room. She glanced around, flustered, one hand holding the cap on her head and the other waving a piece of paper. "I's sorry—I forgot—but I just got this here note! It be for you!" She handed the folded missive to Edward, her hand quivering with excitement.

"For me?" He turned the paper over in his hand and looked at the maid. "Who is it from?"

"I doesn't know—it was give me by the boy as runs errands for the butcher." Her gaze flew from Edward to Charity. "Sorry." She bobbed a curtsy.

"That's fine—thank you." He glanced up at her. "Is the boy still here?"

"No, sir." She shook her head.

A look of disappointment flashed over his face, but he thanked her again and dismissed her before unfolding the note. His brow wrinkled as he read the contents. Then he looked up, his gaze locking on Charity. "They are safe—thank God!"

"Lady Hildegard and Kevin?" Charity asked, sitting on the edge of her chair. Her fingers gripped the cup and saucer in her hands.

He nodded and read, "*Dear Edward, It is difficult to write as we are traveling quite rapidly. I wish I could describe to you what I have seen for you would be quite astounded. The countryside is vast and beautiful, and we are well away from the city now. There are such wonders to behold—you would never believe one tenth of it. As you may guess from my note, we are all safe, and baby Henry travels very well. He is such a dear; I love the little boy so much I wish he were mine and hold him as often as Nell will allow.*

"*Please do not fear for us; my dearest Mr. Stonewright guards us as fiercely as a lion and never falters. I miss you already and will write again when the next opportunity presents itself. Your dearest sister, Hildie.*"

"Oh, Edward!" Charity pressed her hand against her pounding heart. They were *safe*. Relief made her giddy. "I'm so glad!"

Mrs. Maplethorpe nodded and sipped her tea.

"Yes." Edward's eyes burned rich brown as he looked at Charity. "I am relieved they are doing so well."

"She is safe with my cousin—he has traveled a great deal," she said when the brief joy in his face dimmed.

He nodded. "Yes."

"But you miss her," Charity murmured. "I'm sorry."

"She made her choice," he replied heavily, holding out his empty cup for her to refill. "I simply wish—" he broke off and shrugged.

"You wish she hadn't gone so abruptly," Mrs. Maplethorpe finished for him. "It is natural, but these little fledglings must learn to fly at some point or another."

"Yes," he whispered as he accepted his refilled cup from Charity.

Mrs. Maplethorpe studied him for a moment before she said, "Well, I'm sure Mr. Archer has business to attend to, Miss Stonewright. We can't sit here all afternoon chatting about the weather." She placed her hands on the arms of the chair to assist her in rising to her feet, then waved at the doorway. "And I have been working on the last of the cerulean silk. I have not decided which lace to use. You must decide. Will you join me?"

Another ball gown. Why did she need yet another pale blue gown?

To go to all those balls.... The words whispered through her mind in Mrs. Maplethorpe's disgustingly pleased voice.

She flicked an uncertain glance at Edward, but his face was shuttered. She forced a smile and stood. "Will you excuse us, Mr. Archer?"

Standing, Edward nodded and gave her a distracted smile. "Of course. Until dinner."

Though it took an effort, she nodded and followed Mrs. Maplethorpe out of the sitting room. Her back straightened as she climbed the staircase.

They still had a few days, and she would make the most of the time. A few moments she was sure to treasure in the long years ahead of her.

Chapter Twenty-Three

"My client wishes the matter to remain private, so I am relying on your discretion, Mr. Tarte," Edward said as he placed a heavy leather purse in the center of the lawyer's desk blotter.

"Of course," Tarte frowned and poked at the bag with one finger, looking for all the world like a small boy prodding a possibly venomous snake. "However, it is a trifle unusual, is it not?"

"Perhaps." Edward shrugged. "It is a distasteful transaction, and I have no wish to involve myself any further. You may take two percent of the purse for your troubles. Another two percent goes to Officer Carmichael as a finder's fee, and the remaining goes to a Mr. Farnham. For his, em, *property*. Is that understood?" Edward stood, wanting nothing more to do with a transaction that was an abomination and offended every moral scruple he possessed. Simply talking about it made him feel tainted.

"But Mr. Farnham—"

"I trust you to handle it. And I believe we have determined that Miss Stonewright is the owner of Oldwood. There, too, I leave you to prepare the appropriate paperwork to support that conclusion. Is there anything else?"

Mr. Tarte gaped at him, his eyes blinking. He pushed his glasses up to the bridge of his nose and stood abruptly, holding out his hand. "Of course, yes—that is—no. There is nothing else. You can rely on me, Mr. Archer."

"I hope so." Edward shook his hand and turned abruptly on his heel.

Much as he disliked it, the money should ensure the safety of his sister and her friends. This was the last thing he could do for her.

The thought filled him again with anger born of his frustration and worry. Hildie should never have come here. *He* should have kept her away from such terrible things as the abomination of slavery and unjust laws. His hands fisted at his sides before he deliberately relaxed them and increased his pace. Charity was waiting for him, and at least he could still assist her to find peace.

When he arrived at Oldwood, she was already waiting for him in the sitting room. Her pale face and the dark circles under her eyes revealed her anxiety, and she sprang to her feet when he walked into the room.

"Are you ready to go?" she asked, picking up the thick shawl she'd draped over the arm of her chair. "Or would you like a cup of tea, first?"

He smiled reassuringly. "I am quite ready." He replaced his hat and bent around her to open the front door. "There is nothing to worry about, Charity."

"I know." She looked up at him with a shy, sideways glance and gave the ghost of a laugh. "We already know the truth, I suppose." She slipped her hand around his elbow. "I almost wish we are wrong, though."

"To be honest, so do I."

Charity seemed lost in thought, so they walked in silence the rest of the way to Mrs. Eggerton's house. The butler opened the door and asked them to wait in the hallway, his impassive face revealing nothing, except perhaps his boredom.

The tight grip on his elbow revealed to Edward that Charity was increasingly nervous. He patted her hand and smiled at her.

"We were just here yesterday—perhaps we are taxing her far too much," Charity whispered.

"If we were, I'm sure her butler would let us know." He laid his free hand over her fingers and pressed them reassuringly.

"If you will follow me?" The butler bowed and waved them toward the same sitting room where Mrs. Eggerton had received them the day before.

The room had not changed, and neither had she. Mrs. Eggerton was propped up in the same wing chair in front of the fire, with her red blanket draped over her knees. Her tiny feet were propped up on a footstool, and she gripped the hem of the blanket in her gnarled hands.

She turned her head toward them and studied them with faded blue eyes. Her head bobbed forward in a sharp nod, and she waved one hand to the two chairs opposite hers. "So you know. Well, sit. Anthony will bring the tea."

"I'm sorry to disturb you again so soon," Charity said as she moved around the low maple table at the older woman's elbow.

"Sit, please." She waved again at the blue brocade wing chair.

Gaze fixed upon Mrs. Eggerton, Charity sat on the edge of her seat, her hands clasped tightly in her lap. Edward took the seat next to her, his glance going from Mrs. Eggerton to Charity and back. The tension between the two women felt like the suffocating stillness in the air when the sky turns yellowish-green before a storm.

Silence reigned until the butler deposited the tea tray on the maple table at Mrs. Eggerton's elbow and left, closing the double doors behind him.

At a gesture from their hostess, Charity leaned over and prepared the tea, pouring each of them a cup.

"You must have questions. What do you wish to know?" Mrs. Eggerton asked. She took a sip from her cup and peered at them over the gold-edged rim.

"What happened?" Charity blurted out. She paled and straightened, holding her cup in her lap with white-knuckled fingers. "How did you know we found my grandmother in the cellar? What *happened* to her?"

Mrs. Eggerton gave them a small smile. "I should think that would be obvious."

"She had brown hair in her hand. I assume that was yours?" Edward asked.

"Lenore had a temper, and she liked to pull hair." Mrs. Eggerton nodded. "Yes, I suppose it was mine."

"You shot her?" Charity asked. Her cup rattled against the saucer in her hands.

Mrs. Eggerton's gaze fixed on her. "Shot her? I see." She took another, longer sip.

"Perhaps we should start from the beginning. What were you and Mrs. Stonewright arguing about?" Edward asked.

"The same old thing." She smiled and shook her head. "Henry, of course."

Charity stared at her. "But you were—"

"Old? Do you believe the middle-aged and elderly lack feelings? Don't feel love?"

"No, of course not," Charity hastened to say. Some of the milky tea in her cup sloshed over onto the saucer. She bent forward to place the cup on the tray and wiped her handkerchief over the skirt of her brown walking dress.

"Lenore was a jealous woman—very jealous. And greedy." She eyed Charity with a malicious light flickering in her eyes. "Somehow, she'd wormed the story of the Stonewright fortune out of your grandfather. She was determined to find it while he was gone. Then she hoped to leave without anyone the wiser."

Edward caught Charity's gaze. Her face grew pale, and her eyes seemed to plead with him to contradict Mrs. Eggerton's words.

"I have some letters from Henry and Lenore—it appears they loved each other very much," he said in a low voice.

Mrs. Eggerton chuckled. "So it would appear. Henry certainly seemed to love her—he babbled to her about the fortune after all, didn't he? Revealed all his family's secrets, the old fool."

"Are you saying she didn't return his love?" he asked.

"She certainly loved the family name, and their supposed fortune. Henry was a handsome man, as well— so Lenore had a great deal to love."

"Her letters—everyone said she admired him," Charity said. Her voice shook, and she glanced from Edward to Mrs. Eggerton. "She *must* have loved him."

"Perhaps she did." Mrs. Eggerton shrugged.

"So what happened in the cellar that day?" Edward asked.

"Henry had written that he was on his way home. She didn't have much time, if she wanted to find the gold first. When I came to visit, I found her down in the cellar, searching. There was a hidden room." She set her empty tea cup on the table next to her and pulled the red blanket up more securely around her. "Well, you found her, so you know all about that." Laughing, she shook her head. "She was so sure the treasure was there. She'd even managed to open the door to a small room at the end of a tunnel. Hideous place. It smelled of the grave, even before... Well. She was not pleased when she saw me. Accused me of spying for Henry, ruining her surprise." Mrs. Eggerton waved her hands in a vague gesture. "I told her *someone* had to protect his interests. I suppose I shouldn't have said that—I knew she had a temper—and she attacked me. Pulled my hair—you discovered that much."

"But what happened? Why would you bring a pistol with you? Why did you shoot her?"

"*I* didn't."

"What?" Charity leaned forward, staring at Mrs. Eggerton.

"I told you, Henry was on his way home—"

"My grandfather *loved* his wife. He would never have shot her! He was afraid of firearms, you said so yourself!"

"Yes, he loved her, and he was afraid of firearms. But his son wasn't. And he'd been out with his friends, shooting. I suppose when he came in, he saw that his father had just arrived home, and he didn't want to be seen with his pistol, so Bart came in through the kitchen. I suppose he wanted time to hide his weapon in the cellar before his father discovered him. For whatever reason, he came down the stairs to the cellar and heard us fighting. His mother had a knife with her—I suppose she used it for testing the walls—and he came down the corridor." A strange, coquettish look crossed her face. "She stabbed me, sliced my shoulder clean through." She studied Charity. "I

257

can show you the scar, if you wish. It was quite painful. In any event, he tried to stop her, but he couldn't. So he shot her."

"My *father*? I don't believe you—what a horrid thing to say! He would never shoot his own mother—you're lying!"

"Are you sure? Even if she was trying to murder someone? No matter what she was doing?" Mrs. Eggerton smiled bitterly, her gnarled hands brushing the soft blanket over her lap. "Bart was a lovely boy, so loving...." She sighed. "And I was still attractive." She laughed at the appalled look growing on Charity's face. "You don't believe me, do you? Oh, I loved Henry, too, but he would have none of me—too besotted with his dear Lenore. But lovely, delectable Bart—he looked so much like Henry when he was young."

Charity leapt to her feet, her hands fisted at her sides. She leaned over Mrs. Eggerton, her face flushed with anger. "How *dare* you! I refuse to believe my father would do such a thing! You're lying—you have to be!"

"No. I'm sorry, Miss Stonewright, but your father was as besotted with me as his father was with your mother. I doubt he truly realized what he was doing until..." Her hands shook as she smoothed the blanket repeatedly. "He was horrified when he realized—well, you can imagine. We had to hide her there; we could not move her with Henry upstairs. Fortunately, no one heard the shot—the thick walls took care of that. We did what we had to do. Bart ran out—I don't know where he went—and he got rid of his pistol. I slipped out the kitchen door, as well, after I managed to shut the hidden door. Never saw any of them again. I heard later that Henry had had a stroke, and the whole family went to Philadelphia." She chewed on her bottom lip as she stared at the fire beyond Charity.

"I can't—I can't believe you...." Charity hid her face in her hands.

Edward rose and put an arm around her, holding her against his chest as he gazed down at Mrs. Eggerton. "From the position of the shot—"

"You believe I shot her." Mrs. Eggerton nodded. "I am sorry for the girl, having to hear this, but it is the truth. I was trying to get away. Lenore had raised her arm to strike again, half-turned toward Bart. He shot her, not I. I did not carry a pistol with me for a social call, even when I was young and silly." She rubbed a shaking hand over her wrinkled face, every one of her years painted in the bruised circles under her eyes and gray lines. She leaned back and closed her eyes. "It is such a relief to tell someone—all these years—it has been a terrible burden. No matter what you think of me, I was filled with grief for Bart—to kill your own mother—how horrible! I was not surprised when he could not return. I could not have done so, myself. I never set foot in that house again—not after that." Her shoulders shook with a shiver, and when she peered at Charity, her eyes glittered with tears. "I—I heard it was haunted. Do you think...? Is it Lenore?"

"No. Superstitious nonsense." Tightening his arm around Charity, Edward shook his head.

There were other reasons for the noises at Oldwood, other horrors and causes for fear.

Pride welled within him as he remembered his sister's glowing face. His chest tightened. Hildie had been braver than he ever realized and far more mature. She'd done something to end the terror for two people and a newborn babe, and he couldn't think of her now without a sense of awe and the hope that she was happy on her journey to Erie.

At least her note said they were safe. And she'd sounded happy.

A strange, gasping noise came from Mrs. Eggerton, and he realized it was laughter.

"Superstitious," she gasped. "Perhaps so. But at least she will rest easy now, and it is done. What will you do?"

"Do?" Charity stared at her, her cheeks wet and her face pale.

"Will you stay, or run away to Philadelphia like your father?"

Edward felt her stiffen beside him, and she took a step away. Cold air filled the space between them.

"I will stay, of course. This is my home," Charity said.

The firmness in her voice twisted like a knife in his gut. He'd known all along that Charleston was Charity's home, just as London was his. It had always been unlikely that she would leave. It should not have come as a surprise to hear her state it so unequivocally.

The chill seeped into him, hardening to brittle ice.

He had a purpose, and that purpose was almost complete. A few days—no more—and he would be gone.

And Charity would have her home, here.

It was over.

Chapter Twenty-Four

A cold distance surrounded Edward—Charity was aware of it—but her attention was fixed on the tiny figure of Mrs. Eggerton. Her mind whirled over what the old lady had admitted.

Is it true? My father killed my grandmother? How could he? A small, painful wail tore through her mind.

He couldn't have done it, and yet she was sure he had. She couldn't forget how prematurely old he'd seemed, how distant—with bowed shoulders and a faraway, fearful look in his eyes. *Guilt.* He'd spent so much time in the graveyard—she assumed it was his grief over her mother's death. But she realized now that he'd gone there to unburden himself to the only person he could safely tell, his dead wife.

Unfortunately, the dead couldn't grant forgiveness or ease a troubled conscience.

Disappointment, anger, and pity roiled within her. Her father's behavior showed he'd cared deeply about his mother and what had happened. He must have been horrified at what had occurred, and his part in it had been a source of terrible pain to him until the day he died. He had not been without conscience, then.

The thought lessoned her anger at him, both for his part in killing his mother and for keeping it a secret from her, his own daughter. He should have told her—he should have said something instead of falling into such a deep silence that there were days he hardly seemed to do more than grunt in response to her questions.

A snapping sound from the fireplace interrupted her thoughts. She glanced over to see a shower of sparks and fresh burst of flames. When she looked up, Edward and Mrs. Eggerton were both watching her.

"I'm sorry—it is ... difficult," she said. She rubbed her temple. "Perhaps we should go."

"You will return?" Mrs. Eggerton studied her. "I have so few visitors these days. I'm sorry about your grandmother, but that is in the past, now. You must forget."

Charity nodded and flicked a glance at Edward. His handsome face softened momentarily as he said, "Thank you for allowing us to visit."

"Come back?" Mrs. Eggerton's gnarled hands gripped the arms of her chair.

"Yes. In a few days," Charity agreed, hoping it didn't sound like a lie. "Perhaps next week."

Mrs. Eggerton slumped in her chair and fixed her gaze on the cheerfully burning fire. Her thin mouth disappeared in a mass of tightening wrinkles. "You won't come. Well, I can not blame you." She sighed and shrugged, her hands running over the chair arms repeatedly. "You dislike me—I knew this would happen— but it had to be said. You had to know. *Someone* had to know. I couldn't die without telling someone."

On impulse, Charity leaned over and patted one of her small hands. The skin felt dry and papery under her palm. "Thank you for telling me. I do appreciate your honesty."

"Honesty?" Mrs. Eggerton laughed and shook her head. "Yes, well, what else could you say? I'm tired now, and you must leave."

"Goodbye," Charity said, a sudden sadness washing over her.

She'd never see Mrs. Eggerton again—she knew it as surely as she knew what day it was.

Mrs. Eggerton raised one gnarled hand and waved it, her gaze fixed on the fire.

"Good day, Mrs. Eggerton," Edward said. He gripped Charity's elbow and guided her toward the door.

Outside, the air felt fresh against her face, tightening her skin with the drying salt of her tears. She rubbed her cheeks with a free hand and walked rapidly beside Edward, who seemed to be lost in his own thoughts. His square chin was set at an obstinate angle, and his face looked hard. Distant.

"It is so hard," she said in a soft voice, flicking quick glances at him. "My own father... Do you think he really shot her? His own mother?"

His arm stiffened under her hand before he patted her fingers. "You must remember that we have only her view of the events. She would want to present herself in as good a light as possible."

Charity stumbled. Only her grip on Edward's arm saved her from sprawling over the sidewalk. "You think *she* shot my grandmother?"

"No," he responded in a slow, thoughtful voice. "I suspect your father was returning from shooting with his friends, just as Mrs. Eggerton said. And the gun was most likely his. There may have been a fight, and his weapon may have gone off by accident. I'm sure he never meant to kill his own mother, no matter what he felt for Mrs. Eggerton."

"He was never right," Charity murmured. "My father— he was never right. I thought he was consumed with grief over the loss of my mother, but now..." Her throat closed painfully, and she blinked away a new flood of hot tears.

Again he patted her hand. "You can not dwell on it. Mrs. Eggerton was correct about one thing, the matter is in the past. Best to forget."

"I suppose." She gave him a watery smile. "So you don't believe my grandmother was haunting the house?"

His crooked grin made her catch her breath, her pulse racing with love and desire. "I believe your cousin haunted your house."

"But you couldn't hear any sounds from the cellar. Even when the baby was born, you couldn't hear anything. Surely she couldn't have given birth in complete silence."

"There is a great deal of wind in Charleston, and Oldwood is old." He assisted her up the front steps and opened the front door for her. "I don't believe your grandmother's spirit was trapped here until her body was found."

Untying her bonnet, Charity sighed. "Well, she's gone now. Have you noticed? We haven't had any odd noises at night for several days now."

"The wind has died down."

"Oh, you are impossible!" She turned away to find Mrs. Maplethorpe coming down the stairs.

"So you are back already?" Mrs. Maplethorpe asked. "I have finished the last morning gown. Would you like to try it on?"

When Charity glanced at Edward, he nodded. "Go on, Miss Stonewright. I have a few more business items to see to before everything is settled."

"Settled?" Her heart thudded against her ribs. "Then you are leaving?"

"Yes. I expect to be on the packet leaving for New York at the end of the week. I hope that will suit you?"

Her hand pressed against the base of her throat. *Don't go!* She wanted to throw herself at him and plead for him to stay with her, but the implacable look was back on his face. He looked unapproachable. The air of a decision firmly made clung to his broad shoulders and straight back.

"Of course," she agreed.

Mrs. Maplethorpe gestured toward the landing above her. "Come then, Miss Stonewright. I have a few more lengths of fabric that we have not designated for any project, perhaps we can manage one more evening gown and a walking dress from them."

Trapped by the restrictions of ladylike behavior and her own pride—she refused to beg—she ascended the stairs. *A prisoner on his way to the gallows.* The feeling turned her limbs to lead. There was nothing to do but continue on her selected path with dignity and grace.

The afternoon passed, as did the next few days. Edward brought her several documents to sign before he announced that Oldwood was finally and officially hers. No one could take it from her any longer. She should have been pleased by the news, but instead, she greeted his announcement with a sigh as she looked around the large rooms.

While they were no longer dusty, they echoed without their proper compliment of furnishings. So much had been sold, so much was gone. The emptiness gave the house a forlorn feeling that depressed her.

Half of the gold had been deposited in the Second Bank of the United States and the other half, as well as the jewels, placed in a safe Edward acquired and had installed for her in the house. Somehow, she couldn't bring herself to place the entire fortune in the hands of a bank, even a very good one. There were always unforeseen circumstances. It gave her a sense of security and connection with her family's past to know the small tin box was nestled safely behind the thick door of the safe.

In the small upstairs room Mrs. Maplethorpe designated as the sewing room, the colorful pile of expensive new fabric had dwindled to just a few scraps. Charity had given the last of her old, threadbare gowns to Janet and Kitty for rags. Most women would have been delighted by the changes, but it only seemed to add to the gray despair gripping her.

A hush had slipped over the house, intensifying with the departure of Lady Hildegard and Cousin Kevin. The silence grew more and more oppressive with the sense of Edward's imminent departure. The life that had filled Oldwood was slowly receding like the water evaporating after a hurricane. With each passing day, Charity found it more difficult to speak above a whisper, or view the future with anything other than dismal acceptance.

Dawn was on the cusp of painting the blueberry-colored sky a pale rose when she climbed out of bed, just as weary as she'd felt when she blew out her candle the night before.

It was Friday.

She could already hear the sound of Edward's low voice and the clatter of heavy boots as he and his valet carried out the remainder of his luggage. The day before, he'd sent a large trunk to the port for loading.

He was leaving. Her eyes burned, and she rubbed them angrily, wiping her damp cheek on her sleeve.

This was her *home*—she'd made her decision, just as Edward had made his. Everything would settle down once he was gone, and she'd find peace again. *Eventually.* Nonetheless, she washed her face in icy water, hoping it would erase the signs of her tears, and after a moment's hesitation, she dressed in a pale blue walking dress. The day promised to be a busy one, and she didn't have the energy to dress in a delicate morning dress and then possibly have to change later.

"Good morning, Edward," she said as she stepped out of her bedchamber.

"Good morning. You are up early," he commented.

Despite the light from a lamp sitting on the hallway table near his door, the corridor seemed dim and filled with shadows. She stepped closer, noting that he was dressed for traveling. A plain, black wool jacket stretched across his broad shoulders, and he wore blue breeches and well-worn boots. A crooked smile stretched his mouth when he noted her examination of him, and she saw that although he was freshly shaven, his handsome face was haggard with deep lines around his mouth and shadows around his eyes.

"I was afraid you would leave without saying goodbye," she said impulsively, stepping closer.

"No—never." He dropped the leather portmanteau he was carrying and turned toward her, his eyes searching her face. "Charity—" He stopped abruptly, placing a hand on her elbow.

She stared up at him, desperate to step into his arms and feel the strength of his heartbeat against the palm of her hand. The clean scent of soap and his warm skin made her take a deep breath, wanting more of him before he departed and left her with nothing but this cold, empty house.

Her hand went of its own accord to press against his broad chest.

His right hand caught hers and held it more tightly against him. "Charity, you must know how I feel." His gaze flickered between her eyes and her mouth as his crooked smile grew more wry. "I know I am hardly a figure of romance like your cousin—most lawyers are old, prosy bores at the best of times—but I can not leave without trying." He pulled her closer. "I love you, Charity."

Dipping his head, he wrapped her in his arms and kissed her. The pressure of his lips increased as he shifted his hold to caress her neck and slip his fingers into her soft hair and cradle her head. Heart pounding, she felt deafened by the urgent sound, unable to tell if it were her racing pulse or his. Her hands tightened, straining to pull him ever closer, not wanting to let him go.

"I love you so much," she murmured into his neck when he freed her mouth. His skin felt warm against her lips and tasted faintly of soap mixed with a salty tang that made her breathe more deeply and tighten her hold.

He grasped her shoulders and gently pushed her back, locking his gaze on hers. "Then—would you consider—will you marry me? Come to England with me, Charity—I promise you won't regret it."

Her smile faltered. Cold washed through her, dousing the flames she'd felt burning inside her. "Leave?" She glanced around the hallway. A pale, pearl gray light was growing around them. "But this is my home—can you not stay?"

The gap between them widened.

"I am sorry. I knew...." He shrugged and ran a hand through his hair, staring over her left shoulder. He nodded. "Of course—I knew. That is why I did not say anything earlier, though I was sure you must have known how I felt. I apologize." His wry grin returned, though it was much colder and cynical. "My duty and my home lay in England while you have the same here. It was inconsiderate of me to place you in such an awkward position."

When he turned away, she reached out to grab his arm. "No—not at all. I love you."

He again placed his warm palm over her hand to hold it in place on his arm. "Then come with me, Charity. Please. The captain can marry us on the crossing to England."

Her heart pounded, yearning to say yes as she gazed into his eyes. But what of her house? And there was Mrs. Maplethorpe, Mrs. Granger, Janet, and Kitty to consider. She could not turn them out with less than a day's notice.

And most of all, Charleston—and Oldwood—was her home. She fought so hard and for so long for it. How could she throw it all away? This was her security, her fortune, and her future. In England she'd be a foreigner. Society would snicker at her, the ladies laughing behind their white hands at the awkward colonist. She didn't belong there. She couldn't hope to fulfill her role as the gracious, well-bred wife of a man like Edward Archer. And whether he admitted it or not, a lawyer needed a wife who would be an asset to him socially.

Doubts and increasingly dismal objections whirled faster and faster around her like the sharp, pricking grains of sand caught in the wind of a gale. They whipped through her, scraping her raw.

"I'm sorry," she said, her gaze falling to the floor. She took a step back and wrapped her arms around her waist, trying to hold in the last bit of warmth from his embrace. How could she explain how difficult it had been in Philadelphia after her father had died? How Oldwood had become a refuge for her when she fled the loneliness of the city in search of a place where she could belong? "I can't. I can not leave—I wish I could—but I can not. I'm sorry." Her voice broke, and she blinked away bitter tears.

"I understand. And I wish you nothing but the best. Truly. If you ever need anything—all you need do is write," he said, his voice thick. He nodded again, picked up his portmanteau, and strode away.

She took one step after him, her hand outstretched, before she stopped. She squared her shoulders and then slowly followed him down the stairs.

Her decision was made. Now she had to learn how to live with it.

Chapter Twenty-Five

The Charleston docks were teeming and noisy, masts as tall as trees forming a bobbing thicket on the water. Edward made his way to the small clipper ship that would take him from Charleston to New York. From there, he would board the ship to Liverpool.

The prospect did not fill him with pleasure. Quite the reverse. Part of him had wanted to throw Charity over his shoulder and forcibly take her to England with him.

She'd professed her love, he'd felt it when he'd kissed her, and yet she refused his offer. That refusal burned bitterly, even though he'd known she was likely to do so. Even the deepest love might balk at being uprooted and carried off to another country. Not everyone was as tempestuous as his sister, or willing to risk everything for a new life.

Charity had found her fortune and owned her own home. She was settled, and her life was stable here in Charleston. Why risk it for the unknown?

He'd been a fool to think she'd throw away so much for him; he'd known he was hardly the kind of romantic figure of a man that would inspire such risks. Still, it burned as bitterly as frostbite, blackening his life.

"They are ready to board, sir," Atwood said, taking the portmanteau from Edward's hand. "I will be relieved when we arrive home."

"Will you?" he asked absently. He glanced over his shoulder. Amongst the tangle of roofs, chimneys, and the occasional tree, a small corner of Oldwood's roof was visible.

"Are you coming?" Atwood moved closer to him, gently encouraging him to step onto the gangplank.

A wiry old sailor stood at the other end, impatience making a thin-mouthed raisin of his face. His fluffy gray hair fluttered in the wind beneath a faded blue cap, but his dark blue jacket and cream colored trousers looked clean enough.

The memory of his sister's disgust at finding a small crop of mushrooms in a dark corner of her tiny cabin on the last trip brought a small smile to Edward's mouth before a pang of loss took his breath away. Double loss. He might never see his sister or Charity again.

Grimly straightening, he took a step forward, only to have someone grab his sleeve.

"What is it, Atwood?" he asked impatiently, turning back. "Have you forgotten something?"

Except it wasn't Atwood gripping his sleeve.

Atwood stood two yards away, staring at him.

And at *her*.

"Charity?" He choked on the question and reached out to grip her arms. "What are you doing here?"

Her beautiful face glowed with a smile, her rounded cheeks rosy from the sea breeze, and her blue eyes as brilliant as the sky above them. "Are you surprised?" Her voice vibrated with laughter.

"Surprised? What are you doing here?"

Her gloved hands gripped his lapels, her gaze fastened on his. "I thought I couldn't—" Her words broke under a surge of strong emotion that shook her. She swallowed and blinked several times, tears shining in her eyes. "I realized when you left that Oldwood was just a house. I was born in Philadelphia—I never actually lived here until last June. This was never my home, never a place where the people I loved had lived." A frown of frustration wrinkled her face, and she gently tapped his chest with a fist. "Oh, I am not explaining this properly, but Oldwood wasn't my home until you and your sister arrived. And it wasn't until you left that I realized it would never be my home now, not without you."

A wave of love filled him, and his grip on her tightened. He swallowed, but his voice was thick when he forced out the question, "What are you saying? Are you...?"

She nodded and stared at his neckcloth, her fingers picking invisible lint off his waistcoat. "If your offer still stands?"

"Oh God, yes!" He pulled her against him and kissed her, hard, dimly aware of Atwood's shocked intake of breath.

Cheers from the sailors and dock workers echoed around them. Even Nodcock yowled from his traveling basket on the deck, although his cries seemed to be indignant howls about his continued confinement instead of pleasure at Charity's presence.

Finally, Edward hugged her to his chest. She felt so right in his arms, so dear.

Another small punch in the shoulder made him raise his head from her neck. "We are in public," she protested in a half-shocked, half-laughing voice.

"I don't care." He brushed her pink cheek tenderly. "Do you?"

Laughing, she shook her head. "No, I can't say that I do."

"Sir!" Atwood said in agonized tones. "Please. They are waiting for us to board."

He paused to study her brilliant eyes. "What about Janet and Kitty? Mrs. Maplethorpe?"

"Ahem," Mrs. Maplethorpe cleared her throat and stepped forward. "I agreed to accompany Miss Stonewright. It appears to be a good thing that I did. Really, Mr. Archer, have you forgotten where we are?"

"Not in the least," he replied.

"I gave a quarter of the gold to Mrs. Granger—for her, Janet, and Kitty. And I wrote a letter to Mr. Tarte to ensure they are all right." She peered up at him, biting her lower lip.

"Brilliant, my love, as always. You have managed beautifully." He smiled at her and moved to place a hand on the small of her back. "Are you ready to board?"

She flashed him an echoing grin and picked up her skirts. "I am, and I'm sure I can trust you to hold to your promise, as well."

"Mrs. Maplethorpe will no doubt ensure that I do," he replied dryly.

"You can rely on that!" Mrs. Maplethorpe said, pushing in front of Atwood to follow them up the gangplank. "Marriage at sea—it shall be quite lovely, I'm sure. And I packed your new rose silk gown, Miss Stonewright." She prodded them to move more quickly onto the clipper's deck. "You shall look lovely."

"She *does* look lovely," Edward murmured. "And always will."

The blue skies above them suddenly seemed to promise smooth seas and a bright future ahead. Edward helped Charity and Mrs. Maplethorpe onto the deck and turned to greet the captain.

"A word, Captain," Edward said. "We have some arrangements we wish to make."

"Very good, sir." The captain's sharp gaze took in Charity and Mrs. Maplethorpe, and the hint of a smile broke through his stern expression. "As soon as we are out of port, I am at your service."

Charity smiled at Edward and held out her hand.

They were going home.

THE END

Your Opinion Matters: Thank you for reading my book. Your opinion is important to other readers searching for new authors, as well as to me. Authors are always desperate to obtain reviews because 4 and 5 star reviews are required to advertise and promote our books. I know that the time and effort required to write a review can make the task daunting, but even a few words are helpful. So if you have time to write a review, I would really appreciate it.

Thank you again for taking the time to read my book.

Other Titles by Amy Corwin

The Archer Family Regency Romance Series
The **Archer Family series** are traditional Regency romances spiced with a mystery.

While these books do not need to be read in order, the list below presents them in the series order.

The Necklace (Prequel to the series)
The Unwanted Heiress
A Lady in Hiding
The Earl's Masquerade
A Stolen Rose
En Garde, My Love (or Fencing for Ladies)
Love Across the Pond (this book)

Second Sons Inquiry Agency Regency Mystery Series
The **Second Sons Inquiry Agency series** are traditional historical mysteries set in the Regency period in England. The books all feature the Second Sons Inquiry Agency.

While these books do not need to be read in order, the list below presents them in a series order.

The Vital Principle
A Rose Before Dying
The Dead Man's View
The Illusion of Desire
Honeymoon with Death

A Second Chance Paranormal Romances
The **Second Chance Paranormal Romances** are paranormal tales spiced with mystery, danger and an "Urban Fantasy" feel. They do not have to be read in any particular order as each book stands alone.

Her Vampire Bodyguard
A Fall of Silver

Paranormal Suspense
Month of Judgment

Mysteries

A new series of contemporary, cozy mysteries is underway, set in fictitious towns near the Outer Banks of North Carolina.

Whacked!
Deadly Inheritance

About the Author

Amy Corwin is a charter member of the Romance Writers of America and recently joined Mystery Writers of America. She writes historical and cozy mysteries with a touch of romance, as well as paranormal romances. To be truthful, most of her books include a bit of murder and mayhem since she discovered that killing off at least one character is a highly effective way to make the remaining ones toe the plot line.

Her books include the historical mysteries, Regency romances, paranormal romances and mysteries.

Join her and discover that every good mystery has a touch of romance.

Connect with Me Online

Website: http://www.amycorwin.com
Twitter: http://twitter.com/amycorwin
Facebook: http://www.facebook.com/AmyCorwinAuthor
Blog: http://amycorwin.blogspot.com

www.ingramcontent.com/pod-product-compliance
Lightning Source LLC
Chambersburg PA
CBHW030114180626
46812CB00002B/418